BEYOND THE FLASHBACK

*Being the Collected Tales of the
Flashback/Dinosaur Apocalypse,
Volume Three*

by
Wayne Kyle Spitzer

Contents

We would have been quite the sight had there been anyone left alive to see us, rumbling up N. La Brea Avenue in *Gargantua One*—we'd disengaged the electric motor and were running the 16.1-liter diesel only, but that's another story—the expedition vehicle's stainless steel hull glinting back at us from the shop windows and its parabolic antenna whirling; its great pistons rattling.

"Rollin' down—the Imperial Highway, with a big, nasty redhead at my side," Sam sang along with the stereo. "Santa Ana winds blowin' hot from the north, and we were *born to ride ...*"

"Jesus, not again," moaned Lazaro. He reached past her toward the deck but she batted his hand away.

Nigel, meanwhile, had to shout over the music: "You want to follow La Brea all the way to Hollywood Boulevard—then hang a right. We're looking for *Gower Street.*"

"Looks like it's going to be smooth sailing," said Sam.

I glanced out the side window as we passed Pink's Hot Dogs—the awning of which was covered with moss and vines—saw startled Compies scatter like mice. "Let's hope Roman's mission is going as well."

Black Mr. Fantastic—please; he'd nicknamed himself—was skeptical. "At a big base like Lewis-McChord? I doubt it. That place is one big Army surplus store now. You really think he's going to just waltz in there and fly out with an Apache?"

"Hard to say," I drawled. "But I do know this: If he succeeds, and if we're successful in securing Eagleton's bunker, nothing will be able to touch us again. That is, if it's still, how shall I say it? *Available.*"

"It will be," said Nigel. "Because nobody knows it's there."

"Except *you,*" sneered Lazaro. "His former lawn guy. Isn't that it?"

"Ya, mon—that's right. I told you: he showed it to us while we were working. Just rolled up in his 1947 Packard one day and started jabbering like we were best friends. Nice guy—sharp as a whip. I knew it was him right away because I'd seen him on *The Tonight Show;* and because he was wearing those same tinted glasses he likes so much."

"Well, what if he's there?" asked Sam.

"He won't be. He never actually lived there, as I said. It was just one of his passion projects—like this rover was for Steve Dannon." He fell quiet as though in deep thought. "Ain't it a shame. All those luxuries—the swimming pool, the indoor park, the gourmet galley—not to mention the food stores and hydroponics—all of it just sitting there, collecting dust. Meanwhile, there's people living in cardboard boxes."

"Or was," said Sam.

"Yeah, but, he *gave,* too. Like, a lot," I said. "I went to college on one of his scholarships. Read him all the time when I was younger—he was kind of a hero to me. Never thought I'd be barnstorming one of his homes."

"You never thought you'd be running from dinosaurs, either," said Sam. She reached over and wiggled my cheek—roughly. "And now look at you go."

"Okay, here it is," said Nigel. "Take a right."

I took a right—swinging the giant rig onto Hollywood Boulevard, watching the big streetlights pass absurdly close to the windshield. "It won't be long. We're going to want to—"

"Whoa, whoa, whoa," said Mr. Fantastic, having noticed the thing—its startling blue, its clean, perfect white—even before I did. "Slow, slow, slow. Go back."

I left off the gas and applied the brakes—which hissed and squealed, like scythes—bringing us to a complete stop. Then I backed up—the different torque causing the gears to rap and wind—until we had drawn alongside the banner and the cycad trees supporting it.

At last Sam said: "Okay, Batman, riddle me this. What's stranger than a Donald J. Tucker banner in the middle of L.A.?" She turned to face Mr. Fantastic.

We all turned to face him—our very own Reed Richards; the Nutty Professor to our Desert Isle. Our Dr. Zarkov.

"How about a Donald J. Tucker banner that was put here recently; as in, after the Flashback," he said—and nodded at the trees. "Because those are cycads—bennettitales, to be precise, from the Upper Jurassic—*not* palms. And what *that* means, kids, is—we're not alone."

We drove on in silence, Sam having killed the music (*The Best of Randy Newman,* as I recall), past the TCL Chinese Theatre—where a pack of raptors were picking over the corpse of a diplodocus calf—past the Capitol Records Building (whose round, spired roof was crowded with seagulls and pterodactyls), then left on N. Gower Street and up to Scenic Avenue—which would take us to Beachwood Drive and on to the Hollywoodland hills. That is, had its shoulders not been choked with cycads and its roadway blocked by a black allosaurus (we were all pretty much experts on dinosaurs now): which had simply lazed over in the middle of the asphalt as though it were sunning itself—its long, sinewy legs stretched luxuriously and its tail straight and unfurled, its great, blood-red crests glistening.

"Oh, for fuck's sake," I said—and brought us to a gradual halt.

I honked the horn—taking note of the dead triceratops in the reeds (which was partially eaten), as well as the allosaur's obviously full belly—but there was no response.

"Just go, man," said Lazaro. "It'll move. And if it doesn't, so what."

"He's right, Jamie," said Sam. "I don't think we have time for this."

I put it in gear and inched forward—revving the engine even as I laid on the horn, moving to within a few feet of it.

Still it did not move—only twitched a little as though it were dreaming; maybe flicked its tail once slightly.

"Jesus, are you kidding me?" I was beginning to lose my patience. "Let's go! It's time to pick 'em up and move 'em out."

I inched still closer—until one of the thing's outstretched feet vanished beneath what passed for the hood. Then it *did* move, rearing its head and gnawing at the push bar—only gently, playfully, like a cat disrupted from a nap—before getting up suddenly and shuffling aside; at which I stepped on the gas and we lurched forward—turning wide as we passed through the intersection; rumbling up Beachwood like an out-of-control freight train; breaking off heavy branches like twigs.

I looked into my sideview mirror even as Sam did the same, saw the thing bounding after us like a leopard, like a wraith, gaining rapidly.

"What is it?" snapped Mr. Fantastic. "What's going on?"

I glanced between it and the road, accelerating rapidly. "It's chasing us. *Fuck.* Better get up into the Crow's Nest, Lazaro. Just don't get trigger-happy; we're gonna need the ammo. Nigel, I'm going to need you to—"

"It'd be best to just let it go," said Mr. Fantastic. "I mean, what's it going to do—bite through solid steel?" He put a hand on my shoulder, comfortingly, reassuringly. "Save the ammo, Jamie. It'll give up before we get there."

I looked around the cockpit: at the banks and banks of instrumentation, the suffocating array of dials and switches—before focusing on a glowing blue toggle; and flipped it. "I don't know about you, Doctor ..." There was a *thump-thump-thump* as I turned to face him. "But where I'm from—they call that 'borrowing trouble.'"

And then the smoke grenades had detonated and we were crashing through their clouds—at which I hit the brakes hard and hung an immediate left, skidding onto a side street, and whereupon we quickly circumnavigated the block to burst back onto Beachwood. Where we instantly realized—just before swinging north—that we could no longer see the street south of us; nor, for that matter, any evidence whatsoever of a pursuing allosaurus—black with red crests or otherwise.

I'd be lying if I said I hadn't already felt uneasy—even before we rounded the bend and saw the big pickups. Deronda Drive was that kind of road: the kind that started normally but then began to twist and turn, and to narrow, climbing all the while, so that the houses on both sides (some nearly palatial while others seemed little more than glorified hippie shacks) closed in all around us. Add to that the fact that we'd run out of places to turn back, and you can imagine how on edge we (already) were when we saw the crashed gate and the occupied vehicles beyond it.

Nor had those occupants taken long to train weapons on us—about 4 seconds, by my count—snapping them out through side windows and an open door even as the men in the payloads (one of which was equipped with a large-caliber machine gun and the other some type of rocket launcher) did the same.

And then there we were, faced off like the Hatfields and the McCoys—only we weren't ready—there beneath the sun in the Hollywoodland hills with the Santa Ana wind blowing and *Gargantua* idling and their blue and white Tucker flags fluttering, proclaiming "Keep America Great" and "No More Bullshit." As though there was still somehow a recognizable government—a recognizable *enemy;* something they could project all their fear and loathing and frustration onto, just as before. As though nothing had changed since the Flashback at all.

I reached up for the targeting goggles slowly, knowing the new windows were tinted but not wanting to take any chances, but didn't put them on. "Nobody get excited," I said. "It's just … it's just a precaution."

"Oh, Jesus," whispered Sam.

"No, he's right," said Mr. Fantastic. "Because—see that rocket launcher?" He pointed at the truck furthest back—a black Dodge Ram with pig ear exhaust stacks and a custom lift. "That, my friends, is what you call bad news. Now, I don't pretend to know what that is, exactly, but what it reminds me of is the French MILAN ..." He got out of his seat and crouched in front of the windshield. "Okay. Yuh. See that dome just inside the barrel? That's the warhead. Big, right? Nasty, right? That's because it's an *anti-tank* weapon." He looked at Sam suddenly—to make his point, I guess. "It *kills* tanks, see. Stops them dead in their tracks. They've even been confirmed to have taken out a U.S.-supplied Abrams—that's the main battle tank of the U.S. Army—in Iraq, in 2017, during their conflict with the Kurds."

He turned to me before making eye contact with each and every one of us. "And you better believe it when I say, people, that that thing will cut through this hull like it's tinfoil. So Jamie's doing the right thing; providing he keeps his focus on that missile launcher. The question is, do we shoot first and eliminate the threat preemptively—by taking out the operator and anyone else who dares to go near it—or do we try to talk to them? Reason with them? Convince them we're not a threat?"

"But we are a threat," said Sam—softly, gravely. "We're here for the bunker. And so are they, obviously. Or they've seized it already. I mean, look at what we're driving. There's a machine gun on the roof, for—"

"I say we shoot first," interjected Nigel—after which he seemed shocked that he'd actually said it. "She's right, I mean—S-sandahl. Sam. We are a threat; and there's no point in trying to deny it. So are they. I mean, come on. You *saw* the banner. If that's not a territorial claim, I don't know what is. And they're white trash, anyway, mon. Stupid and dangerous on—"

"Yo, pound sand!" snapped Lazaro. "I voted for Tucker, too, you know, and I'm not some crazed redneck you can just ..." He trailed off suddenly and looked around—as if for approval—but nobody said a word.

"—on the face of it," finished Nigel, succinctly. He looked at Mr. Fantastic and then at me. "And you know it as well as I do."

I looked out through the long, narrow windshield: at the armed, thickset men—most of them were at last partially overweight—and their dirty, dark-colored trucks; at the poised rifles and trained, glinting machine gun, the rocket launcher with its big, tank-killing warhead.

Mr. Fantastic, meanwhile, had gotten back into his seat. "What's it going to be, Jamie?"

I unbuckled my harness and leaned forward, elbows on my knees—began rubbing my temples.

At last I said, "And this is the only way in? The only road that can be used?"

Paper rattled as Nigel shifted. "Mount Lee Drive, that's right. Winds all the way up to the City of Los Angeles Communications Facility, which is right above the Hollywood sign."

"And beneath it? The sign, I mean? *That's* our bunker?"

"About 50 yards down from it, that's right. Only accessible by air or on foot from there, since the private road from below was removed."

I peered out at the trucks, which shimmered in the heat. "How in the hell did they find out? That's what I want to know."

"Does it matter?" asked Mr. Fantastic. "Besides; we don't actually *know* that they have—we don't know anything, really. Not why or how long they've been here, nor how many of them there are, we don't even know if—"

"That's bullshit, mon. We know it's a train because that's how they roll; and we know there's more of them—probably up there rooting around because they've never actually been here and don't know what they're looking for. No, scratch that—they're probably on their way *here,* because these assholes have already radioed them while we sit here and have a goddamn debate about—"

"Nigel."

"About—"

"*Nigel.* Shut the fuck up."

"But ..."

"Here." I handed the targeting goggles back to him. "Put them on. *Shut the fuck up.* And put them on."

"Wait, what?" Lazaro just glared at me; it was almost as though I'd stabbed his mother. "Is this a joke?"

"I know, you're checked out on the internal gun control. But let's be honest, Dwayne. You don't want to hurt these people. Hell, they're like family, right?" I clapped him on the shoulder briskly. "Just one, big, happy Tucker Train. One big tent from Cabela's. Isn't that right?"

"What the hell are you talking about?"

"Sam, get the ramp," I instructed, and watched as she flipped the toggle—reluctantly.

"Because we're going to go meet your friends with our hands up," I said. "And you, sir, are going to do all the talking."

"Ready?"

I looked at Lazaro and he looked back. "Ready." He squinted at me suddenly. "Why wouldn't I be?"

I shrugged. "No reason." I took a deep breath. "Okay. Remember, hands in the air."

He put his hands in the air.

Then we moved out; stepping into the sunshine from the cool shadow of the expedition vehicle, raising our hands as though we were surrendering.

"Easy does it ..."

There was a rattle of arms as they noticed us and hurriedly re-trained their weapons.

"Halt! Who goes there?"

Both of us froze. "A-Americans. Two of us," said Lazaro. "We want to talk."

The wind blew; the sun beat down. Nobody said anything.

"Daryl," snapped one of them at last—after which a skinny blonde dude stepped out (he couldn't have been more than 17) and seemed to hesitate; looking at us over his rifle, shifting his weight from one foot to the other, before shuffling forward quickly and giving us a pat-down—briefly, hurriedly. "They're good," he said.

The man who'd directed him to frisk us—he looked like John Goodman, I swear—motioned for us to come forward.

"That's close enough," he said, after we'd closed the gap. "Trent, Brady, Mitchell—cover us. Everyone else, hold your positions." He seemed to relax—slowly, grudgingly. "Americans, you say." He handed the skinny guy his weapon—some kind of long rifle, who knows. "That doesn't really feel complete to me. You say you're Americans. Which one?"

Lazaro and I glanced at each other.

"Both of us," said Lazaro, and straightened a little. "Born and bred."

Jesus, I thought, and rubbed my brow.

The man stiffened. "Hands in the air."

I raised my hands—after which he seemed to lighten, and just chuckled. "No, I mean: *Which America?*"

I looked at Lazaro, who hesitated. "The—the only one," he said. "The only America. Tucker's America." He feigned confusion. "What other is there? I mean; since the Flashback, that is?"

The man didn't say anything, only glanced at the skinny kid, whose face was a wreck of pimples.

That's when we heard it: the sound of diesel engines— lots of them—coming down the hill, coming down Mount Lee Drive.

He snatched the radio from his belt. "We're over here— in front of the trucks. We've got two of them," he said.

And then the trucks began to appear, rumbling down the service road like a cavalry, like an armored support column, black smoke billowing from their exhaust stacks and Tucker flags flying; their huge, aggressive-looking front grills gleaming, the radio and C.B. antennas whipping—until they'd made a parking lot of the base of the hill and their drivers had begun getting out—many of them wearing red hats and loud shirts, campaign buttons, red, white and blue leis—and all of whom headed our way and partially surrounded us; at least, until a singular personage—a towering man in blue jeans and a black T-shirt, who wore a strikingly-sculpted beard and a gleaming white Stetson—parted them like the Red Sea: the MAGA Nephilim, the "No More Bullshit" Moses, and joined our little drum circle.

"They say they want to talk," said the first man, "but I wanted to wait until you got here. We, ah, we don't know anything yet."

The man in the Stetson just looked at us, his hands on his hips. Then he took a few steps toward *Gargantua* and paused, his great, broad back facing us.

His silence seemed to make the first man uncomfortable. "What do you think? You, ah, ever seen anything like it?"

The towering figure didn't move, didn't budge, only continued staring at the stainless steel vehicle, which gleamed beneath the sun.

At length he said: "Devin tells me you want to talk." He paused to clear his throat. "That you—that you got something to say." He reached up slowly and stroked his beard—thoughtfully, meditatively—before turning to face us. "So say it. *Talk.* You can start with your names. I'm Denton."

We both just looked at him, unsure how to begin.

"I'm Jamie," I said, and held out my hand. "Jamie Klein. This here is Lazaro."

He looked at my hand as though he was uncertain what to make of it. Then he gripped it; gently at first, but then squeezing suddenly and briefly, crushingly—if only for an eyeblink. *Message received,* I thought.

He shook hands with Lazaro.

I chose not to waste any time: "We're here for one of the parabolic antennas," I lied. "From the Communications Facility. Our engineer thinks he can use it to replace our existing one, which is malfunctioning."

Denton raised an eyebrow—as though that wasn't what he'd expected. He glanced at *Gargantua* and then back to me. "For that?"

I nodded, saying nothing.

"I see," he said. He raised his chin abruptly. "So you're not—affiliated with anyone? FEMA? Red Cross? The United Nations?"

I shook my head.

"NATO? EUFOR?" He looked us up and down, first me, then Lazaro. "No. I don't suppose you are." He indicated *Gargantua* again. "And the rig?"

I told him the truth: that someone in our group had known about it before the Flashback, in Seattle, and that after the time-storm we'd stolen it. And that that was all—

"Seattle?" exclaimed the first man, 'Devin,' incredulously. He harrumphed. "I thought you said you were *Americans.*"

Denton suppressed a smirk. His eyes had lit up at mention of Seattle too. "That where you're from, Jamie Klein?"

I could see where this was going. "Originally—yes. But we left the shithole to seek a warmer climate, a *southern* climate." I looked him directly in the eye. "And better people. Loyal people. Like you." I looked around at the others. "Like *all* of you."

He followed my gaze, seeming to appreciate the sentiment (although it was hard to tell, really, because he was squirrely, this Denton: a sidewinder dressed as a straight-shooter). "Well, I'm glad you feel that way, Jamie. I really am. But we've got a problem—several of them, actually. The first is, we can't let you do that: take the antenna. As part of the Array, it's got to go—it's got to be destroyed. Second, we're not currently accepting—which is to say, if you're looking to join our train, we can't take you. And the third is— we've already claimed this land. Hollywood, that is. Everything from Beverly Hills in the south to the Santa Monica foothills in the north—it's, ah, it's ours now. I'm thinking you probably noticed our banners. Oh, yeah. And the fourth." His blue eyes met my own, piercingly, unflinchingly. "You're trespassing. And you need to leave. Like, now. Also—if we see you again," He shrugged, real cute-like: "We'll execute you."

I looked from him to Devin and onto the pimply kid. "So that's it. No discussion, no compromise; not even a reason why."

"There's a reason. It's because there's important work that needs to be done." He half-turned to face the others. "Isn't that so? Isn't there important work to be done?"

"*Important* work," said a woman in a foam campaign hat, and smiled. "*American* work."

"To end the Chinese Flashback," said someone else.

"And detonate the charges," said another. "To knock down the Array."

I must have looked confused. "I—Okay. What's the Array?"

He raised an eyebrow sharply. "You mean you don't know?" He looked from me to Lazaro. "Neither of you?"

"Yeah, I know," said Lazaro. "It—it's a secret high-power, high-frequency transmitter ... said to be somewhere in the U.S." He looked at his shoes as though vaguely ashamed. "Some say it's Chinese. Others say deep state. You know ... conspiracy stuff."

Denton just looked at him. "Conspiracy stuff," he said. He began pacing around us. "Well, let me tell you—Lazaro from Seattle—we've been up there, to this so-called 'Communications Facility,' and there ain't nothing normal about it; all right? Fact is, it's been *designed* to look like just another antenna farm, that's how it's stayed hidden all these years. Another fact is: it's home to the second High-frequency Active Auroral Research Program, or HAARP[2], which just happens to be what caused the Flashback."

He circled back around to face us and paused. "Got it? That's what started it all, see. That's what brought hell down upon us." When neither of us said anything, he added, "*They were messing with the ionosphere, man, don't you get it?* That's what let Them in ..." He indicated the lights in the sky, which hadn't been particularly active since we'd left Seattle. "That's when They became aware of us. When They—how did H.G. Wells say it? 'Drew their plans against us.'"

Everyone seemed to look at me, I have no idea why.

"You're fucking crazy," I said. "You—you've totally lost it."

"Have I?"

"It's a fucking *antenna farm,* Denton!" I glanced around us at the throngs of people. "I mean, is that what you people actually *believe?* Christ, did it steal the election, too? Is that what kind of bullshit you're trying to pass off?" I glared at Denton. "We're done here. Let's go, Lazaro."

"Now wait just a fucking—"

And he lunged at me—which was followed by the sound of *Gargantua's* .50 caliber swinging around, locking into position. Which was followed by it ratcheting down, down, until it was trained on Denton alone.

"Nobody move!" he shouted, splaying his hands, even as there was a riot of shifting arms. "Is that clear?"

But nobody did; move, that is, not even when Lazaro and I walked back the way we had come and ascended the ramp into *Gargantua;* where I gave the order to retreat and go back down the hill and Sam did, operating the rover like a champ—even though she'd only driven it twice before— backing into a driveway (one I hadn't even noticed) to reverse direction, taking us all the way to Rodgerton Street and beyond.

"Wait, *that's* Hollywood Park?"

I looked out the windshield as Sam pulled over on Canyon Lake Drive and killed the engine, which dieseled and rattled, briefly. "It's a park, what did you expect?"

Lazaro cupped his eyes, peering out the side window. "I don't know. Like, a statue of Marilyn Monroe; or somethin'. You know, with the wind all up in her shit and—"

"That's Palm Springs," said Nigel. "'Forever Marilyn,' on Museum Way. You'd like it."

"How the fuck would you know what I'd like?"

"It's an up-skirt. Just your speed."

"Hey, *fuck you, Jamaica.* Why don't you just—"

"Alright, knock it off, both of you," I said. "Nigel, let's have a look at that map."

We all gathered around as Nigel spread it between himself and Sam.

"I'm afraid it hasn't changed much," he said. "There's still no road other than Mount Lee Drive. And you saw the terrain; Gargantua can't handle that."

"What about on foot?" I circled a tangle of residential roads with my finger. "So we know these are blocked; what if we headed northeast straight from the park and just circumnavigated the whole mess?"

"Could work, but it would take time, and we don't know what's in those—"

"Hills, precisely," interjected Mr. Fantastic. "Look, see these? All these peaks and valleys? It's like a great big washboard, right? Well, see, that's precisely the kind of terrain welterweights like Utahraptor and Phorusrhacos love, because it allows them to herd prey into the lowlands and trap it there."

He looked at me gravely, solemnly. "In other words, we'd be walking straight into a kill box."

I sat back in my seat and exhaled, wondering why Roman had put me in charge in the first place, why I'd accepted. Why I'd made the decisions I'd made. Why we'd come over a thousand miles on such a fool's errand. What I was going to tell the others back in Issaquah ...

"If we could ... if we could just *move* faster, maybe," I said. "Get there before anything could triangulate us."

Mr. Fantastic only shook his head. "No, man. *No.* You're smarter than that. Turn us around, Jamie. Turn us around ... and let's go home."

I took off my glasses and rubbed the bridge of my nose.

At length Sam said, "I can drive—if you're not up to it. I don't mind, really."

I must have nodded. All I remember for certain is hearing the engine start and Lazaro grumbling before Nigel said, unexpectedly, "Wait a minute. Wait a minute. *The Ranch.*"

"Forget it," I said—irritably. I didn't want to hear it, whatever it was.

"Holy shit, I forgot all about it." I heard the map rattle as he tapped it. "The Ranch. The Ranch, mon, Sunset Ranch."

Lazaro cursed as he swiveled in his chair. "What the fuck are you even—"

"What do mean, 'Sunset Ranch?'" I glanced at the map and quickly back to him. "Talk to me, dammit!"

He only shrugged, carelessly, nonchalantly. "It—it's a tourist attraction, sort of a barbeque joint, but with a riding stable and a corral full of horses. It's right here." He indicated a spot on the map. "Yuh, see, there's even a trail, here, which intersects with Mount Lee Drive."

"And follow that right into an ambush?" Mr. Fantastic harrumphed.

"Horses," I muttered. "Holy *Christ.*"

I slouched over the map and pointed. "If there's horses left alive we could follow the trail to Mount Lee Drive and then cross it—right here, then cut through the hills north by northwest until we come straight to the bunker." I looked at everyone one by one. "Not only that, but if we get attacked ... they'll go for the horses. Not us."

I tried to smile as Sam glowered at me. "More meat," I said, and shrugged.

The cockpit fell silent as everyone thought about it.

"I've never even rode a horse," said Mr. Fantastic. "How the hell am I going to—"

"You'll stay with *Gargantua,*" I said. "And cover us with the .50 cal for as far as you can. How about the rest of you?"

"4-H Blue-ribbon, Poulsbo State Fair," said Sam. "2007."

"Used to ride 'em right there at Sunset," said Nigel, "when we were working for Eagleton."

I looked at Lazaro, who seemed to hesitate.

"Of course I've ridden a fucking horse," he grumbled. "I'm from Idaho." He added: "What about you?"

"Never in my life," I said, and looked at Sam—I don't know why. "But I'll manage. Don't worry about it."

I looked at Mr. Fantastic, who just shook his head.

"Okay ..." I breathed. I held my hand out to the others, palm down. "Who's in?"

And Sam slapped her hand over mine, after which Nigel slapped his hand over her's—and Lazaro topped us all off.

"Great," said Mr. Fantastic, disappointed. "All right ..." He picked up the targeting goggles. "Let's hope there's some horses."

And then we were off, making a U-turn in the middle of Canyon Lake Drive and rumbling toward Sunset Ranch—all of us, I think, wondering if we were really up to it, and if we could actually pull it off. All of us, I think, frightened out of our wits.

As it turned out, there *were* horses: fourteen of them, to be exact, all of which were healthy and had been well-maintained—thanks to a woman named Shawna, who lived at the Ranch. Nor had our meeting been a confrontational one, in part because she'd been riding out in the field when we'd first rumbled up and had hardly been in a position; but mostly because she was a woman of singular grace and beauty who wouldn't have hurt a fly—even if her life and wellbeing had depended on it. In this case, fortunately—it hadn't.

"Well now, if that isn't a posse," she said, and took the picture—even as our horses grew restless and mine most of all: nickering and neighing, clearly wanting to go. "The Apple Dumpling Gang rides again."

She waited as the Instamatic developed the snapshot and pushed it out—humming in the silence, groaning as though its batteries were low. "Ah, see?"

She quickly approached and handed it to me. "That'll be a buck ninety-eight."

I took it but didn't look at it yet, smiling down at her from "Rusty," liking the way the sun fell on her face and hair. "Just add it to your Lifetime Protection Plan," I said, and glanced at *Gargantua.* "You're going to like having that parked here, I think."

"If it means I'll be seeing you again, I will," she said, and beamed up at me, earnestly, unguardedly. She seemed to grow somber. "Take care of my horses, Jamie. Bring them back safe."

I looked at the picture, which showed the four of us mounted in front of the trailhead, our rifles slung across our backs—and smiled. "I will do everything in my power, Shawna. I prom—" I left off, feeling as though a cold hand had gripped my heart. *"Oh, no."* I looked from the picture to the trail.

"What is it?" Her previously lilting voice had lowered an octave. "What's wrong?"

I gripped the reins, dropping the picture—even as Rusty whinnied and squirmed—wanting to reach back and unsling my rifle; wanting to have some kind of defense. But it was already too late; too late for fight or flight. Too late for anything but to hold perfectly still. *"Shhh,"* I whispered, "nobody move. And don't reach for your weapons. Don't even breathe."

I indicated the trail—the horses snorting and shuffling about—even as Shawna followed my gaze, and gasped.

"Oh, my God."

"Shhh ..."

We didn't budge, didn't blink, as the allosaur approached: its leg muscles working beneath black and pebbled skin; its blood-red crests gleaming (for, indeed, it appeared to be the same one we had encountered earlier in the day).

"No way, man," moaned Lazaro—quietly, unsteadily. "No fucking—"

I waved him to silence even as Shawna worked the horses—stroking their manes, rubbing their snouts; trying to calm them—as I recalled something about horses and predators in the wild, something I'd read: which was that they didn't fear predators so much as the *act of predation*—meaning, I suppose, that those who hadn't encountered dinosaurs before (which these hadn't, according to Shawna) would have no reason to fear them—unless, of course, they (the dinosaurs) behaved in a threatening way. Which, curiously, this one wasn't doing.

I carefully reached behind me and pressed the emergency button on my radio. "Here's where we find out if Mr. Fantastic is right ..."

I glanced at Shawna, who looked back at me questioningly.

"About their vision," I said. "Predatory dinosaurs. About it being movement-based."

To the others I mumbled: "I just alerted Mr. Fantastic; we gotta give him time. He'll hear it and then arm the .50 cal. Just hang on. And keep your horses steady."

"Here it comes," said Sam, indicating the allosaur.

And it came—but did not attack; striding instead to a nearby trough (or rather a bathtub on blocks) and beginning to drink—deeply—before plopping down in a cloud of dust and beginning to yawn and stretch ... after which it laid its chin flat and just stared at us—as though we were friends. As though we were one big, happy family.

I exchanged glances with Shawna, who smiled earnestly, unguardedly, even as something whirred—*Gargantua's* .50 cal, which swiveled and lowered, training itself on the allosaur.

I shook my open palm, indicating he shouldn't fire.

"Shawna," I said—breathlessly, tensely—eyeing the animal carefully, "Walk back to your house. Don't be afraid. Just ... walk. Slowly. Non-threateningly. Go."

"Oh, my God, Jamie. But—"

"Do it," I said, feeling for my rifle, touching its wood stock. "We've got you covered." I gripped the weapon and brought it around—slowly, non-threateningly—saw Sam and the others doing the same. To them I said: "Don't fire unless I tell you to."

Lazaro harrumphed, sneering. "What should we do, then, introduce ourselves?"

I looked at the allosaur: at its golden eyes, which were entirely free of the glow—"the Color," as we often called it, the mysterious light by which we always knew an animal had been affected, been swayed, by *them,* by the Others—which seemed almost passive, meditative.

"Easy ... He's not a threat." I watched as Shawna went, cautiously, reluctantly—then motioned again to *Gargantua.*

Do not engage, I repeated, staring at its tinted windows. *Hold your fire.*

"This is ridiculous," cursed Lazaro, and pumped his long gun—slowly, smoothly, with hardly a sound. "Are we going to leave it? What—so it can come after us the moment it starts to feel hungry? Are you kidding?"

But I'd already decided; the allosaur would be spared.

We weren't going to butcher it—even if it meant facing it later, and increasing our risk. Because it was important, somehow—keeping it alive. It was ... I can't explain it, not really—I couldn't then and I can't now. I just knew that we couldn't kill it. That it—had a purpose, somehow. A *mission.* Just as we.

"That's exactly what we're going to do," I said, and patted Rusty's shank, encouraging him forward. "Now let's move."

And we moved, trotting up the orangish-tan clay like Chieftains, like a posse, our rifles in one hand and the reins in the other (the allosaur closing its eyes and seeming to doze as *Gargantua's* cannon hummed and realigned, following us as we went), Shawna watching safely from her window.

It was at once garish and sublime, hipster and gauche, a burnt-orange relic of a bygone era with a tip of the hat to Frank Lloyd Wright and a debt to Googie architecture—a thing as righteous as it was ridiculous, which sat amongst its desert like an outsider, an intruder, as out of place as the transplanted palms and piped-in water, as artificial as L.A. itself.

"They weren't kidding when they called it the Lost Aztec Temple of Mars," I said, as Rusty fidgeted and nickered, and shook flies from his ears. "But what's with all the high fencing and concertina wire—only to leave the entire front-perimeter open? There's just a hedgerow. No fence at all."

Nigel sat up in his saddle and looked on, the sweat beading along his forehead. "Be damned if I know; it wasn't like that before." He looked around the area—skittishly, I thought. "Maybe he had it removed when they took out the road. He was like that, you know. All about the visual." He pointed at the house itself. "Wouldn't have been a problem, though, even if it *were* there—there's a man door in the fence just beyond that breezeway."

I held out my arm as everyone started to move. "I—hold up. I—ah, I don't like this."

I scanned the overgrown yard and the cosmetically-placed boulders (some of which were the size of moving vans); looking for traps, looking for threats. "It doesn't feel right."

Lazaro got off his horse and approached the hedgerow—then turned to face us, splaying his arms. "What? You heard Jamaica; dude was all about the visual. Probably figured there was no need—once the road was taken out. For a front fence, I mean." He let his arms slap to his sides. "Now are we going to go check it out, or what? Or are you all just going to sit there all day?"

And there was a growling noise, a deep-throated snarl, which sounded from behind one of the rocks even as a shadow fell across the knee-high grass—at which a great cat padded out which was easily the size of a pickup, and *hissed* at us: its huge pallet showing pink and pale, its black lips stretching, its whiskers and curved fangs—which were like tusks—gleaming in the sun.

"Lazaro, *don't!*"

But it was too late; he'd already drawn his pistol and squeezed off a few rounds—which went *pop, pop, pop* in the late afternoon sun and echoed along the hills; which reverberated across the valley like the sound of a car backfiring.

"Goddammit, man," I cursed, even as my horse and everyone else's leapt up in a panic and started to bolt; as Lazaro's trotted into the scrub and didn't look back, as the saber-toothed cat advanced several yards toward us—and stopped.

"You—you just let that entire army know we're still here; and exactly where we're at," I snapped, having wrestled my horse back around along with everyone else (although Nigel was still struggling), and finally climbed off, tossing the reins into the scrub. I looked at the cat, the Smilodon, which paced back and forth furiously. "Now just back away, *slowly. And hold your fire.* It's not advancing. Come on!"

But he didn't; back away, that is—all least not right away; choosing instead to creep closer ... advancing several feet before pausing in front of the hedgerow and leaning forward—looking down.

"Yo, Jamie! You got to see this!" He turned to face us, his face lit up like a child's. "Come on! It's completely safe."

I looked at Sam, who got off her horse and looked back at me—tentatively, hesitantly. And then we moved forward, Nigel having gained control of his steed and dismounted and quickly run up to join us.

"It's a moat," said Lazaro, "like the kind they have at Woodland Park. Check it out."

I looked into its depths, amazed at its cleverness and ingenuity; at its ability to follow form with function.

"A perfect illusion," I said, shaking my head, and added: "Leave it to a sci-fi writer, I guess. To come up with something like this." I peered through the breezeway at the house, which seemed wide open to us now. "My friends ... it is time."

I looked at the others and then to Sandahl—to Sam. "Let's go check out the world's most well-appointed basement, shall we?"

"It's more than that," she said, and beamed; our beautiful and only female (in the away team, that is, since we'd lost Joan); our very own Heather Locklear. "It's home."

And then there was a burst of gunfire and she fell—just slouched face-first into the dirt; and we all followed the sound to the Hollywood sign where an array of trucks had fanned out above and behind it—all along the ridge—trucks with blue and white flags flying from their beds.

After which we scooped Sam up by her armpits and scrambled for the nearest rock formation: where Nigel and Lazaro began shooting back while I leaned over Sam and the blood poured from her mouth and down her cheeks. Where it trickled into the orangish-tan clay even as she looked up at me—trying but failing to form words; trying to tell me something but wholly unable—and pooled around her head like dark, red wine.

"Jesus, Jamie, *look.*"

It was Nigel—catching his breath with his back to the rocks, peering beyond the hedgerow. I followed his gaze to where the cat had begun backing up—crouched low like a puma, swinging its hindquarters. Focused on us like a laser beam.

"Jesus, shoot it!" I snapped, cradling Sam's head in my arms, unable to do it myself. "Hurry, before it—"

But it was too late—the Smilodon had already launched itself at the moat: clearing it but only barely, snatching the hedgerow in its forepaws, fighting its way up and over.

And then we were pinned: Nigel and Lazaro firing at the Tucker train as I cradled Sam and the Smilodon approached; as the Communications Center exploded and there was a tremendous fireball—which rose, curling, into the clear, blue sky—as the cat hunkered down yet again (as if to pounce) but was disrupted by a hiss and a snarl from behind me; from behind the rock formation, at which the black allosaur stalked out and crouched low—its foreclaws splayed, its eyes rolling back in its skull—and launched itself at the cat—like a cobra, almost, or a barracuda—the force of it spinning the tiger in the dust and pushing it onto its back, where it thrashed and snapped its teeth—but quickly rebounded.

I snatched up my radio and toggled it: *"Gargantua One* this is Mobile, do you copy?"

Sam stirred as I waited, reaching up and touching my face, trying desperately to speak, as guns crackled all around us.

"Gargantua, go ahead."

"Listen up: We are pinned down at the bunker and are taking heavy fire. I need you to double-time it back to the gate and engage those targets. Engage them—and then move right up the road, all the way to the Communications Center. Use your smoke screen; it'll disorient them. But you need you to hit 'em with everything you got, understand? *Gargantua. Do you copy?"*

I heard it across the hills even before he acknowledged: the rapid-fire of *Gargantua's* Gatling gun—tearing up targets, hopefully taking out the missile operator.

The radio hissed and squelched. "I heard it and I am already there, *and* engaging," said Mr. Fantastic. "Stand by."

I put my hand over Sam's own and held it against my cheek, holding her as tight as I could, rocking her gently. "Hang in there, kiddo. We're going to get you to that medical bay, you just wait and see. *But you've got to hang in there."*

I watched as the animals spun around in a deathmatch, kicking up orange dust, causing clouds of it to overtake us, growling and gnashing their teeth.

"It's no good, mon," said Nigel. "I'm down to my last clip."

"Here," said Lazaro, and tossed him a fresh one. "I brought extra."

But Nigel was right: We weren't going to last, much less get Sam to a medical bay—not the one in *Gargantua* and not the one in the bunker. I just didn't see it happening before—

Before—

And there was a sound, very faint at first but growing, intensifying, coming closer. Getting louder—and I mean exponentially. Chopping the air like a string of firecrackers, like a machete, seeming to eclipse everything as a shadow passed over the ground and I peered skyward—following the thing as it briefly blotted the sun, tracking it as it pounded toward the Hollywood sign.

A helicopter. An Apache. The most beautiful thing I had ever seen, before or since. Our own Roman Malone—Black Stringfellow Hawke, as he jokingly referred to himself (in deference to Mr. Fantastic and that old TV show, *Airwolf*). Our Eye in the Sky—who had gone into Fort Lewis and come out with a tiger in his pocket. Who had somehow managed the impossible and brought it all the way here—to save us in our most desperate hour; to save Sam before she bled out.

"Well hello down there," came his familiar voice over the radio—followed by a loud burst of static, which crackled and popped. "Looks like you've made some friends here already ..."

I watched as he circled the mountain: being a good Eye in the Sky, taking in the lay of the land. "Is that something I might be of assistance with? We got rockets."

"Hot-damn, that crazy bastard did it," shouted Lazaro—gripping Nigel's shoulder, giving it a shake. "Flyboy comes through again!" He howled at the sky.

"We're the posse that can't be stopped, man," said Nigel, and gripped him back. "The Issaquah Five has struck again. Can you believe it, James? I mean, can you—"

But I wasn't looking at him anymore, Sam's hand having relaxed and slid slowly from my cheek, her head having slumped, heavily, it seemed, deeper into my arms.

"Is she—?" began Nigel, as Lazaro grimaced.

"Fuck no, man ..."

But she was gone, and there was nothing else to say.

Nothing else to do.

I lowered her to the dirt—slowly, gingerly—as small arms continued to rattle and pop. Nor did I notice the absence of combat from the animals—although, looking back, it must surely have been over. Nobody said anything for several moments.

At last my radio squelched. "Jamie, this is *Gargantua*—and the road has been cleared ... to within about a quarter mile of the Communications Center. I can see it from my location. Thing is, that Apache's got them seriously spooked, and they seem to be heading out ... heading this way. What do you want me to do, over."

But I just remained slumped over Sam, feeling responsible for it—all of it—feeling as though I'd failed her. Feeling as though I was to blame.

"Second that, Jamie," came Roman, followed by another burst of static. "We got them in a pincer, a real kill box. This is your call."

I looked at Nigel and Lazaro, my eyes brimming with tears.

"We'll have to deal with them eventually, Jamie," said Nigel—softly. "I think you know that as well as I do."

I must have focused on Lazaro, who said, "Take it from someone who knows them. They'll be back."

At last I toggled the mic: "Sam is dead," I said, and gave it a moment to sink in. "So here's what we're going to do. Mr. Fantastic, I want you to hold the line and prevent any of them from escaping, okay?" I waited for him to acknowledge. "But it's going to fall on you, Roman, to neutralize them. Because they're too dangerous to leave standing. Just ... use everything you have. There's no children. There are, however, woman and young people. It—it's a tribe, you understand Like ours. But—they've made it clear: we're not welcome. Nobody is. Under penalty of execution. And they've claimed all of Hollywood." I looked at Sandahl's lithe, crumpled form. "And, well ... they killed Sam."

I lowered the radio and stood, now that the firing had stopped, and looked at the ridge, where the Tucker trucks were evacuating. "This one's for you, Sam." Then I raised it again. "Play something for her, would you, *Gargantua?* The

Randy Newman album. And pipe it over the loudspeakers so we can hear it. Otherwise ... fire when ready."

And then we waited, watching the trucks with their billowing flags slowly move along the ridge, watching them go.

Last night I saw Lester Maddox on a TV show / With some smart-ass New York Jew / The Jew laughed at Lester Maddox / And the audience laughed at Lester Maddox too ...

I heard gunshots—nothing major, just some idiot in the Tucker train shooting at the sky.

So I went to the park and I took some paper along / And that's where I made this song ...

And then it started, the Apache firing two Hellfire missiles which hit a group of pickups at the start of the train and instantly blew them to pieces, glass and shrapnel flying, a body tumbling in the air.

We talk real funny down here / We drink too much, we laugh too loud / We're too dumb to make it in no northern town ...

Two more missiles fired, this time at the other end of the train, blowing pickups and blue flags into the air, sending a cab higher than anything else—like the turrets of those Iraqi tanks in the first Gulf War—hurling a Rugged Terrain tire along the ridge, which eventually rolled down the hill.

We're keeping the niggers down ...

More missiles, like scaled-up bottle rockets: hitting the column like hammers, making fireballs of King Cabs and beds of people; spitting from the chopper's hardpoints like fireworks, like flairs, incinerating skin and catching hair on fire, I knew, and didn't care, obliterating pennants and banners.

We're rednecks, we're rednecks / We don't know our ass from a hole in the ground ...

Until he'd finally fired everything: Hellfires and Hydras, Stingers and Spikes, all of them hissing and screaming, finding their targets; all of them lighting the ridge up like the Fourth of July, or maybe the volcano at The Mirage, in Las Vegas, each making our world safer and saner and more secure—more righteous, more lost.

Each bringing smoke and silence and peace—like the lights in the sky themselves—to the war-torn hills of Earth.

By the time Roman had finished mopping up and landed the Apache, we'd covered Sam with a tarp from *Gargantua* (Mr. Fantastic had parked it next to the Hollywood sign) and I'd closed the allosaur's eyes—having said a prayer for him first in appreciation of his sacrifice (for he'd surely saved us from the saber-toothed cat, which also lay dead) and even piled stones.

"I don't know why he took to us like that," said Lazaro, walking over to join me, "but I'm sure glad he did."

We looked down at the beast as the sun continued to sink and everything took on a golden hue.

"You were right, you know. About not killing him." He looked at me as the breeze tousled his hair. "And I'm sorry."

I stared at the allosaur, which looked oddly at rest, oddly peaceful, and thought about Sam. "Yeah. Well. I was wrong about a lot of things too."

I looked up to see Roman walking toward us across the scrub. "If that look means what I think it does you can knock it off, right now," he said, and paused. "We all knew the danger; Sam perhaps most of all. She died doing what she believed." He looked at the allosaur and then to me. "Don't take that away from her."

I rested my hand on his shoulder. "Nor you, Roman?"

He straightened suddenly and looked me in the eye. "Nor me. We both did exactly what we had to do." He gripped my shoulder and shook it slightly. "It wasn't the first time, as you'll recall. And it won't be ..."

I must have squinted at him. "What? What is it?"

But he only stared beyond me—toward the bunker, toward the breezeway, at which I turned around and saw an old man creeping toward us holding a shotgun: a man as bloated and pale, as unhealthy, as I had ever seen; a man in silk pajamas and a monogramed bathrobe, who's dark hair was parted as if with a knife and who wore yellow-tinted glasses through which you could clearly see his eyes—a man I instantly recognized as Hugo Eagleton.

"Take off your weapons," he said, continuing to approach, "All of you. *Right now.*"

But nobody did, only moved back slowly to give him space—holding their arms at their sides, ready for anything.

"I'll fill you full of shot, don't think I won't. Now drop 'em. *Now."* He hurried toward me suddenly, I have no idea why, and stuck the shotgun in my chest. "Who's in charge here? Huh? Is it you, you bespectacled little shit? Answer me!"

"It—it is," I said, sensing everyone stirring, and added, "Everybody just chill, okay? I'm all right."

He used the double barrels to raise my chin. "I'll be the judge of that. Now, listen. I want you to say something—all right? I want you to prove to me you're *human.* Got it? It can be anything; a quote from a book, a humorous aphorism, a dirty joke; hell, we can have a Socratic dialogue, for all I care. Just entertain and enlighten me; prove to me you're human and not one of these animals wandering the city like a saw-boned coyote—just looking for something to eat. *Or fuck.* And make it snappy, yeah? 'Brevity is the soul of wit,' they say. I don't have time to dawdle—one look at me should tell you that." He pushed the shotgun hard against my throat. "And go. You're the Oracle at Delphi."

I rolled my eyes, looking around. "Nobody try anything, all right? I—I got this. I think." I took a deep breath and exhaled. "Okay. Fine." I cleared my throat. "The Dreaming City ... by Hugo Eagleton. Ch-chapter One, paragraph one." I paused to collect my thoughts. 'It ... it was the first night of the Sacrificium, a night of sacrifice and death, a night when the black coins tendered in the Lottery would be tendered back. B-but it ... it was also the *Hora Mil—Mille Semitis,* the Hour of a Thousand paths, for that is the day the Sacrificium had fallen on this year, an hour when best friends might become enemies, when lovers of longstanding might betray oaths, in which anything and everything was possible. A night—in other words—for dreaming; but also for something else. Something elusive but impossible to ignore—nebulous—but as real as the River Dire; and which seemed to have stolen into the world on the wind itself ...”

I opened my eyes—having closed them in order to concentrate—and saw that he was crying. Weeping.

“Bullocks, of course,” he said, finally, and lowered the shotgun. “Pure, undiluted bullocks—as stupid and naïve as the young man who wrote it.”

He let the weapon fall to his side. “Ah, well. Such are the things men busy themselves with.” He cocked his head as though thinking of something, as though it were standing right it front of him, whatever it was. “And yet the thing is, I can still remember when I wrote that. Isn’t that the damndest thing? It was in that first shithole apartment in New York, the one in Flatbush, Brooklyn.” He smiled a little, thinking about it. “Susan was there, still young, still beautiful, but had long since fallen asleep. I was wearing comfortable shoes—funny I should remember that—and I’d eaten not long before. Nothing fancy, just—food that fit my stomach. And there was a good dog; Bruno, a Bull Terrier, laying right at my feet. And that part—that part was not bullocks. That part—well, it’s what I should have been writing about, isn’t it?”

He looked at me somberly, lucidly. “You’re here for the bunker ... aren’t you?”

I just nodded, slowly, firmly.

“And if I don’t freely give it, I suppose you’ll take it—isn’t that about right? That about it?”

I nodded again, slowly.

He looked at the dead; at the allosaur and the Smilodon, which must have been some sort of pet, and poor Sam, with one foot sticking out of her tarp.

“Is this all of you? Just you five? There’s no women? No kids?”

“There’s 28—27—of us ... in total,” I said. “Got a settlement in Issaquah ... that’s in Washington State, at an old drive-in theater. It’s been good, but ... we’re running out of things. Out of supplies. And it’s getting harder and harder to make excursions into the city, into Seattle. It, ah, it gets more treacherous every day. We ... we've lost a lot of good people."

He seemed to think about that, scratching at his stubble. He leaned forward abruptly. "There's food enough here to last a decade," he said, conspiratorially. "Maybe longer. Not to mention the hydroponics, and a modest medical facility. *There's even a bowling alley.*"

"We'd love to see it," I said. I looked at Sam. "But I don't want to leave her like that. Do you have a shovel—or a spade? Maybe some blankets? Or a pillow?"

He reached up and gripped my shoulder—the dude was definitely short—gave it a little shake.

"Son, we'll give your friend all the honors she deserves, and more, or my name isn't Hugo Eagleton." He slapped my arm harder than was necessary. "You just follow old Uncle Hugo to the shed."

And then we went, Lazaro, Nigel, Mr. Fantastic, Roman, and I, through the orange breezeway and into the back yard—which was populated with stone beasts—into his private world; which he'd decided to share.

Needed to share, I'm certain.

FLASHBACK TWILIGHT (2018)

I

<The abandoned drive-in, we'll hide there. Move your ass, Will. They're right behind us.>

Williams gazed down the long, overgrown slope at what had once been the East Mirabeau Drive-in Theater. "That's a pretty steep decline, Ank. You sure you can handle it?"

He was doing it again. Responding to the imaginary voice.

The armored dinosaur examined the slope, flies buzzing about his eyes. *<The gear on my back might slow me, but I can do it. Just don't walk in front of me, in case I lose my footing. Hurry ... we're sitting ducks out here in the open.>*

Williams gripped his rifle and looked behind them: Sure enough, the marauders were coming, the wheels of their trucks and ATVs and motorcycles kicking up great plumes of dust as they motored across the plain. He quickly joined Ank who was already descending, his great hooves sinking into the earth like anvils, the water containers and camping gear and boxes of ammo strapped to his shell sloshing and clanking.

"Those prints are going to be a problem," said Williams, falling back to rub them out.

Your sanity is going to be a problem, he thought to himself, *if you keep this lunacy up.*

<Never mind them. It won't take them long to figure out where we went. We'll lose them in the tall grass when we reach the bottom—I'll hide behind the snack bar while you ascend my back to the roof. With luck, you'll be able to pick them off from there.

"Good plan ... even if I do say so myself."

<You didn't say so yourself. Now is not the time for this!>

"It's been the time for this since I started hearing your voice in my head. My voice, I mean. I mean—"

<Later, Will. We're almost there. You should climb onto my back now and start gathering up your ammo.>

"Yes, sir, Mr. talking dinosaur!" He ascended Ank's tail using its spikes for hand grips until he'd gained the crest of his shell, then tore open a box of ammo.

<I tell you, a telepathic connection has formed between us—don't ask me how because I don't know myself. And I am no longer merely a dinosaur, in case you haven't noticed. If you listen to nothing else I say, listen to that. These continued attempts at self-deception serve no one and will only hinder our search for—"

"What? What are we searching for, Ank?" His frustration with himself and the situation had begun to boil over at last.

<You know as well as I do what we're searching for.>

Williams sighed, giving into the hallucination and its comforts as he had done so many times before. "Yes, I know. We're searching for Tanelorn, where my great lost love awaits and they'll be fields of green, supple plants for you to eat and all this, this Flashback, will be explained. I know, Ank. I haven't forgotten. It's just easier to believe sometimes than others."

A shot rang out suddenly and Williams jolted as the bullet ricocheted off Ank's armor. He peered at the top of the hill. The marauders had arrived and dismounted their vehicles, and were even now sighting them with an array of rifles and pistols. There was a pronounced *crack! ka-crack!* as more rounds bounced off Ank's shell.

<Climb forward onto my head, you'll be protected beneath the lip of my armor. Hurry!>

He did so, rolling onto the beast's great, horned skull and coming up firing, his elbows resting on the edge of the shell. *Crack! (Ka-chink). Crack! (Ka-chink).*

The marauders began to fall as he pumped and fired again and again.

And then they were down and into the towering overgrowth, and Williams thought he saw a were- raptor flit past before a hail of gunfire forced him to crouch lower beneath the shell.

"We're not alone here, Ank. Were-raptors, two o'clock." He could tell by their unmistakable pale coloring. He pumped and fired as one of the marauders clutched his chest and tumbled down the slope. "How close are we?"

<We're almost there now. Don't shoot the raptors, whatever you do. If they were after us, we'd already know it.>

Williams jerked his head left and right as the predators began pouring past them on both sides, snarling and gnashing their teeth. And then they were there, they were behind the snack bar, which was dilapidated and covered in creeper-vines, and he scrambled over Ank's shell and dove onto its roof.

<The marauders only! The raptors will do most the work.>

Williams shimmied forward on his elbows and braced his rifle against the building's cornice. The brigands were working their way down the slope, completely ignorant of what was coming—until the raptors began leaping from the overgrowth and knocking them down, tearing out their throats, gutting them with their sickle-claws.

"They'll come for us when they've finished," shouted Williams, scrambling to his feet. "What's the plan?"

He skittered to a stop at the edge of the building and saw Ank preparing to strike the rear wall with his club tail.

"Is that a good—"

But it was too late, and the cinderblock wall collapsed at the impact as though it had been struck by a wrecking ball, after which Ank lifted his tail so that Williams could climb on and lowered him to the ground.

Williams peered into the gaping hole. The '50s-themed interior was mostly intact, it would make a good campsite if they could find a way to stop up the ingress. He moved forward, stepping over the rubble, his rifle at the ready. Ank lumbered in after him, the spikes of his shell scraping the edges of the hole and making it still wider.

"The pizza oven," he said, scanning the kitchen. "And that refrigerator. What do you think?"

Ank looked at the big, commercial appliances, a bass grumble rattling his throat. *<I'll take care of it. Check out the rest of the building. Make sure there's no compies or prehistoric centipedes or ... God knows.>*

There was a crash upstairs followed by a scratchy shuffling and Williams froze, staring at the ceiling.

"God knows there's someone or something up there."

<Go check it—>

"Don't say it," snapped Williams, and pointed at him. "I'm not going to be bossed around by a figment of my imagination. And so long as I've got even a little sanity left, that's exactly what you'll remain."

Ank only stared at him, his big, dark eyes impossible to read.

"Now move this ... this shit, and I'll be right back."

And then he was shuffling up the stairs—and the only sounds were those of the marauders screaming as the raptors tore them limb from limb; and the rumble of storm clouds as they collided high above.

Good Lord, what a mess, he thought, easing open the door to the projection room as the smell of decomposing flesh assailed his nostrils. *What on earth happened—*

But he knew what had happened, just as he now knew what had happened to the rest of the world (despite having no memory of who he was or where he was from). The projectionist had been going about his life when a storm-front full of strange lights had rolled in and changed the rules of reality forever—scrambling time so that three quarters of the population had simply vanished, and causing prehistoric animals and plants to begin materializing out of nowhere. And now all that was left of him was a rotting husk with only half its arms and legs, wedged into the corner of the blood-splashed and overgrown room (although the blood had long since dried), and seeming almost to twitch—which was impossible, of course. For if there was one thing Williams was sure of, it was that the projectionist was, in fact, dead, and so would not be returning as a were-raptor or anything else.

Were-raptors, he thought, and chuckled bitterly to himself. *Time storms. A fucking talking ankylosaur ...*

He had turned to go back downstairs, realizing, for the thousandth time, that his eyes, like his ears—indeed, his very thoughts—could no longer be trusted, when there was a sudden squelching sound followed by a snippet of music—AC/DC, to be exact, although he didn't know how he could know that—which stabbed at the air briefly before reducing in volume quickly and vanishing altogether.

He whipped back around, rifle at the ready, as the corpse twitched again—this time noticing something he had utterly missed the first time: a child's shoe, filthy white with pink laces, protruding from beneath the stiff, dead form. A shoe which *moved* as he watched, attempting to conceal itself.

Someone was hiding beneath the body. A child—*or a midget,* he thought insanely, and lowered his rifle. The wind gusted and the blinds of a nearby window rattled. At last he said, "It's okay. I'm not going to hurt you." Flies buzzed about the dead man in the near total silence. "But hiding beneath a corpse is no place for a child, do you understand? You could get very, very sick. I'm sure your parents wouldn't want that."

What the hell are you even saying? he reprimanded himself, not knowing if he'd been a parent in his previous life but fairly certain he had not. And this voice was joined by another, a merciless, pragmatic voice, which whispered: *There's still time. It's not too late. Time to pretend you haven't seen this. Time to leave this place and its potential burdens as far behind as you can.*

"You'll take my radio," came a little girl's voice, stunning him somewhat, for it was the first human voice he had heard since Devil's Gorge and the western theme park turned survival compound. "The last grownups I saw wanted it too, but I got away from them. And my parents are dead; I seen them killed myself."

A radio, he thought. *Holy mother of God, a radio!* He thought of the snippet of AC/DC he'd heard. *And a signal!* Someone, somewhere, was broadcasting. And that meant power, electricity, lights. It might even mean an entire city had survived.

"I would like to listen to your radio, I confess," he said, trying not to sound too eager or overly interested, "but I would never take it from you, do you understand? I presume you found it amidst the rubble ... that makes it yours, and yours only."

He lowered his rifle. "My name is Williams. I have a friend downstairs I'd like you to meet—his name is Ank." He watched the corpse, listening, but there was no movement and no response. "Do you have a name?"

The wind moaned forlornly and the blinds rattled again. At last she said, "Luna. Because my hair is white."

"Luna ..." He smiled in spite of himself—in spite of the situation. "Because your hair is white." He took a tentative step forward and paused. "May I see it? I've never seen a little girl with white hair."

There was a brief silence. "You promise you won't take my radio?"

"Promise and hope to die," he said, and gently moved the rest of the way to her.

The corpse shifted slightly and the filthy white tennis shoe reappeared. Then she began pushing outward and upward and he quickly laid down his rifle and began assisting—until the body had been rolled over completely and he could see her in her entirety.

The first thing he noticed were her extraordinarily light violet (almost pink) eyes, which stared out from their dark recesses with an eerily penetrative gaze. The second was that, beyond them, she had no pigment whatsoever: her skin, her eyelashes, her brows—all were white. And the third was that she appeared dreadfully malnourished and was filthy from head to toe, like a porcelain teacup left out in the elements too long.

But it was the eyes that held him, haunted him, for they were the eyes of an old woman trapped in the face of a child.

"I'm an albean, albin—albino," she stammered, as though apologizing in advance. "Do you still want to introduce me to your friend?"

"Why yes, I do, very much," he said, even as his eyes dropped to her radio, which was red and had a large hand-crank.

She pressed it to her chest possessively, crossing her arms.

"Yours," he repeated. "And yours only. Promise."

She seemed to think about this, eyeing him uncertainly. At last she said, "Can your friend come up here? There's blood roosters down there."

He plucked the hair away from her eyes gently. "They're called raptors. And no, he can't, he's too big." He picked up his rifle and stood, swinging it by its loop lever and cocking it. "But don't worry. Raptors—blood roosters—are our specialty."

The first thing she did upon seeing Ank at the bottom of the stairs was to scream, nor was it just any scream, but the kind which could only come from a particularly agitated little boy or girl—the kind that bore through one's skull like a long, thin drill bit. Then she promptly scurried back up the steps and cowered behind the wall, shaking her head and saying, "No dinosaur, no dinosaur."

"Luna, it's okay," stressed Williams. "He isn't going to hurt you. His name is Ank. He—he doesn't eat people. Especially little girls. Isn't that right, Ank?"

Ank merely looked at him from beneath his horny brows. *Yet. I haven't eaten anyone yet, Will. What is this?*

Williams straightened somewhat awkwardly and gestured at Luna to come down. "Well, I ... This is Luna." He looked back and forth between the two. "Luna, because her hair is white. Luna ... meet Ank."

"Who are you talking to?" she asked. "I can't hear anything."

Ank snorted. *‹Because I'm a figment of his imagination.›*

Williams was temporarily at a loss. "No, I guess you wouldn't ... would you?" *Of course she wouldn't,* he thought. *Because in spite of what she's been through, she hasn't gone stark, raving mad, like you.*

"Let's just say that Ank can communicate with me without actually speaking, and that he can understand what you say to him." He gestured for her to come again. "Luna, come here! He's not going to hurt you. I promise. Show him your radio."

She descended the steps tentatively and held out the device, and Williams couldn't help but to notice that her entire body was trembling. "That's it, that's a good girl," he cajoled, then pointed at one of her hands and raised his brows as if to ask, May I?—before taking it in his own and guiding it to Ank's snout, which she began to stroke slowly, cautiously.

‹Is this really necessary? Just tell me about the radio. Does it work?›

"I'm getting to that." And to Luna Williams said, "Your radio. Can you play it for us? We—we've been travelling for a long time, and we miss the sound of other voices. Would you mind?"

She didn't respond right away but only continued to stroke Ank, who's stony texture seemed to fascinate her endlessly. At length she said, "Okay," and turned one of its dials, and the room was immediately filled with the slightly raspy voice of a woman, who continued, "... if you're heading our way through Shadow Canyon, following that beautiful river, perhaps, be advised there's a pair of allosaurs operating in that area we call Lenny and Squiggy, and stay alert. And while we'd prefer you didn't kill them if in fact you are armed, we wouldn't recommend you get too friendly with them either. Once again this is Radio Free Montana, nestled just south of Paradise at Barley's Hot Springs Resort, where we've got power, lights, food, and about three-hundred survivors who'd love nothing more than to meet you. But be advised as always: if you're a marauder or a carpetbagger, you won't like what we've prepared for you. So take a little advice from Bella Ray and don't even try it. And on that it's another round of AC/DC ... for those struggling to get here even now, we salute you!"

It would have been difficult to overestimate the swelling in Williams' chest as he looked to Ank and the armored dinosaur looked right back, for both of them sensed that this could be the destination they'd searched for—Tanelorn, as they called it. The place where both of them might find comfort and possibly even some answers to the riddles they each embodied.

"My God, Ank," Williams stammered. "Do you think—"

<I think it's the best lead we've had since coming north ... and that a bath in a hot spring would be divine beyond, well, my ability to imagine. Regardless, there's the girl to think about ...>

"Yes, we could drop her off there if nothing—"

"You're crazy, aren't you?"

Williams came out of his thoughts as if from a dream and just looked at her. At Luna. Because her hair was white. "Maybe," he offered, and then winked. "And you're an albino. So what's your point? If you ask me, I'd say a crazy man, an albino, and an ankylosaur make a pretty good team."

She looked at him a little quizzically, as though unsure whether he was having her on or not. And then she just grinned infectiously, and Williams knew she'd accepted it—as he had finally accepted it: Ank as a possible talking reality, the Flashback, all of it. And then the spell was broken by a voice both familiar and alien, a voice which was human and at the same time serpentine, a voice which called out amidst the brewing storm: "Come out, Williams!"—and was instantly joined by another, which chimed in, parrot-like, "Yes, come out!" And another: "Eggsucker! Pig-fucker!"

And they knew the were-raptors had zeroed in on them at last.

"Those I can hear," said Luna—and began retreating up the stairs again. "They only talk when they're about to attack."

Williams, meanwhile, had focused on Ank. "Jesus ... it called me by name."

Ank stared at him from beneath his brow. *<A survivor of Devil's Gorge, maybe?>*

Williams nodded slowly. "But how in God's name? The only one who knew our names was ... Unless—"

<Unless the town was attacked by another pack of were-raptors after we left. Which would mean those outside could be anyone—Sheriff Decker, Katrina ...>

Williams misted up as he thought of the saloon girl who had shown him such affection. "I won't shoot them, then."

<Now listen, Will. Don't let your personal feelings—>

"I said I won't shoot them," he snapped, and turned toward Luna, who was cowering at the top of the stairs. "We'll have to find another way." To Luna he said: "It's all right, sweetie. Everything's going to be all right."

<Dammit, Will, I can't handle an entire pack on my own, and you know it. Now are we serious about making it to Tanelorn, or at least Barley's, or not? Or have all our plans changed because a saloon girl threw a leg up on you in a town we will never see again?>

"Meh," Williams sighed angrily and moved toward the building's front windows, which Ank had blocked with pinball machines and video games, with only partial success.

<Don't walk away from me when I'm talking to you, dammit!> He lumbered after him, the tiled floor cracking beneath his elephantine feet. *<We made a pact. And what about the girl? Would you see her torn to pieces by those things while you simply watched?>*

"Go away!" Williams hissed. He peeked around one of the machines and saw the raptors lined up in the gathering dark, waiting to make their move, waiting to rush the snack bar and overwhelm them, waiting to kill them or, worse, to turn them into creatures like themselves.

"Are you talking to me?" whined the girl, her voice seeming to bleed as if cut by invisible knives. "Why would you want me to go away all of a sudden?"

"No—that's not what I meant—I ..."

<*I can't do it, Will. They'll swarm in beneath my armor and ... they'll tear me to pieces.*>

Williams held up his rifle—pressed his forehead against it.

<*We need your magic with that gun, Will. I need it. And if you don't step up I'm going to have to ... and, I won't make it. Not this time.*>

"Come out, Williams!"

"Yes, my love, come out!" A new voice. *Her* voice. Katrina.

Williams squeezed his eyes shut.

And then they were coming, he could hear their growls and the tapping of their awful sickle-claws against the cracked and broken pavement, and Ank was charging past him, breaking through the windows and walls, roaring defiantly, and when Williams looked up he saw the dinosaurs collide like thunderheads, heard Luna scream her piercing, drill bit scream, and knew they'd never make it to Barley, to say nothing of Tanelorn.

II

"Dammit, just dammit," Williams cursed as he gripped his rifle and scrambled over the rubble toward the battling dinosaurs, then shouted over his shoulder, "Luna, take cover!"

And then he was sighting were-raptors with non-lethal precision (even as the thunderheads collided and the sky boomed and the rain came down in merciless torrents), targeting them in their legs, their thighs, their tails: fearing with each squeeze of the trigger that he might inadvertently strike a killing blow; that he might destroy the very people who had shown him such kindness, that he might murder the woman with whom he'd formed such a powerful and inexplicable bond—worse, that he might wound or even kill Ank.

He zeroed in on the thigh of one of the animals that had gotten too close to Ank's unprotected underbelly, a thigh that looked like so much uncooked chicken, and fired, blasting a hole the size of a teacup in it ... and causing the creature to drop instantly and to scramble away. *Was that you, Katrina?* he thought as he cocked and sighted another—this time the head of a raptor trying to close its jaws about Ank's neck. He fired and its skull blew apart. *Was that you?*

Ank, for his part, was putting up one hell of a fight: clubbing one of the beasts with his tail and sending it flying, ramming another with his horns so that it was crushed against a rusted and overgrown automobile. But Williams' presence had not gone unremarked, and he shuffled backward as several raptors, four, to be exact, broke from the pack, and began stalking toward *him*—for they were pure raptors only in form, and the parts of them that were human understood guns and bullets full well. He cocked and fired almost instinctively as the animals approached, hitting one in its shank so that it fell like a sack of potatoes and began crawling away through the rain, then, just as the rest were preparing to leap forward all at once, he shouted, "The next shots will be kill-shots—one for each of you—if you don't break off your attack. You know I can do it."

The animals paused ... tapping their sickle-claws, cocking their heads. At last one of them said, in a perversion of Katrina's voice: "But you won't do it—how can you? We are your friends, remember?"

And another, also in Katrina's voice: "Why don't you join us?"

And still another: "Yes, join us!"

Williams hesitated. One of them was Katrina, but which one?

And then they were leaping, all three of them, and he cocked and fired twice, debilitating two of them instantly with non-lethal blows while delivering a shattering kill-shot to the third—even as it knocked him to the ground and pinned him there beneath its hemorrhaging dead weight. And such was the force of the impact that he dropped his rifle and found himself gripping the creature's snout—a snout he knew could morph back into a human face at any instant—Decker's face, *her* face. And he shoved it off with a violence that shocked him—even as Ank cried out in pain and he looked to see a final raptor attaching itself to his friend's exposed neck, just beneath the armored plating, and fired from where he lay.

And then the thing dropped and it was over, and neither Ank nor Williams could do anything but to try and catch their breath as the surviving raptors fled and the storm slowly subsided.

‹Thanks, Will. I—I really appreciate that. I ... understand how conflicted you must have been.› He exhaled heavily. *‹But, the ones you spared, they'll be back. You know how fast they heal.›*

Williams only nodded, staring at the corpse at his feet, which had finished reverting to its human form.

"Decker," he said.

Ank looked down at the body nearest him. *‹I don't know who this is. It doesn't matter anyway. Where's the girl?›*

Williams stirred as if from a trance and hurried back to the snack bar, Ank loping after him, where they found Luna standing straight as a board amidst what was now essentially a ruin—her violet eyes empty and eerily glazed over, and still staring at where the battle had taken place.

"You smell that?" Williams asked Ank. He waved a hand in front of her face.

<Affirmative. Smells like smoke. Or something on fire.>

They looked around; nothing was on fire. Williams kneeled before her and gently rubbed her shoulder. When at last she began to come out of it he asked, "What were you seeing just now? Can you tell us?"

"I was ... thinking about something I killed once. An ant. His name was Fred. He was my friend ... but I burned him all up."

Williams moved to speak but hesitated—it wasn't just because he was both charmed and disturbed by her words. No, an image had come into his mind with a vividness that was startling: an image of a black ant crawling beneath the thick lens of a magnifying glass—a lens in which he discerned the reflection of a boy—and which had been positioned so that it caught the sun and focused its rays upon the insect, which caught fire and curled upon itself and was immolated as the boy watched. Then it was gone and he was left, despite the cruelness of the act, with a distinct feeling of euphoria. For the boy, he knew, was himself.

"Ank ..." He turned to face the ankylosaur incredulously. "I—just had a memory. I'm sure of it."

Ank regarded him from beneath his bony brow. *<Maybe you should tell me about it. Quickly, before you forget.>*

He told him about it. At last the dinosaur communicated, *<It isn't much, is it? But it is something. By God, it's something. Hold onto it, Will. Hold onto it as though your life depended upon it. It just may.>*

"I will, I promise," he said, and ruffled Luna's hair. "As for you: you burned an insect with a magnifying glass, I think." He stood and patted her shoulder. "We all did. It's like, a rite of passage. Doesn't make you Hitler."

He paused, looking at Ank. "How do I know that? Old books, historical figures ..."

<I told you. We can both remember the world, just not who we were, not before the Flashback. Please don't overthink things.>

"You talk to yourself a *lot,* don't you?" said Luna.

Williams looked at her and finally smiled in spite of himself. "Or it just may be that he's really talking to me, and you just can't hear it." He tweaked her nose. "Yet. Either way, you need to eat something and get some sleep. We all do. We've got a big day ahead of us tomorrow."

"Why a big day?"

"Ank, camping gear," he said, and the dinosaur folded his front legs with a groan. "Because we're going to head out for Barley's in the morning." He loosed his bedroll from the supplies strapped to Ank's back and tossed it to her. "The place where the sounds on your radio come from. We've—we're searching for something. A place we call Tanelorn. And we think that might be it."

"Tanelorn," she repeated. "What's that?"

Williams rested his arms on the bundles of supplies, thinking about it. "I don't know, exactly. I reckon it's just a place someone feels drawn to ... even if they don't know why. A place where the homeless can find a home, maybe." He looked at the lights in the sky, the Alien Borealis, as Ank called it, and wondered. "But it may be that it's something else—a kind of Omega Point. A place where all the colors of the spectrum meet, like a prism. And become focused into a single, burning light. Maybe that's what people mean when they talk about the power and the glory." He tugged on a rope, releasing a waterfall of pots and pans. "Meh. It's just something to keep us going."

"Like a magnifying glass," she said, ignoring his last statement.

He paused, thinking about it. "Like a magnifying glass," he agreed. Then he added, "Now, what'll it be? Beans or beans?"

Williams spread the map out in the sun as Ank and Luna looked over his shoulder. "Here's where we're at." He tapped the map as the shadow of a pterodactyl passed over it, then another. "Montana Highway 200, at Mirabeau Park. We were taking it to Spokane instead of the more obvious Interstate 90 for one simple reason, even though we'd have to double back ..." He indicated a winding blue line. "The Clark Fork, which runs its entire length—clean water being job one, always. Now, if we diverge here, and take 382, we can cut across the Camas Prairie—badlands, essentially—and hook up with 28. Here." He tapped the map again. "Then it's clear sailing all the way to Niarada—there's even a reservoir, here, at Dry Lake, in case we don't find any running water in Benton or Lonepine." He took off his hat and wiped his brow. "After that it would be back into what amounts to badlands, but with no road to guide us, all the way to Barley's—for a total distance of, I'm going to say 80 miles."

"What's this?" asked Luna, and pointed.

"It says Shadow Canyon. And look here, see? A river runs through it, the Santiago. So, more water. The only problem I can see is that we'll have to ford it."

<I'm not an amphibious vehicle, Will. I'd direct you to the last time we tried that.>

"The last time we tried that was with a bigger river. This looks like little more than a creek. Besides, we'll need the water after crossing the badlands. And look here, see, Barley's is right on the other side."

"I can't swim," said Luna.

"You can ride on Ank's back," said Williams, and stood. He redonned his hat. "As for travel time, well, that's anyone's guess. There's three of us now," He ruffled Luna's hair. "One with short legs."

She beamed up at him.

<We usually do about 20 miles a day,> communicated Ank, *<With the girl, we'll be lucky to get ten. Could take a week. And we'll be going through more food and water. You sure this is a good idea?>*

"No," said Williams. "But it's the only one I got.

<And there's another thing. The radio broadcast said there's a pair of allosaurs working the area—or did you forget that? There's limits to what I can do, Will. And there's a limit to what you can achieve with that rifle, especially with ammunition running low. Allosaurs are nothing to trifle with.>

Williams patted the air as if to say, *When we get there, Ank. When we get there.* "For now, let's get some food in her. And in us too." He turned to Luna. "So what'll it be? Potatoes or potatoes?"

"Potatoes!"

"Potatoes it is," he said.

And then a cry rang out that made them all freeze, for it was the cry of a were-raptor, just as clear as day, nor was it particularly far away. And it was followed by a shriek—a human shriek, a woman's shriek.

Katrina.

"This is Radio Free Montana, coming at you from the soothing, steaming pools of Barley's Hot Springs Resort just south of Paradise, and I've got another string of hits just raring to go—plus some travel tips and advisories for all you nomads still working your way through the Big Not-So-Easy ..."

Williams looked around for Luna and her radio and quickly realized she had fallen behind yet again; nor was it her fault, he was walking too fast, as always. "Sorry," he said, and cooled his pace. He added: "Can you turn that up, please?"

She did so, hustling to catch up. The announcer continued: "But first we're going to check in with Felix the Fixed-wing Wonder, who's airborne and on the air and milking those extra fuel tanks for all they're worth, as he tracks a herd of brachiosaurs near beautiful Billings, Montana. What say you, Felix? Are they playing nice like normal herbivores, or are they showing signs of having been touched by the lights?"

"Jesus, Ank, are you listening? An airplane!"

<I'm not particularly surprised. You'll remember the helicopter we saw over Pocatello.>

"Yeah. The bastard that swung back around as I waved—then high-tailed it out of there just as fast as he could. I remember." He listened to the radio:

"Seem pretty harmless to me, Bella. Just your normal herd of migrating sauropods, probably heading for the ponds around Eastlake. Still, all the usual warnings apply. I'm going to swing around Billings and check for survivors ..."

"Roger that, Felix. As always, fly careful. You're not alone up there. And while we're on the subject, a word of advice for those in vehicles using sauropod herds for cover: It's not a good idea. At 62 tons, it only takes a single step for you to have a really bad day—whether they've got the blood fever or not. And on that, it's back to the music, and another ditty for all you weary travelers trying to get here even now. It's Roger Miller, and "King of the Road," on KKRP Radio Free Montana ..."

Trailers for sale or rent, rooms to let, fifty cents ...

Williams looked at the sky, a sky completely devoid of contrails, fancying what a would-be pilot might think if he were to look down and see them now: an ankylosaur whose great armored back was laden with supplies, a man in a poncho and wide-brimmed hat, and a little girl as white as the sun, all of them traipsing along secondary highway 382 as though they hadn't a care in the world. And he wondered what they would find when they finally arrived at Barley's—a welcoming family of friends at last, or a hardened clic of distrustful survivors, as had initially been the case at Devil's Gorge—and he wondered, too, at his own sense of contentedness, for it was days like today, when he had someone to talk to and a clear destination in mind, that he felt he could handle anything. That, in the end, the universe would simply unfold as it should. And for just now, just this one, small moment, that was good enough.

I'm a man of means, by no means, king of the road ...

The campfire crackled and popped—something Williams normally would have found soothing after a long day on the road. But now its loudness and intensity only reminded him that the radio had gone silent around noon and had been broadcasting dead air ever since. He tried to assure himself that this was normal and to be expected: the station couldn't have been more than a make-do operation; surely it would crackle back to life when they least expected it—probably in the middle of the night after they'd just gotten to sleep. Still, it *was* peculiar, and Ank himself had expressed his concern more than once, something he did again as Williams lay with his head propped up, watching Luna watch the fire (from a good distance away), and wondering what she might see in it that she could simply stare into it for such a lengthy period of time.

<Maybe they switched frequencies. It's unlikely, I know. But a search of the dial couldn't hurt.>

Williams looked from her colorless face to the bright, red radio, which she held clasped to her chest like a teddy bear, and shook his head. "I made her a promise that the radio would remain hers and hers alone. I think she'd view my manhandling it like that as a breach of trust. It can wait, Ank. We'll know what the situation is soon enough." He continued looking at her, noting for the first time that there were tears crusting her cheeks and that her mouth was moving slightly, almost as if she were whispering to the fire. "What's wrong with her, you think?"

<Hard to say. Post-traumatic stress, maybe. Didn't you say she was a witness to her parents' death?>

"Yes," said Williams, then shook his head. "And no. No, this—seems like something predating that. Something she was born with. Whatever it is, it weighs on her. P.T.S.D.? Maybe. But from something other than her parents' death." He laid his head back against one of Ank's folded legs and nudged his hat down. "Meh, beats the hell out of me."

The fire crackled and popped but otherwise the world was silent.

At length he said, "But I know this. We've got to get her to Barley's. It's weird, I know. But I haven't felt so certain of something since we first headed north. It's important, somehow. It's necessary."

Neither of them spoke for what seemed a long time, and it wasn't until Williams was nearly asleep that Ank communicated, simply and succinctly: *<I feel it too.>*

And then they both slept, even as Luna laid down and finally did likewise.

He awakened suddenly, having dreamed—or thought he dreamed—of footsteps and breaking branches. A scan of the camp revealed nothing amiss: a smoldering fire, the clutter of dinner, Luna curled up in her sleeping bag. And yet—

He heard it again, not in dream—the breaking of branches, the shuffling of steps—and sat up with a start. He listened intently: something was moving through the scrub beyond the camp. He reached for his rifle instinctively (thankful he had cleaned and loaded it before supper) and eased the blanket from his legs, then nudged Ank.

"Ank, hey, *pssst.*"There was no response.

He stood slowly, gripping the rifle in both hands, peering into the blackness. Ank's words from the previous night had not gone far: *The ones you spared, they'll be back. You know how fast they heal.*

He moved into the dark carefully, wondering if it was just one were-raptor or the entire pack; wondering if he could do what finally needed to be done. For he was responsible now—not just for Ank and himself but for the girl; for delivering her to Barley's and her ultimate safety. And for something else he was only just beginning to divine.

And then he came face to face with the maker of the sounds—and the boy, who could have been no more than eight, froze like a statue, his eyes wide and wet, his skinny legs trembling, before dropping his gathered sticks and bolting into the night.

"Hey, wait ...!" Williams shouted, and promptly pursued, dashing through the sagebrush, acting without a care, chasing the boy relentlessly until they both burst into a clearing in which another campfire burned and a battered police car sat with its hood propped up—at which instant a woman barked, "Freeze! Drop it!" and he trained his rifle upon her ... only to see a revolver pointed directly back at him.

III

"Who are you? What do you want?" she snapped, and shuffled forward a step. "I'll fire this thing, don't think I won't!"

Williams didn't budge, only continued to sight her. "Yes, I believe you would ... if you had to. But you don't have to. I—I heard the boy foraging ... it woke me up. I wanted to tell him he had nothing to fear, but he was already gone. I'd suggest just now ... we both lower our weapons. Can you try that for me? Please? I'll start and you follow, okay?"

It was difficult to gage her reaction as he remained focused on her trigger finger. He began to lower his weapon ... and, to his surprise, she began to lower hers as well.

And then there was a *crack, ca-crack!* somewhere in the blackness, and she raised the revolver again, snapping, "What's that? What was that?"

"What's what?"

There was another *crack!*

"That! You're not alone! Tell them to—"

He had barely had the chance to see the blur of Ank's clubbed tail before she was knocked into the air and sent flying to the far side of the clearing, dropping her pistol along the way—which Williams snatched up instantly and tucked inside his pants. "It's okay, Ank!" he shouted as the ankylosaur lumbered toward her, "I've got her weapon. She's just scared ..."

The armored giant ground to a halt and turned to face him. *‹There was a boy also. I saw him by the police car ...›*

"He's my son, Erik," the woman groaned, holding her side, rocking forward and back. "Please don't let him get too far away."

Williams hesitated before shouting, "Erik! We are not going to hurt you! Please, don't wander far. We're going to get this sorted out." He hurried to the boy's mother and kneeled, placing a hand on her back—which she swatted away, causing her to gasp in pain.

"Easy does it," he said, and added: "We're not going to hurt you, you have my word." They locked eyes briefly. "My name is Williams. This here is Ank—"

She started to scramble to her feet and he stilled her with a firm hand. "He's harmless, I assure you. Most the time. He was just trying to protect me—easy now ..."

"Whoever heard of a friendly dinosaur?" she spat, stringy hair hanging in her eyes. "Even the plant-eaters, they'll turn on you like that. Where's my gun?"

"I've got it right here, and you can have it back. *After* we've established a few ground rules. Now, first things first. Like, what's your name?"

"Sheila," she cursed, and groaned. "Sheila Were. We were heading for a place called Barley's—they've been broadcasting ... a welcome message. But I haven't heard anything since—"

"Since about noon, I know," he said. "We've been listening to the same thing." He held out his hand. "Friends?"

She looked at him warily before her expression softened in a rush and she took his hand. "Friends. Now, can we find my son, please?"

"Of course, I'm sure he hasn't—"

More cracks, more shuffling amongst the sage. "Oh, Jesus," Williams mumbled. He loosed the pistol from his waist and handed it to her. "Were-raptors, I think. How many bullets do you have in that thing?"

"All of them," she said. "The car's been our weapon. Were-raptors; what are—"

"*Shhh,* they're coming. Ank?"

<*I'm ready. Let's finish it this time.*>

The rustling intensified. Whatever it was, it was almost there.

"Get ready," said Williams, and sighted the dark.

And Luna emerged, holding Erik's hand with one arm and cradling her radio in the other, and everyone sighed. But their euphoria didn't last long—for it was immediately obvious there was something terribly wrong with her, something rattled, something haunted.

"Something's happened," she said, and sat the radio by the campfire. "I thought you'd better hear it."

She turned up the dial as everyone gathered around:

"... hence the dead-air, and for that I'm sorry."

—Bella Ray, her tone dark, sober, pensive.

"But now you know, and it's up to you to search your hearts and decide what to do next. Once again ... Felix is gone. He was shot down, yes, *shot down,* at approximately 11:45 am, Mountain Daylight Time, near Billings, Montana, during what was a routine broadcast. I'm going to play his last transmission again for those of you just tuning in; you'll want to sit down, all of you. Once more, I'm sorry. Dear God, I am so sorry. This broadcast was my idea, and it seemed like a good one at the time, although we always knew we were rolling the dice. Well, the dice have come up snake eyes, at last." There was an extended silence. "So here it is ..." She sounded as though she were crying. "Take it away, Felix."

There was a burst of static which quickly resolved itself into the pilot's voice. "Coming around ... coming around ... and there it is. Good Lord, Bella—I literally can't see the end of it. Once again: I'm tracking what appears to be a kind of caravan—I'd count the vehicles but there are too many. I'd say a thousand, maybe more, rolling across the plains amidst a cloud of dust, following Interstate 90 but not confined to it. As for Billings, which the tip of the caravan has already passed through, I'll say it again: It appears to be burning. I'm sort of crop-dusting the length of the column now; I'm seeing semi-tractor trailers, motor homes, construction equipment, but mostly military hardware, and not the stuff you see at the Interstate Fair. I'm talking tanks and mobile artillery pieces. Lots and lots of motorcycles. Wait a minute—okay, you're not to believe this, but I'm seeing cages, big ones. They—it's like they're transporting—roger that: count 'em, one, two, three, four; they're literally transporting carnosaurs. T. rexes, allosaurs, a smaller species I haven't seen ... I don't know how many there are, a *lot.* I *still* haven't reached the end of the column. There's troop transports, both covered and uncovered, plus—okay, I've got trouble. Someone's sighting me—" Static exploded, drowning him out. "... a shoulder-fired—" More static. "... he's behind me now ... okay, here it comes, hold on ..."

All of them listened as the plane could be heard straining and shuddering, as though he were attempting a maneuver it clearly wasn't designed for, and then there was what sounded like an explosion, which was followed by dead air.

A few moments passed and none of them said anything.

At last Bella Ray said, "As for us ... we've decided to stay." There was more dead air. "More music after this moment of silence."

Williams stayed kneeled for what seemed a long time. At length he stood and began pacing slowly. And then he began walking, just walking— into the dark, into the sage.

<Will? You all right? Hey—>

He waved a hand in the air. Not now, it said. I need to be alone.

He walked until he came to a brushy rise which overlooked the prairie, which was bathed in moonlight now that the clouds had parted some, and looked out at it in silence. At length he heard movement and turned to see Sheila looking at him in the dark.

"Are you all right?" she asked. She took a step closer and paused.

"I don't know," he said.

The breeze kicked up slightly, blowing her dirty hair sidelong across her face. "I've got to go," she said at last. "I don't know where. Somewhere Erik can be safe."

He turned away and stared out over the plains again. At last he said, softly, "You were heading north before you ever heard the broadcast ... weren't you?"

"Yes. I—I lost my husband and a daughter to the Flashback in a town called Anchor Rock ... a long ways from here. A Sheriff tried to help us ... we lost him too. After that I just—I can't explain it. It's like, when you spend enough time alone, or nearly so ... when the whole world is quiet ... you grow an antenna you never knew you had. Like the land itself is talking to you, trying to tell you something. It's—it's always been talking to you. You just couldn't hear it, not through all the noise. Is that what you mean?"

"Yes," he said. He didn't elaborate.

"Where will you go?" she asked.

The silence was deafening. At last he said, "Come with us."

She laughed, a little too harshly, she felt. But then she had become a harsh person. "To where? To Barley's? No ... absolutely no. They're on their own. I've got a kid to think about. You ... you're not actually going to continue on there. Are you?"

He turned to face her slowly. "There's nowhere else to go. I think you know that. Come with us. You know as well as I do there's nothing back the way we came. You said so yourself, your car's been your primary weapon. What will you do when a pack or raptors or worse finds you on the open plain—kill them all with your six bullets? And what then; what will you do when the bullets run out, when there's not even enough to put your kid out mercifully, much less yourself?"

She moved to slap him and he dropped his rifle and took her in his arms, hugging her almost violently, holding her fast as she resisted, squeezing her tight against him, until at last her efforts subsided and she began squeezing him back, and they stood beneath the moon for what seemed a long time, listening to one another's breaths, feeling each other's hearts, knowing they could no more walk away now than they could go fly to the moon. Knowing that the die was cast and the road was set, and that they'd both been dying since the start of the Flashback, possibly even before, and that whatever lie ahead, it represented, in a very real sense, life itself. Short, brutal, but not a limbo. Not entropy.

Not a vacuum.

And when they returned to the campsite they knew that the others knew, as well. For there was no going back from this point forward, something Ank acknowledged when he said to Williams, <We've always known, even though we

didn't talk about it, that the road to Tanelorn wouldn't be without cost. But I'm glad we're still on the same page. And we are still on the same page, I can feel it, else you would have already said something. Will?>

But he'd already fallen asleep, rolled up in his blanket not far from Sheila, even as the moon shone down and the fire crackled and the radio played Louis Armstrong.

At first there was only the blackness, as silent and total as anything he had ever known.

"He's coming to," said a voice, a female, confident, clearly in charge, adding, "Mind your monitors."

"I've got him," said another, his voice eager, alert. "He's lighting up like a Christmas tree."

"Heart-rate normal, blood pressure good," said another, also female, but younger, less confident.

He stirred against his restraints. Where was he? How long had he been here? He remembered a prison made of flesh and bone; a prison he had lived in for a very long time (but which had been compromised suddenly and violently), as well as a kind of rising ... so that he had found himself looking down upon the body of a man—a very old man—who lay with his face in a small pond in a clearing which was as wide as it was green and verdant. Nor was he alone, for an armored dinosaur stood nearby and drank from the very same pool.

"Cerebellum is active but not overly so, frontal and parietal lobes nominal," said the man.

"And the occipital? The temporal?" —The older woman, her voice full of anticipation.

Ank opened his eyes in time to see the man glance at her and smile. "Occipital and temporal are, as predicted, essentially on fire. Congratulations."

There was a round of applause as Ank drifted back into memory. For the rising had not stopped there, had it? No, it had continued on until he was virtually amongst the clouds—until he had been engulfed in an array of lights the likes of which he had never seen, at least not up close—alien lights, foreign lights. Lights which pulsated and bled in and out of each other and seemed at once both physically alive and utterly abstract. And then he was being lowered, back through the clouds and the blue nothing of the air, back toward the pond and the body and the passively drinking dinosaur, back into a prison of flesh and bone and blood.

"So he's not just some random amalgam of the Flashback," said the older woman. "Not just ..."

Her voice trailed off. Ank looked around the room, at the complicated technical apparatus and the bubbling tanks, recognizing in one what appeared to be the body of a man, a man merged with a small dinosaur ... haphazardly, messily, so that neither could have survived long. A snippet of memory flitted through his mind, an image. It was of a stand of cycad trees with human arms and legs.

It was of two different lifeforms who had been standing in the same place when the Flashback had struck.

He pushed it from his mind, focusing instead on the calm that had come over him when he'd returned to his prison of blood and bone; a prison which was the same but different, which was hardy and robust. A prison which didn't feel like a prison, not yet, but an extension of the world itself—which stood on all fours and breathed slowly and fully and which had nothing on its mind but the sweet taste of the water it was drinking.

"As for what it proves beyond that is anyone's guess," said the woman, sounding suddenly tired. "That they're experimenting on us as well as exterminating us? We don't even know who *they* are, much less what their relationship to the Flashback is. We don't even know if 'they' applies; or if they're just a force of nature, like the weather." She pulled down her mask. "It just feels so pointless sometimes, this whole operation." She shook her head. "I'm sorry. I'll be all right, I just ..."

The man reached out to her and touched her shoulder. "It's been a long day, Maggie. Why don't we just ... retire to the Tiki Tent." He tried to sound optimistic. "There's still enough vegetables for Bloody Marys—I'll be the bartender." He looked at her hopefully.

"Please, *God,*" said the younger woman. "I'm dying here."

Maggie looked back and forth between them and then at him, at Ank. She stroked the side of his snout gently. "So we know now that you're thinking ... we just don't know what. Nor what to do with you."

At last she powered something down and said to the others, "Lisa, can you change out his I.V.? Tom? If you'll get the lights?"

And then they were gone and the room was dark save for the lights of the instruments and the glow of the tanks. And the next day there were two; nor did Ank know where the younger woman had gone other than, "she vanished while she was drinking, may we all be so lucky." And three days later there was one—the man, who trashed a portion of the lab while screaming and talking to himself before stumbling off toward what they called the Tiki Tent ... after which Ank heard a single gunshot.

And then the days and nights became one as he lay paralyzed by the steel restraints, the I.V. no longer providing sustenance, the room sprouting cycad trees and creeper vines and mossy growths, the air becoming stale. And it was as he lay dying that a man in a black coat and carrying a guitar case emerged one day and began foraging amongst the ruins, a man as pale and gaunt as a ghost, a man who, finding a bottle of liquor and some cigars in the Tiki Tent, sat down next to his head and decided to have himself a little fiesta, and to talk to himself, and to him, as he did so.

A man who released him from his restraints and brought him some shrubs from outside and plied him with water from a plastic tub until he was strong enough to walk again.

A man whom Ank followed when at last he left, and who, by the time they'd come to the Old West-themed resort turned survival compound—Devil's Gorge—he had formed an unmistakable bond with. A man the dinosaur had come to love.

A man who was not there when Ank at last awoke from dream.

<Will? Is that you?>

He'd heard laughing and what for all the world sounded like water splashing. Now he was investigating with two children in tow, and when he crested the rise of a scrub-covered berm to find Will and Sheila frolicking in a largish water hole, he was quite frankly annoyed. <I'm not going to play babysitter for you two, Will. Bringing along the girl was your idea. Plus there's the boy, and if his mother won't—>

"Ank! Ank, buddy, can you believe it? A water trap!" He splashed Sheila back playfully. "It was just sitting here all along. We were both camped right next to it."

Ank looked at their clothes, which they'd laid out across several scraggly bushes. <You might want to tell Miss Wonderful there to cover up. Her son's here. And you ... Jesus, do I need to see this? Now come on. We've got a lot of miles to cover.>

Williams just looked at him, suddenly sobered. "What's gotten into you? You sleep on the wrong side of your shell? It's fresh water. And cold!" He looked at Sheila. "Let's get out of here and let the kids come in one at a time."

She looked back at him, clearly smitten.

<Dear God, not again. I would remind you that your one, true love supposedly resides in Tanelorn, about 80 miles from here. I would also remind you that there's a whole lot of hell heading its way. Now I don't know about you but I'd like to actually see it before it gets raised to the ground. Besides, the kids need breakfast, or does your submerged hard-on not care about that?>

Williams paused, looking down into the water. "It's no longer an issue, Ank. Don't worry about it. Fine. Take the kids back to camp and we'll ..." He glanced at Sheila. "We'll get dressed."

<And I suppose I'll just tell them to!>

"Kids, go with Ank. You can come in after breakfast."

"Ah, but I want to come in now!" shouted Erik.

"After breakfast," said Sheila curtly. "You heard the man."

<Jesus, gods, please!> Ank turned around and headed for the campsite, and, to his surprise, the children followed.

It was fortuitous timing. For Bella Ray was back on the air. And she sounded positively terrified.

IV

As it turned out, Bella Ray sounded so frightened because it was a replay of the previous night's broadcast. And so after a breakfast of pemmican and beans—and after Erik had cannonballed into the reservoir while Luna demurred—they set out, continuing along Montana Highway 382 until it connected with Highway 28, where the landscape turned green again but also more primordial, more prehistoric. It was funny and impossible, how the geography of the world had been affected by the Flashback—randomly, inconsistently, so that one region might appear virtually unchanged while another teemed with landforms not seen since the Jurassic—frightening too, for it was amongst the latter that the danger level was always the highest. But it was not a dinosaur that appeared in the hazy distance and brought them to a near standstill on the overgrown side of the road—it was a jet airliner: its fuselage covered in creeper vines and metastatic patches of lichen, its great nose angled into the earth in what must have been a violent crash landing, its wings shattered and broken.

"I'm seeing it, but I'm not sure I'm believing it," said Sheila, as her pace slowed to a crawl and she checked for Erik's whereabouts, who was lagging as usual, just sort of lost in his own world. "Hey, buddy. We're up here. Come join the party."

"I'm seeing it too," said Williams. "Ank?"

Sheila looked at him, concerned, nor was it for the first time.

<*I see it. And I'm seeing something else. Phorusrhacos. Terror birds. Three of them. Looks like they've got someone cornered.*>

Now wasn't the time to ask him how he knew that, nor why a herbivore should have such sharp vision, much less teeth.

"Jesus—are there still survivors?"

Ank peered into the distance. *<Only one that I can see. Middle-aged white male, holding some kind of spear. Wait— there's a female, she just emerged from the wreckage. But ... the fuselage ... it's broken in half. They're wide open, Will.>*

"Sheila, stay with the kids," said Williams. He swung his rifle by its ring lever so that it snapped to at the ready. "We're gonna get them out."

"Wait, get *who* out? And who's 'we?' You and the dinosaur?"

"They talk to each other," said Luna. "Or at least he talks to Ank."

Sheila paused, taken aback. "Whatever," she said. "I'm not staying here alone. And I'm not leaving Erik here alone. Nor you," she added, and glanced at Luna.

Williams looked back and forth between her and Ank.

<We can't do it, Will. We can't take on three of those things while worrying about our flank at the same time.>

"We're going to have to," said Williams at last. "Things have changed, Ank. You better get used to it." He looked at Sheila. "Okay. We'll tip the spear while you guard the kids in the rear. Everybody ready?"

And everyone nodded.

The so-called terror birds were aptly named, resembling emus with the heads of bald eagles and each standing no less than 10 feet high. Nor did they deign to simply stand around and be picked off, for two of them broke off from the other the instant Williams fired—whereby, in a blunder so uncharacteristic as to be virtually unbelievable, he missed his target entirely—before charging him and Ank across the clearing even as the third predator snatched up the end of the man's spear with its beak and snapped it into.

"Ank!" shouted Williams, wary he might hit the man or woman, suddenly distrustful of his gift, as he sighted one of the rapidly approaching beasts and fired, skewering its brain like a lance and causing blood and tissue to explode out the back of its head.

<I see it. I'm almost there,> communicated Ank, even as Williams sighted the second animal and, somehow, missed again. And then it was there, it was upon him, nor did it pounce as he'd expected but rather flicked its great beak suddenly—so that both he and his rifle were sent flying—and continued on ... toward Sheila. Toward the children.

Ank, meanwhile, had struck the bird closest to the couple with a devastating roundhouse blow of his tail—knocking it clean off the aircraft's broken wing—before completing his spin and seeing that Sheila and the children were under attack. And then he was snarling, snarling and charging—even as the terror bird righted itself behind him and quickly gave chase. What happened next happened very fast, as Ank pounced upon the bird closest to Sheila and the animal behind him swept near enough to beak him just below his armored shell. And then the beasts were tangled up in furious combat, two against one, as Sheila attempted to shield the kids and Williams, his head spinning, his vision blurry, staggered to his feet.

He searched for his rifle quickly and, finding it nowhere, drew his revolver. He tried to sight one of the birds—but they only swam in and out of focus as he squinted. At last he squeezed off a round and one of the things fell, opening and closing its beak, thrashing its limbs. He cocked and sighted the other, feeling the magic returning, sensing its dark energy reawaken in his hand and arm and eye. And then Ank cried out as though suffering a major wound—and he fired.

In truth, it wasn't until he saw Ank begin to stir amidst all the kicked-up dust that he knew he'd pulled it off. The terror bird was dead. What remained unclear was the extent to which Ank had been injured. He ran forward suddenly and knelt beside his friend.

"How you doing, buddy? Talk to me ..." He ran a hand along the back of his head. "What's the damage?"

<They ...> He grunted as though experiencing a spasm of pain. <They got a couple good ones in. Once in the neck ... one in the ribs. I'll be all right. Just a little—can you check my side? It ... hurts to move my neck.>

Williams did so and was distressed to see that the wound was more than superficial—not life threatening, at least that was his hope, but not minor, either. "You'll need a dressing on that," he said. He rushed around to the other side. "This one's better. A lot better." He stood and ran his hands through his hair—he was missing his hat as well as his rifle. "Okay. Now. Let's see ..." He looked around before focusing on the supplies strapped to Ank's back.

Sheila spoke at last. "It—he saved us. And just now, I could of swore I heard ..." She stared off into empty space. "A voice ... and it wasn't the first time. I heard it last night, too. Right after he knocked me across the camp." She laughed. "Now, are you going to tell me what's going on?"

Williams moved to speak and paused, hearing voices. It was the man and woman from the airliner, heading their way.

"Okay," he said, then looked at Ank, who seemed to be wavering in and out of consciousness. "But first I'm going to need some help. Quickly. Luna? Erik? I'll need you, too."

Sheila climbed out of the natural trench they'd been hiding in and stood next to him. "If you don't mind me asking, what for?"

He pulled a rope and let loose a tumble of supplies. "Leverage." He looked at her over his shoulder. "Because we're going to make the biggest tourniquet in history."

By the time they'd patched Ank up using a series of ropes and blankets, not to mention disinfecting his wounds with what remained of Williams' liquor stash, introductions had been made and the sun was high. The man and woman—Peter and Samantha—were the only survivors of a flight bound for Houston when the Flashback had hit. Peter had been deadheading to his next assignment (but was forced to take control when the on-duty pilots vanished) while Samantha had been enroute to visit her father. They'd been living in the downed plane ever since, during which time Samantha had gotten pregnant and was now six-weeks along.

"What I don't understand is how you ended up crash-landing in the middle of Montana," said Sheila. "You said the plane was bound for Houston."

"Yeah, well," Peter glanced at Samantha. "That's the damndest thing. Because both of us just had a sense that ... we should head north. Don't ask me to explain it, because I assure you, I can't." Williams and Sheila looked at each other. "And so, with what fuel we had, we did exactly that: leaving Texas for Wyoming and finally entering Montana, where we began to catch snippets of a broadcast. Radio—"

"Free Montana, yes," said Sheila. She shook the hair out of her eyes. "We've been listening to it too. The girl, Luna here, has a radio, one of those Red Cross ones with the hand crank." She glanced at Williams warily. "I don't suppose you've been able to listen to it lately, have you?"

"No," said Samantha. "Not since the crash." She looked suddenly troubled. "Why?"

Williams and Sheila exchanged nervous glances again. At last Williams said, "Because they've got trouble—big trouble. Trouble in the form of an armed armada heading their way right now ... burning everything in its wake." He put on his hat, which he'd found near his rifle in the middle of the clearing. "And we're going there, anyway. Me, Sheila, the kids, you and Samantha. And we should probably get going before we lose the day completely."

"Well now wait just a minute," protested Peter. "An armada? What do you mean?"

Williams knelt by Ank. "I mean every bad apple survivor from here to New York has somehow found each other and his heading this way." He stroked the ankylosaur's head with what Sheila thought was surprising gentleness. "And that you aren't the only ones to have had, I don't know, a feeling, an impulse, to head north. All of us have." To Ank he said: "Can you travel, old boy?"

The dinosaur stirred. *<I don't know. I think so. Just— give me a minute.>*

Williams patted his back and stood. "And that ..." He thought about it and shook his head. "We've got a responsibility, somehow. Like you said, don't ask me to explain it because I can't."

Peter and Samantha looked at each other, uncertain how to respond. "I suppose we don't have much of a choice, do we?" she said at last, and shrugged defeatedly.

"How far is it, this Radio Free Montana?" asked Peter. "Is it based in a city, a town, what?"

There was a clattering of supplies as Ank rose up off the ground and shook the dust off.

"About 60 miles, give or take," said Williams, and began re-securing items to the giant's back. "I'd say we'll arrive in about 5 days. Maybe four."

"Just in time to die, I take it," said Peter.

"Yeah. Maybe," said Williams. He pulled the revolver from his holster and indicated Peter should catch it before tossing it to him. "You know how to use one of these?"

"Never fired one in my life," he said, then handed it to Samantha. "Sam here, on the other hand, is a kill-shot from hell."

They walked. Nor did they stop until they'd reached Lonepine, which wasn't so much a town as a pair of houses—both of them ramshackle and overgrown and completely devoid of power—one of which Williams, Sheila, and the kids set up camp in, while Peter and Samantha sequestered themselves in the other. Ank, meanwhile, had to make do with a yellowed patch of lawn between the two. Fortunately, there were several small ponds nearby from which he could drink, which was what he was doing when Williams stepped out onto the porch to have a cigar.

He wondered what the great beast was thinking that he should now seem so sullen and withdrawn, but supposed his injuries, along with the added burden of having travelled so many miles with the supplies on his back (which Williams had relieved him of once they'd gotten there), had contributed to most of it. And yet it wasn't like him to shut off communication entirely—which was precisely what he'd done since leaving the site of the plane crash. And thus he watched, smoking, as the ankylosaur lapped at the water and the pink sky continued to darken, until at last a hand touched his shoulder and he sensed Sheila standing nearby, who said to him, softly, "You're worried about him, aren't you?"

Williams didn't turn around. "Yeah. I guess I am." He exhaled cigar smoke. "It's not like him to be so ..."

"Morose?"

"Yeah. I guess that's it. You know, he's been at that pond almost since we got here ... just drinking and staring ... completely oblivious. Remember how I told you that neither of us could recall our previous lives? Well, maybe he's recalling ..." He paused, struggling to find the right words. "A different state of being. A different incarnation. I think he was a man once. A man who lived for a very long time."

"A lonely man, then ..."

"Yes. Sort of a last man standing. And I think when we met ... he rediscovered something he'd been missing for a long time."

"Friendship. Someone to talk to," she said.

"More than that. A reason to live. I—I've felt it myself. All those weeks, months, spent walking alone. I told you about Tanelorn. Well that was what we called our reason to live ... our reason for putting one foot in front of the other. Because without that ..."

"'Gazelle Theory,'" she said.

"What?"

She laughed a little. "Something my husband used to say. It means, 'move or die.'"

He laughed a little himself. "That's good. 'Move or die.' Whether it's a physical death or an emotional one." He stared at Ank in the gloaming before another hand touched him, this time Luna. "Is Ank all right?"

Sheila put a hand on Williams' other shoulder and laid her head against his back. "We don't know, honey. We think he's just lonely. Where's Erik?"

"He's sleeping," said Luna. "He snores, did you know that?"

Sheila laughed. "Oh, God, *do I,*" she said. "But you should try and get some sleep anyway. Long day tomorrow." She rubbed Williams' upper arm as she spoke.

"Okay. I'll try," she said, and trotted back into the house.

Sheila kissed Williams' back gently. "You should, too," she said. "I—I made a bed for us. That is ... if you want to."

He turned to face her slowly. "Sheila, there's something you should—"

"Shhh," She placed her fingers to his lips. "We both have ... someone. Out there. I've gathered that. But we also have right here ... right now. And maybe Tanelorn is ... what we make it."

He looked into her dark brown eyes, feeling he could fall into them and never come out. "I've wanted you since the moment you pointed a gun at me," he said, and they both laughed a little.

And then they went in to their dingy little room and closed the door behind them.

<*Will ...*>

Williams paused, unsure whether to respond. The timing was—less than optimal.

<*Will, are you awake?*>

He laid his head on the inside of Sheila's leg, breathing heavily, and wondered if she could hear it too.

"What's the matter?" she asked.

Apparently not.

"Nothing," he sighed. "Just a kink in my neck. I'm all right." He kissed her along the belly. *Now, let's see, where was I?* He kissed and nibbled down her skin and she gasped once, twice. *You like that?* he thought. *Well, just wait.* She wrapped his hair up in her hands as he closed his lips about her vulva.

"Oh, Will, Will—"

<*Will. Will!*>

Williams ignored him, reaching down to see if he was still ready—still showing that he wanted her. He was, at least for the—

<It's vitally important that you respond to me. I'm sorry I haven't said much since the plane wreck. But, well, I'll explain it all later. What's important just now—>

—the—

<—is that you respond. Please, Will ...>

And the moment was gone. He rolled onto his back and exhaled.

"That bad, huh?" she said, sounding vulnerable and embarrassed. "Sorry. But the Wasteland Food and Drug was fresh out of feminine—"

"It's not that," he said, and sat up with a groan. "It's just that, well, *it's Ank.* I better see what's going on."

She curled up in a ball as he stood and looked out the window. But nothing was amiss. He simply saw Ank laying with his tail toward him on the patch of dead grass between the houses. "It's nothing," he said. "He might be dreaming. It's happened before."

"Well, that's a relief," she snapped, and threw the covers off. "Maybe you should go check on him. I'm going to check on Erik."

And then she was gone, and Williams lay back on the bed wondering what it was a dinosaur-man could be dreaming about to cause him to reach out like that.

But he wasn't dreaming. Of that Ank was certain as the branches rustled again and a smattering of pinecones rattled across the ground. *Something* was moving—out there, just beyond the tree line. Worse, something seemed to be moving on the opposite side of the house, something light-footed, something cautious.

He blinked and one was there, standing in the moonlight at the foot of the yard—its pale skin as wan as the dead, its purple-rimmed eyes focusing on him as he looked.

Ank narrowed his lids, feigning a deep sleep, as two more were-raptors emerged from the trees. He watched as they exchanged glances and crept forward across the lawn. There were six of them now, not counting whatever was creeping around on the other side. He glanced at the house in which the newcomers were staying and saw that whatever they'd been using for light had been snuffed out since last he'd looked. Which meant they were sleeping, as was Will, clearly. That or he was banging Miss Wonderful. Either way it meant he was alone, more alone even than he'd already felt, nor could he possibly hope to defeat them in his present condition. He remembered the ravine they'd passed before arriving in Lonepine and wondered: Could it work?

The raptors crept still closer, taking great care not to wake him, and three of them split off from the others. He lay perfectly still as the three passed him on both sides and, presumably, began stalking toward the houses.

The ravine. A stampede. It just might work, and it was the only thing that had any hope of success if he was to save the others as well as himself. The question was, could he do it in the shape he was in? Could he run fast enough to even reach the ravine before the bloodthirsty bastards caught up to him and tore him to pieces?

A part of him was convinced he could not. And so he communicated, or tried to communicate, one last time, ⊲*I don't know if this is going to work, Will. But I hope you'll understand I've got to try. If all goes well, I will see you shortly. If not, just know this. I—I love you, Will. You have been, and will always be, my best friend.*⊳

And then he was up, trying to roar to alert the others but finding his wounded throat uncooperative, and he was loping as fast as he could toward the ravine even though he knew, in his heart, that he would never make it in a thousand years.

V

It flowed through his fingertips somehow; even he didn't understand it. He understood the thing as he understood his rifle and his pistol, as he had understood Sheila's lithe body and small shoulders. He understood its strings and its frets, its tuning knobs, its symmetry, and he knew just how to hold it, with its waist on his right leg and its back against his stomach and chest, its neck horizontal to the earth. He played it as Ank lay in the tall grass beyond the porch: picking and strumming, pausing occasionally to tune its strings, as the wild blades of grass blew all around and the thin wood of the guitar and porch creaked. For they were home; they had made it—Tanelorn was real, as they had known it would be.

So, too, was *she* there, in the cabin's kitchen, preparing dinner not out of any sort of obligation or duty but simply because she enjoyed it. Nor was she one person but three; sometimes she was Sheila, as sun-browned and gaunt as the badlands themselves, other times Katrina, still others a woman he somehow knew but could not recognize.

Otherwise the day had passed without event and without so much as a slightly increased heart rate, a day in which the grass had blown in hypnotic, predictable patterns and the eternal present had continued to unspool and the sky had looked down upon them mildly. A day which had lasted and would continue to last forever—without beginning, without end, without even a context in which to exist.

It was a dream-state interrupted only by the appearance of a black dot on the horizon—which grew, by imperceptible degrees, into a human figure ... which walked across the prairie slowly but assuredly and resolved itself into a man. A man holding a rifle and dressed in desert rags, whose face was partially hidden by a dirty bandana, and who stopped when he had closed to within fifty feet or so and simply stared at Williams, his eyes dark, his weapon held at the ready.

A man Williams merely looked back at until his fingers no longer pressed the frets or strummed the strings and he set the instrument aside and stood—slowly, deliberately. Then he walked across the tall grass and faced him, for he knew, in the same way he had known that they must continue moving north, that it was his purpose somehow to do so.

"You ... you're not what I expected," said the stranger, his voice surprisingly smooth and non-hard-edged—a study in contrast to his rugged and weathered exterior. He laughed a little. "So I have met my mirror paladin and he is ... just a man, after all." He paused as though surprised by Williams' non-reaction, and his eyes suddenly lit up. "You ... don't know me, do you?"

Williams shook his head slowly.

"You've ... no seer, no epitome?"

Williams only looked at him.

"I must say, I'm disappointed. Our seer, our epitome, the One Who Commands the Freezing Dark, he speaks so gravely of you. And of your army." He glanced at Ank and then at the cabin and beyond. "But where is it? I see only the beast's counterpart, and even he is not what I expected." His eyes lit up all over again. "You don't know, do you? You don't know what it is for which you've been summoned." He stared off into the distance. "Yes, I see it. You're still operating off a kind of blind intuition, completely oblivious to the larger forces at play. You probably don't even *know* that you've been summoned—much less why—you just, have a feeling. Is that it?"

"Yes," Williams said at last. "Now, what do you want?"

The stranger began to chuckle slightly. "But you do know we are coming, do you not? Surely you must have heard—if not the radio broadcast than a whisper in your own mind. Or could it be that all the heads on pikes have been for nothing? Not to mention the—"

"Gibberish," said Williams, shaking his head. "This is gibberish and I am dreaming. And I think just now—"

He jolted as the man slapped a hand over his face, squeezing his fingers. "Here's some sleep paralysis, to keep you a little longer. I want to show you something."

Williams wanted to swipe his hand away but could not, finding himself frozen in stasis, unable to move. He blinked and the figure was gone, replaced by a panorama of a city—Billings, Montana, according to a sign—a city under siege, a city in flames. He'd been transported somehow to a hill overlooking it.

"This is who we are," said the man in the bandana, who stood next to him on the grassy hill. "And this, fellow paladin, is what we do. Beautiful, isn't it?"

Williams watched as the steeples of a church burned and collapsed, then focused on a woman carrying a child from the wreckage.

The stranger continued: "Don't look to us for the method of carnage—fire is of the Other's design. We only use it as a means to an end. But watch now as I show you what will happen when we descend upon your Barley—and what mercy to expect from us when we finally do. And tell me if it would not be better to simply turn around now, while you still can, and ignore the Call completely."

Williams squinted through the smoke as a motorcycle burst into view and bore down upon the woman, its headlight creating a halo, its rider brandishing a sword. Then, before he could so much as cry out a warning, the rider struck, beheading the woman in one fell swoop before continuing on with a rumble and leaving the child abandoned in her arms.

And then Williams was turning to the mysterious figure with the intent of killing him with his bare hands, but froze when he saw that the man was no longer there: that he had been replaced with something else, something about 9-feet-tall and covered with kinky hair, with a goat's head and six golden eyes, which vanished as he blinked—awakening with a start—and heard Sheila say, with desperation in her voice: "Will, It's Ank. *And he's gone.*"

It was no use. Even under optimal conditions it would have been difficult to track him across the stones and the scrub, but it had rained heavily during the night and a thick fog had settled in, which made doing so now virtually impossible. Regardless, it wasn't until after they'd searched for the better part of a day and reconvened on the porch that the first mutterings of real defeat were heard, and these had come from a surprising source—Williams himself.

It wasn't just because he was privy to information no one else had—information in the form of a kind of telepathic voicemail left by Ank the previous night—a message which said, *<I don't know if this is going to work, but I hope you'll understand I've got to try. If all goes well, I will see you shortly. If not, just know this. I—I love you, Will. You have been, and will always be, my best friend.>*

No, it was more than that. It was the dream and what it had portended. It was the growing suspicion that not only had they been called by someone, *something,* to go to Barley ... but that someone or something else was as equally insistent they *not* go. Viewed in that light, it was difficult to see Ank's disappearance as anything but an attempt to stall them and to prevent them from reaching their destination. Not by Ank, obviously, but by ... by ...

Our seer, our epitome, the One Who Commands the Freezing Dark.

Madness, the rational part of his brain countered. It had just been a dream. There was no *One Who Commands the Freezing Dark.* There was no Bandana Man.

"One thing's for sure," said Sheila, exhaling, "we can't just leave him behind."

"Not if you're as close as you seem to be," said Peter. "And besides, how will we carry all our supplies?"

"Peter's right," said Samantha. "That dinosaur has been the only thing standing between you—us—and a swift extinction."

"I won't leave without Ank!" chimed in Luna.

"Well there you have it," said Sheila, and sat hard upon the steps next to Williams, causing them to creak and to groan. "The Fellowship has spoken. The question is: What do we do now?"

Williams could feel their eyes upon him as he mulled it over.

<I don't know if this is going to work, but I hope you'll understand I've got to try. If all goes well, I will see you shortly.>

He stood and took a few steps into the gloom. *<If not, just know this. I—I love you, Will. You have been, and will always be, my best friend.>*

At last he turned to face the group. "I ... the truth of it is, I don't know what to do. The link between us, between Ank and I, it's ... like a voice. It's clear up close but recedes with distance. And the fact is I'm not hearing anything—nothing, that is, except a final message, which has been repeating in my mind ever since this morning." He focused on Luna; he didn't know why. "And that message seems to indicate that Ank has done something he feels is necessary. Now, I'm not going to pretend to know what that thing is; it may be that it's not for us to understand, just like the Flashback, just like the lights in the sky. But our coming together has not been an accident; I think we all feel that, we just don't know why or for what purpose. I only know this: We have to get to Barley before ... before that armada does." Everyone just stared at him. "Dammit, that's not crazy, is it? Sheila—you feel it, don't you? Samantha? What about you, Peter? And you, Luna, surely you feel—"

"I feel it," she said. "It's like ... it's like God is looking at Barley through a magnifying glass, and—"

"Yes! Like what we talked about. It's like we're, we're ..." He trailed off, feeling suddenly deflated. "It's madness, isn't it?"

No one said anything for several moments.

At last Sheila shook her head. "No. I feel it, too."

"So do I," said Samantha.

They all looked at Peter. "Let's just say I feel something," he said at last. "That—there was a reason I was on that flight. That ... I have a purpose, somehow."

"I think we all do," said Williams. He turned to face the gloom again. "And it just may be that Ank's purpose is out there ... somewhere. I guess what it comes down to is a matter of faith." He turned back around. "Faith in my friend, for example. Because he wouldn't have left us without a damned good reason."

"But, if we push on, how will we carry our gear?" asked Peter.

"We'll just all have to shoulder our share," said Williams. "Even the kids. Even you, squirt." He ruffled Erik's hair. "... and have faith that something will present itself."

As it turned out, something presented itself pretty quickly—in the middle of the night (they'd opted to stay at the homes one more night in the off chance Ank might show), in the form of a battered school bus, which wheezed to a halt in front of the houses just after midnight and belched a cloud of smoke before dying without much ceremony. Nor did the resulting standoff last more than a few scant minutes, for the driver of the bus and Williams hit it off almost immediately, and before anyone knew it there was a line of kids filing from the bus—7 in all—and Williams was introducing Sheila to a man named Sammy, who had inherited the children when the Flashback hit a town called Pine Stump Junction and had been driving them north ever since.

"Trying to, anyway," said Sammy, and added, "The damn thing will only drive in first gear. Plus its breaks have seized up, so you're topping out at about 3 miles per hour even then. Radio works, though, which is how we first knew to head north. Can't say I'm thrilled about what's transpired since then."

"And you're still going? Even with the children?" asked Sheila, who had warmed up to the man ever faster than Williams—for he was nothing if not intriguing, and it wasn't every day one met a leather-clad stranger who looked like he'd be more at home on a Harley than piloting a boatload of children.

"Why, yes," He paused, watching as his children gathered around Luna—making introductions, touching her white hair. "Aren't you? Don't get me wrong, I was torn at first, in spite of the ..." He trailed off suddenly. "But Bella's recent broadcasts have given me new hope."

"We're going," said Williams. "I think Sheila was just curious if you were experienced the same ..." He hesitated, squinting at him. "New hope? What do you mean?"

"You weren't listening yesterday, I take it. Bella calls it 'The Rising'—friendly survivors numbering in the hundreds, convening on Barley from every direction, most of them with weapons. Seems her radio broadcast was picked up by yet another station and re-transmitted, some say as far as the Cascades."

Williams and Sheila looked at each other in stunned disbelief—until she embraced him suddenly and then just as quickly embraced Sammy.

"Sorry, it's just that ..." She swiped the tears from her eyes. "That's the first truly hopeful news we've had since—well, since the start of the Flashback." She jolted abruptly, touching Sammy's outstretched arms. "I've got to tell Erik!"

And then she was gone, hurrying off toward the throng of kids as Sammy watched her go and Williams watched Sammy—who, sensing he was being watched, straightened suddenly and cleared his throat.

"You'll excuse me, of course. I—I didn't realize—"

"That she's spoken for?" Williams chuckled slightly. "Well, that depends on your point of view."

Sammy nodded as though he understood, his mouth hung slightly open. "So is that a 'yes' or a 'no?'"

Williams moved to speak then paused, an image having come unbidden to his mind: an image of an Asian woman in a traditional Vietnamese dress standing utterly alone on what appeared to be an outdoor stage. No—not alone. He was there, too. Himself, Williams. He was seated on a stool some distance away with a guitar in his hands and a rifle at his feet.

And then the crowd began to cheer—for he had begun to pick
and to strum—and the woman had turned to face him
(smiling broadly, toothily), and the vision was over—having
passed as quickly as the boy with the magnifying glass but
having affected him thrice fold.

"It's both," he said at last, slapping Sammy's shoulder.
"Now why don't you tell me about that bus ... because believe
me when I say, we're going to need it."

Morning spread across the prairie warm and clear, as clear as
Radio Free Montana, which trotted out some Loretta Lynn as
Williams ladled beans onto the kids' paper plates and
Sammy prepared the school bus and Sheila bounced back
and forth between the two helping as best she could.

*They say to have her hair done Liz flies all the way to
France / And Jackie's seen in a discothèque doin' a brand-
new dance / And the White House social season should be
glitterin' an' gay ...*

And then they were off, the children in the bus and the
bus moving at a crawl, while Williams, on foot, took point
with his rifle and Sheila followed close behind and Peter and
Samantha brought up the rear.

*But here in Topeka the rain is a fallin' / The faucet is a
drippin' and the kids are a bawlin' / One of 'ems a toddlin'
and one is a crawlin' / And / One's on the way ...*

So, too, did they make excellent progress, travelling all
the way to Niarada before Williams held up a sweaty hand,
indicating the caravan should stop—then just stood there,
listening. At last he knelt and touched the ground, even as
Sheila crept closer and asked, somewhat tentatively, "What is
it?"

He scanned the slopes to their right and seemed to nod
gravely. "That's what I thought," he said, but didn't
immediately elaborate. He stood and faced the bus. "Sammy!
Keep her parked but do not shut it off. Peter, Samantha, one
of you mind the front. We'll be right back."

And then he and Sheila were scaling the slopes until they crested a hill and saw what Sheila at first took to be a mirage—it couldn't possibly be anything else. For what they saw was a convoy—a wagon train—which stretched for miles along the highway and seemed to consist of every type of vehicle imaginable: motor homes and travel trailers, semi-trucks, bulldozers, all of them moving at a crawl and belching fumes, heading along Highway 12 which would become 28, heading to Barley only the roundabout way, which would take them through Rollins and Somers and Kalispell; which would cause them to arrive later, perhaps by as much as a day.

"Jesus—is it ...?"

"No," said Williams. "It's not ... what do we call them? The enemy?"

"The caravan that took out Billings? I'd say so."

Williams shook his head. "It's not big enough, for one. Look, see the lack of military equipment? I mean, there's some, I can see that, a few armored personnel carriers, but nothing like what the pilot reported."

"What's that? There, on the side ..."

He squinted at where she'd indicated, and to his shock and consternation saw what appeared to be a swastika painted on the transport's armor. "Jesus. But look, see? It's like they've tried to scratch it out."

"Either way, it doesn't put me in a mind to amble out and say 'hi.'"

"Not so much, I agree. Regardless, they're taking the long way while we'll be cutting through the wilderness. So we'll be in Barley and amongst friends when they arrive. I say we hold off on contact until then."

"You'll get no argument from me," said Sheila.

"All right, then. Let's go tell the others." And then they climbed back down the hill.

Ank awakened and yet could not see, could not breathe, could not move. Was he still dreaming? No, of that he was quite certain; his head hurt, for one thing, as though someone had hit him with a great hammer. He reared up suddenly, the dirt cascading down the sides of his snout like sand, and looked around: a dead were-raptor lay nearby, half-buried in rubble, and beyond that, another.

He rose his entire body with a groan and shook himself off, causing a great cloud of dust to dissipate on the wind. There were only two of them—the others were either buried where he couldn't see or had fled after the collapse of the cliff face. Either way, they were no longer a threat, at least not for now.

And yet ... the world had changed, he could tell. *He* had changed. Something inside him had awakened, had cleared. It was almost as if the blow to his head had jarred him into a different state of being, a higher level of consciousness. He froze suddenly, unable to process what had just entered his mind ... unable to fully grasp the enormity of it.

For his name was Sebastian—he remembered it with perfect clarity now. And he remembered something else: a place—Paradise, Montana—where everything that had ever been important to him still lay beneath the sun. A place the finding of which was more important than anything—more important than Tanelorn, more important than the army in the east, more important than his best friend.

A place he had to get to right now—to which he would virtually run if he had to. A place from which he never planned to return.

VI

As it turned out, there *was* a road directly north at where Highway 28 bent east—a dirt road. It even had a couple crude signs, one of which read REDNECK HIGHWAY and the other BARLEY HOT SPRINGS: 22 MILES. Williams couldn't figure it, even after consulting his maps; for one, there was the Santiago River, which stood between them and Barley and would need a bridge in order for the road to make any sense. But a bridge for a *dirt* road? It seemed unlikely.

"It does say Redneck Highway," said Sheila. "Redneck Bridge is probably a plywood ramp propped up with cinderblocks."

"Someone's idea of a joke, maybe," said Sammy, and stood up from where they'd all knelt around the map.

Williams remained crouched, squinting down the lane. "But look at it ... it runs just as straight as an arrow, and for a good distance, too. It's not even wash-boarded." He stood and peered down the state highway. "One thing's for sure ... if we follow 28, it's going to take us 2 to 3 times longer to get there."

Peter stepped forward with a quizzical look on his face. "With all due respect, I'm not seeing what the hurry is, frankly. Last we heard the—the enemy, was in Billings. Isn't that a good distance from here?"

"Yes and no," said Williams. "But remember, they're motorized." He glanced at Sammy. "And something tells me they're not stuck in first gear. But it's not just that. We're running low on supplies, the stuff we picked up in Lonepine notwithstanding. Besides, we'll need to get to Barley well ahead of the enemy if we're going to arrive at any sort of battleplan. No," He stared down the dirt road again. "We've come this far on blind faith; we'll make it the rest the distance the same way."

"Faith isn't going to build a bridge if none is there," said Peter.

"And yet it might, Mr. Romero. It just might," said Williams.

And then he was again taking point as Peter and Sheila and Sammy and Luna exchanged nervous glances ... before following him at last onto the dusty byway.

Ank ran—his wounds from the terror birds throbbing and protesting, his tourniquet of blankets having long since fallen off. He wanted to get there before nightfall—before the light receded from the sky and his eyes began to fail, before he possibly even changed his mind. He ran as he had never run previously, testing his new body and its limits under duress, pushing it in ways he had never pushed before, tasking it with what seemed an impossible end: crossing a 30-mile stretch of badlands to reach the town of Paradise by the close of a day almost three-quarters over.

And as he ran, he remembered (or thought he did) the details of a life prior—a life which had been full and interesting and robust, in which he had found his work and his love ... but which he had outlived long before he had ever died and awakened in the beast; which he had outlived long before the Flashback.

Nor did he run the entire distance alone, for as he re-crossed the Camas Prairie he came upon a most unusual sight: a Union Pacific train, dieseling across the wastelands as though there'd never been an apocalypse or a collapse of civilization as they'd known it. And, as it was moving relatively slow, he veered alongside it and kept pace—but he did more than keep pace, really; rather, he made something of a sport of *racing* the thing, pouring on the speed so that he drew even with the engine's cab, where he saw a bearded man in coveralls extend an arm out the window in what seemed a gesture of goodwill.

And then Ank was falling back, back, his armored body growing weary, the calloused pads of his feet aching, so that he was even with the caboose—until it, too, moved on down the tracks without him ... leaving him to pant and thirst in the desert sun.

Exhausted. Dispirited. Alone.

By the time they entered what his map called Shadow Canyon, Williams estimated they had about two hours of light left. As for the Santiago River, they heard it before they saw it (for the world had grown eerily silent since the Flashback), rushing and bubbling, swirling and sluicing, until they rounded a craggy bend and saw it laid out before them—beautiful in its untamed wildness, bursting as though in flood, and, having no bridge, utterly impassable.

"I don't get it," said Sheila, exhausted. "Who builds a road and then runs it straight into a raging river?"

Williams peered at the opposite bank, where the dirt road resumed. "If I had to guess I'd say there's a dam upriver, which would have allowed passage—in, say, a 4x4—whenever it was closed." He sneered and spat. "It's a 'Redneck Highway,' indeed."

"Any chance we could ford it using the bus?" asked Samantha. The look on her face as she studied the boulders on both sides of the river suggested she already knew the answer.

"No way," said Sammy, looking at the same. "We'd be lucky to get a quarter of the way across before a wheel got stuck in the rocks. Then there we'd be ... high and dry and with a boatload of kids."

"There has to be a way," said Sheila.

Peter stepped forward, hands on his hips, and examined the river. "Let's see," He wetted a finger and pretended to draw an equation in the air. "Nope. There doesn't appear to be a way." At last he turned to face Williams. "Any more bright ideas, cowboy?"

All eyes turned toward Williams as the river raged and the sun continued to sink. At length he set down his rifle and eased the backpack from his shoulders. "Just one," he said, retaking up his weapon. "Something I was planning on doing when we reached Barley, anyway." He looked at Sheila, knowing that if anyone tried to stop him it would be her. "See, a mistake was made when we left Ank behind—a mistake I've been trying to reconcile ever since Lonepine. I don't know, but it's like—it's like I had a lapse in faith ... a lapse in brotherly love, something; one we're paying for even now." He paced back and forth with his rifle, trying to figure it out, trying to find the right words. "I read the tea leaves wrong—misinterpreted the entrails—whatever. But the fact is," He looked at them one by one. "Ank was meant to be with us now. He was meant to ford us across that river. And the only reason he isn't ... is because I failed our friendship." He paused as a drop of rain flecked his nose and the clouds rumbled gently overhead. "Surely you can feel it, just as I do. The feeling that ... we're being tested. That the Flashback was not just an apocalypse in the physical sense. It was an apocalypse in the spiritual sense. That there's more at play here than dinosaurs and strange lights in the sky—aliens, whatever—that the battle has now been joined by something else entirely. Something, I don't know-"

"Dear God, he's going to say it," protested Peter.

"Yes, yes, I am," said Williams rapidly, and added: "Something divine. And I guess what I'm trying to tell you all now, especially you, Sheila, and you, Luna, is that ... well, I'm being called to go find Ank."

A silence settled over the group that was hard to define as the river breathed and the sky continued to darken.

"What a bunch pseudo-spiritual horseshit," Peter exclaimed.

"He's right, Will, you can't be serious," said Sheila.

"A damn stupid idea, is what it is," added Sammy. "If someone has to go, let it be me. Anyone can drive that bus. But not anyone can use that rifle the way they say you can." He cocked his pistol in a move that stunned everyone, but didn't raise it. "I won't let you do it, Will. I'm sorry." He glanced at Sheila as if for confirmation and she nodded intensely. "The way I see it is, I've got a responsibility too.

And if you won't hold the group together then I guess I'll have to."

Williams stared at him for what seemed a long time before finally appearing to relent.

"Okay," he said at last, and shrugged. "We'll try to build a raft ..."

"Now you're talking!" said Sammy. He shot a sidelong glance at Sheila. "He's talking now, am I right?"

Sheila began to nod and smile in a flood of relief.

And then a gunshot rang out and everyone jumped—and when the smoke had cleared Williams was standing with his rifle raised, although he lowered it quickly to prevent further alarm. Sammy, meanwhile, lifted his wildly trembling gun hand and merely looked at it, for Williams had shot the weapon clean from his grasp.

"I'm sorry, too," said Williams. "Now here's what I want you to do ..."

He could walk, let alone run, no more, and yet it didn't matter: He'd made it to the cemetery in Paradise. Now all he could do was to collapse beneath its entry arch and catch his breath—as the crows scattered and the sun continued to sink and the storm clouds gathered in the west. Again, it didn't matter: he'd crawl the rest of the way if he had to. He knew precisely where they were—by the maple tree, just a sapling on the day of the last funeral—not far from where he lay. And yet, to his amazement, he *was* able to stand; and thus he used what strength he had left to make his way to their graves.

Nor had anything changed since last he'd been there, including the initial shock he'd always felt when the names upon the markers first jumped out at him: Mary Lynn Crenshaw, Devoted Wife and Mother, 1932-1984; Tamara Ray Crenshaw, Beloved Daughter, 1965–1986, James Roy Crenshaw, Beloved Son, 1968-1991. Actually, that wasn't true: the tombstones themselves had changed—they'd become weathered and eroded by the elements to the point that the inscriptions were difficult to read. The important thing was, they were still there—they hadn't been replaced by a stand of cycad trees or otherwise blasphemed by the Flashback. Not yet, anyway, for who knew what turn the anomaly might yet take, nor what the lights in the sky might still have in store, nor even what powers greater than they might yet deign to do with the world.

For there were powers greater than they, of that he had become convinced. But they were powers that would have to unfold their grand design—if design it even was—without him, for he was through; he was finished. He had come back to this place to die. But also, also, to remember: for he had been a man long before he had become a dinosaur—a man named Sebastian Crenshaw, who had wielded the power of the atom bomb in his soft, pink hands and had worked on projects which might have decided the fate of millions. A man who had found his passion and his one, true love—Mary Lynn—who had fathered two bright and beautiful children; and who had lived a life even the gods might envy ... until time had taken it all away.

Not the Flashback, not the lights in the sky, just Time.

The ultimate equalizer. The ultimate enemy.

Mary Lynn, where are you now?

But the grave markers held no answer—nor the darkening sky, nor the wind which had just begun to blow. And it was only then that a tidal wave of memories at last assailed him, memories of her and of them, of holidays and special occasions, of births and deaths and rites of passage, of flying kites on a blustery autumn day.

He froze under the weight of it all, under the weight of his own body, the armored plating, the clubbed tail like an anvil.

... of love and of making love. And what it meant to move through the world as light as a feather; in a body which was as soft as it was agile; a body which had been his and his alone—not shared with the beast, the animal, the monster. Not a prison of thick, sluggish blood and even thicker bone. And it was here that he would have cried had he only possessed the right kind of tear ducts—would have sunk his face in his hands had he only the right kind of mobility.

And thus he did the only thing he could do, which was to lash out at anything and everything— ramming a nearby tombstone with his armored head, knocking a concrete sphere from its pedestal with his clubbed tail, pouncing upon a box marker with all his weight. And as he did so the rain came down in a veritable torrent, the clouds having burst at long last—spattering his armor, running in rivulets between his spikes, so that he at last crumpled at the foot of the graves and curled into a ball, thinking, with his eyes squeezed shut, that he only wanted to die at last and to join them wherever they were; and thinking, too, about Williams and the others, wondering where they presently were and how they'd ford the Santiago River without him ... and communicating, at last, what he intended to be his final message, although he knew it would never reach them. *Him.* His friend.

<I'm sorry, Will. Sorry that I failed you. God be with you in all the times ahead. I have been, and always shall be, your friend.>

And then there was only blackness and pain and the storm, and the question of how to do it. How to end it.

Forever.

Williams paused, the rain dripping from the brim of his hat. *<I have been, and always shall be, your friend.>*

Where had that come from? He ducked under a stand of pine trees to escape the downpour and knelt, thinking about it. He didn't know rightly, only that it had seemed to be a new message and not merely a memory of the last. As for where it had come from ...

He stared south-west, toward Baldy Mountain, toward the town of Paradise. Was it even possible? Could Ank have just communicated with him over such a vast distance?

The truth was, he didn't know. But it *was* something, something he could use for a north star, something he could follow when all he'd had before was a gut feeling—just the faintest intuition, really—that the answer to Ank's whereabouts lie somewhere back the way they'd came. He stepped out from beneath the branches and hung his head back in the rain, letting it spatter his tongue and the roof of his mouth, knowing there would be precious little water to be found between here and Lonepine.

And then he started to run, not knowing how long he could keep up the pace and not caring, but understanding, somehow, that this was what he had to do. That faith would somehow lead the way. And understanding, also, that time was running out; that the Enemy was on the march and they still had not delivered the girl to Barley. That while he yearned to find his friend he had an obligation to the others, as well, and that they were waiting for him even now, unprotected by anything but a handful of pistols and a half-roofless bus. And that everything, everything, depended upon what happened in the next 24 hours.

It was hopeless, of course, even if Williams had given them the go-ahead to try and build a raft in case he didn't return. They simply didn't have the tools, nor the will, frankly, to do so as the rain came down in sheets and they huddled in the back of the bus.

Nor, given the circumstances, did merely waiting seem like such a bad idea—at least not until a throaty snarl unwound from the tree line and caused everyone to look up ... seeing a pair of what appeared to be small tyrannosaurs emerge just outside the bus.

"Holy shit, we've got trouble," said Sammy, then fumbled for his pistol as the others did the same.

"Yeah we do," said one of the kids—his name was Lucas—adding, "Those are allosaurs. As bad or worse than T. Rex ... because they're smaller, fleeter."

"Small enough to get in here?" asked another, clearly alarmed—Carina, if Sheila remembered right.

Nor was that all Sheila remembered, for she recalled with sudden clarity what Bella Ray had warned about Shadow

Canyon—that there were a pair of allosaurs working the area named Lenny and Squiggy.

"Everyone with guns, look sharp," said Sammy. "We've got nowhere to go."

And it was true; they didn't have anywhere to go.

Unless ...

He stood suddenly and moved toward the front of the bus—even as Sheila protested and Peter snapped, "What are you doing? What are you doing?"

He sat in the driver's seat and turned over the engine. "I'm taking us over Redneck Bridge; that's what I'm doing." He shot a look at Peter over his shoulder which would brook no argument. "Unless you've got a better idea?"

"You crazy—we won't make it ten feet in that flood ..."

"We're about to find out," said Sammy, and ground the gears. "I'd suggest just now that everyone simply hang on."

And then they were rattling forward, toward the river's edge and the threatening rocky terrain, as the allosaurs parleyed and began gnawing on the hull and the children screamed and Sheila and Samantha lowered their windows—each trying to get a shot at the predators.

VII

They'd speak of it in the days ahead as the Santiago Miracle, for that's what it had been, as surely as the sun crosses the sky. Nor would there be a single dissenting voice—not even Peter—or any attempt whatsoever at explaining it away. For the simple fact was they should not have made it: they should not have veritably glided through the water only to meet sudden resistance on the opposite bank, where the boulders snapped the axles and burst the tires, laying the bus low.

"It had been like Moses parting the Red Sea," Sheila would say, and no one would laugh—at least no one who had been there—while still others would claim they had felt the bus literally rise upon the water, fording the river like a hydrofoil.

Lost in the celebration—at least at first—had been the fact that something else had happened that was equally as inexplicable: that the rear window of the bus had literally melted during the crossing—melted as though it had been superheated by an atom bomb—so that it sloughed away like a glacier and all that was left was a little girl, Luna, looking on from the back seat, still staring at the allosaurs who had abandoned their pursuit and smelling faintly of smoke and burnt toast.

But this realization would only come later, after they'd been surrounded by men and women with guns and escorted through fortifications worthy of D-Day to the heart of Barley itself, where they were greeted at last as comrades rather than enemies and treated to a banquet in their honor alone, for it was a tradition amongst its residents to celebrate the arrival of survivors as though they were long lost friends.

Nor did they have to wait long to meet Bella Ray herself, the slight and gray-haired owner of the voice which had both comforted and encouraged and sometimes terrified them along the way—for she emerged onto the covered stage which the rows of tables faced well before dinner was even done, asking the newcomers to stand and introduce themselves and directing leis to be placed over their heads as each of them spoke up.

"Sheila Were, housewife, Anchor Rock. This is my son, Erik."

"Sammy Benson, Harley-riding man-child turned bus driver." He glanced at Sheila and winked. "And these are *my* kids: Lucas, Carina, Sally Meyers, Thomas, Freddy, Malcolm, and Sloan."

"Peter Romero, pilot for United Airlines. This here is my fiancée, Samantha."

"How do," she said, and accepted her lei.

"And who might you be?" asked Bella, indicating Luna.

The albino girl slowly stood. "I'm Luna ... from Mirabeau Park." She hugged her radio against herself. "But this isn't all of us. There's also Will and Ank ... but we don't know where they are right now."

"Oh?" said Bella. "When was the last time you saw them?"

"Ank's been gone awhile," said Luna, and frowned. "But Will went looking for him."

"Just today," interjected Sheila. "Heading south on something called the 'Redneck Highway.'"

Bella looked confused. "Is that on the other side of the river?"

"It is," said Sammy, but didn't elaborate.

Bella glanced at a big man standing near the stage. "That river's impassable," she said. "We've tried it."

"I'd suggest prayer," said Sammy at last. "And a Wayne bus. Look, all I know is ... we did it. Even—even we don't understand it."

Bella looked at the big man near the stage. "It's true," he said. "We found them grounded on the north bank—tires ruined, axles shattered ... They crossed it, all right."

Bella appeared distant as she thought about this. At last she gathered herself and said, "Then you've achieved something we could not, and are doubly welcome. Unfortunately, since the bus is ruined, I see no way we can send a search party. There's no boats here. There is, however, a plane—a small Cessna. It's in good mechanical order but no one here's a pilot." Her wizened eyes fell upon Peter. "Although it would appear that's changed. Can you fly it?"

Peter glanced at Samantha and straightened. "I'd have to look at it, but, yes. I'd say the chances are good."

"In the morning, then," said Bella. "For now I'm sure you are all extremely tired. I just wanted you to know that," she paused, looking at them, at the newcomers. "I just wanted you to know that, whatever awaits us ... you are among friends." She scanned the entire crowd, which Sheila estimated to number in the hundreds. "I'm told that nearly all of you felt compelled to come here even before we started broadcasting. Now I don't pretend to know what that means, only that, that ... we were meant to be here, together, all of us. At this place and at this time. And that ..." She trailed off, unable to find the right words. "Well," she said at last, "here we are. And I think once you've looked around and met everyone," She looked at Sheila and the rest. "You'll agree ... that what we've built here is worth fighting for. That it's the closest we've come to regaining our humanity since the Flashback. And, well, I've said enough. We've already prepared tents for you on the west lawn—but whether you retire to them immediately or party like it's 1999, that's up to you. For now, the bar is open and everything's free. Goodnight, fellow survivors. And welcome home."

And then, to Sheila's utter astonishment, a *band* took to the stage—what they were using for power she hadn't a clue— and she found herself drinking, even dancing! with Sammy as Erik and the children frolicked and Luna wandered the premises alone and the red lights atop the Radio Free Montana transmission tower blinked like hopeful beacons in the night.

Williams collapsed in the mud—the side of his face impacting a reef of basalt, his rifle tumbling before him. In his present condition, the slightest misstep is all it had taken. Behind him, meanwhile, the were-raptors continued to call out—sometimes in their warbling cries while others in their profane speech.

"Give up, pig-fucker," cried one, not Katrina, as Williams turned his head and saw it duck behind a prairie bush.

"Yes, my love! Give up! We only want you to join us!" cried another—and this time it *was* Katrina.

He scooted forward and snatched up his rifle, the chamber of which now contained a single bullet, then swiveled and sat up, sighting her almost immediately before she, too, sought refuge behind the scrub.

His vision blurred in and out as he shifted his gun back and forth between them. *These are the wages of your blind faith!* he thought deliriously, cursing his decision to leave with only the shirt on his back and the ammo in his gun, and all because of a voice he had heard with increasing propensity since leaving Lonepine, a voice that had urged him to act without reflection and make of everything a leap of faith, a voice which was not the Bandana Man but may as well have been, for look where it had led him!

He swiveled back around to face forward and examined the land, seeing nothing that might provide a respite—nothing but ... but ...

A fence.

Holy God, *a fence.* And that meant a house or some other structure, surely—and yet it was not the sort of fence one might expect to find in the middle of the prairie, for it was built of cyclone mesh and topped with razor wire; although he could see even from here that parts of it were collapsed and would allow easy access.

And then he was up with what little strength he had left, delirious, dehydrated, his feet aching from the trek, and scrambling for the barrier, and it wasn't until he was stepping over a downed section that he saw the sign, which was lying askew in a jumble of wire. A sign which read:

WARNING:

Restricted Area
Use of deadly force authorized.

Some kind of government facility, he thought, like the kind he'd found Ank in.

He hustled forward with only the moonlight to guide him, picking his way as quickly as he could through the rubble; for there was indeed a building, a building which had suffered the same fate as so many others in the quake-rocked wake of the Flashback: a building which was covered in moss and creeper vines and partially collapsed. And as he did so he heard the raptors grunting and sprinting across the steppes, having the feeling, he was sure, that their quarry had at last cornered itself in an inescapable kill-box. Nor did he doubt that they were correct in that assessment.

And yet to his surprise he found a door straight away, a door which by some miracle or other circumstance of the Flashback had remained unlocked, and quickly squeezed through it, securing it behind him. And then he collapsed in the pure and total blackness as the raptors met the door and began scratching and barking wildly, as though infused with some sort of blood-lust, and knew in the pit of his stomach that there'd be no escape for him this time.

And yet there was one possible escape, wasn't there? He gripped his rifle tightly, not knowing how serious he was but fearing he was serious enough. They'd all thought about it at one time or another, of that he was sure, especially in those awful first hours after the Flashback, when the world had realized it had lost most its people to a force they couldn't begin to comprehend—a force which had taken their loved ones as surely as a thief in the night, transporting them to some elsewhere and elsewhen even as it transported dinosaurs of a hundred species and from various epochs into the world of men.

He caressed his rifle like a lover in the dark as his mind turned the possibility over in his head. *Indeed, why not?* Why prolong the inevitable when he knew he was cornered and cornered in truth; that the raptors would only wait him out no matter how hard he tried to outlast them and that he was cold and hungry and thirsty and weak. That even worse, he'd lost his faith ... that he could no longer imagine a world in which things might yet work out or the forces allied against them might be turned back or even defeated.

He listened as the scratching at the metal door ceased, but took no heart from it: they'd only refocused their efforts on finding another way in, of that he was certain. Nor could he bear the thought of what would happen when they finally broke through—not the terror and pain of them gutting him like a fish, for Katrina would only wound him, he knew, but the inconceivable horror of walking the earth like *them*. Like a zombie. Like a dead man walking a dead planet.

So, too, would they *know* then, having added his consciousness to theirs. They would know that Barley Hot Springs lay just beyond the Santiago River, which he suspected they could swim, and that nothing in the others' experience would have prepared them for an attack from the rear. No, no, he couldn't under any circumstances allow that—it alone was enough to justify what he couldn't help but see as a surrender under cowardice, a spitting in God's eye.

For there was no God, otherwise the Flashback could never have happened. There was no light to counter the dark, no paladin to counter the Bandana Man, no magnifying glass to focus the sun. There was only the lights in the sky and a world gone mad, only death and pain and suffering without end—and time itself, which had been scrambled like eggs.

He repositioned the rifle so that it pressed against his forehead then slipped his thumb across its trigger.

There was only this: Only ending it at last by his own will and direction ... only the victory that would come in death and its numb embrace.

He jumped as something metal and heavy fell over upon its side, and knew, even before he heard the brutish grunt in the dark, that Katrina and the other raptor had gained entry into the building. And then he refocused on his weapon and steeled himself for the unthinkable, even as their feet padded closer and their breath came and went in bursts, and he was beginning to squeeze the trigger when he sensed a massive head next to his own— Katrina, he knew, who would no doubt profane his final instants with professions of love perverted by a predator's tongue.

And then something happened he could not explain, for he eased his finger away from the trigger as though guided by an invisible hand—for he'd decided, in the eyeblink before committing, that his end would be met with grace rather than cowardice, and that he'd surrender himself to God before he surrendered himself to nihilism, for that is what the Bandana Man wanted, after all, wasn't it?

And it was in that instant that an enormous tongue lapped his face from chin to forehead, knocking his hat off, and that he recognized in the beast's breath a familiar (but no less nauseating) stench that he had nonetheless come to know and love.

For it was the fetid, imperfect breath of his friend.
Of Ank.

Who communicated to him without actual words, *‹You taste of fear and death, Will. So knock it off. We've ... got work to do. Now come on ... I want to show you something.›*

Sheila awakened with a start, her heart hammering, her pulse racing, and rolled away from Sammy so that she faced the tent's flap—which they'd left open to allow for the flow of free air into the shelter (although they'd zippered the bug screen against the mosquitos; one of the drawbacks of being surrounded by hot springs). Erik was fine; she could see the boys' tents clearly from their own—but she could also see, by the light of the gas lanterns, that the air was thick with haze and smelled strongly of smoke, nor was it the kind of smoke one would associate with a structural blaze, but rather the dry, eye-watering fog which could only have resulted from a forest fire. Not close, not a danger to Barley, but many miles away ... in Bozeman, of course.

Bozeman, of which she had dreamed. Or thought she had dreamed, for now it seemed she had experienced something closer to a vision—a vision of a city being shelled without mercy by the tireless war machines of the Enemy.

She sat up abruptly and swung her legs over the side of the air mattress; no, not just shelled—*invaded.* And not just invaded by people with their guns and machetes and hand grenades but by animals, by dinosaurs, which worked in tandem with the people to ensure nothing could remain alive and no one could escape, and this while still others lit the trees and bushes on fire so that the sky glowed red-orange and the smoke piled high like mushroom clouds and the birds scattered in the night.

It had been, in short, a vision of hell on earth—nothing more nor less—and it had revealed to her, in the twilit moments between wakefulness and sleep, a kind of trinity of figures, one of which had been a man bearing an automatic rifle and wearing a bandana, the other a boy whose head was bald as though he'd been a cancer patient before the Flashback, and the third a dinosaur the likes of which she'd never seen: a large allosaur, or something like it, blood-red in color and with arms like a velociraptor, which killed, or so it seemed, not just indifferently but with a kind of practiced glee, as though it had not only been born to it but trained to it, as well.

Nor had those been the only strange aspects to the dream/vision—for they had changed, then, the figures, as personages so often did in dreams, to become Will, Luna, and Ank. Moreover, she had observed herself in the dream—just a fleeting glimpse, really, walking hand in hand with Will, before he once again reverted to the man in the bandana. And yet she continued to walk with him; and it was only right before she stirred that she saw that her dream doppelganger was clearly pregnant. That's when she had awakened, her small frame trembling, her skin bathed in sweat, and moved away from Sammy.

Sammy ...

She turned to face him and found him already looking back at her, his black mop of hair a tangled mess, his stubble having noticeably grown, his eyes seeming to understand. "Are you all right?" he asked. "I guess ... I guess we got a little carried away, didn't we?" When she didn't respond he moved to get up. "I'll go—"

"No, stay. Please," she said, and lay back in his arms. "I had a dream, that's all. A nightmare. But it's over. It's fading. I'm—I'm fine now, really." She toyed with the hair on his chest; there was a lot of it. "You and Will are a lot alike; did you know that?"

He didn't respond for several seconds. "I have *no* idea how to respond to that," he said at length, and laughed.

"I mean you're both independent spirits. He perhaps more than you, but ... you're both cut from the same cloth. It's not a criticism—I guess it's just ..." She laughed a little to herself. "An explanation."

"An excuse, then," he said, and chuckled. He stroked her long, dark hair.

"Maybe," she said.

"It's okay," he said, softly, gently. "I know you belong to him. Like I said, we just got—carried away. That's all."

She lay against his chest in silence for what seemed a long time.

"I don't know who I belong to anymore," she said.

And soon she slept and dreamed once again—in which she found herself making love to her husband in the shitty trailer house in Anchor Rock ... which morphed into the ramshackle house in Lonepine and Will; which bled into the tent with Sammy and the vision ... a vision to which she returned, lost, wandering, until she found the man in the dirty bandana. Until they, too, were making love, or a perversion of it, and she knew not in truth who she even was anymore, but sensed that she had become not just a woman but a focusing point, an epitome, a river of menstrual blood as dark as it was unpredictable—the mother and whore to the entire world.

VIII

It hadn't been easy securing the massive, black bomb to Ank's back—even with the heavy-duty ratchet straps they'd found elsewhere amidst the ruins. They'd had to wait for daybreak, for one (for the complex was as dark as it was impenetrable, even with its roof half-collapsed); moreover, the thing was *heavy*—so much so that the only thing to do was to have Ank lay on his side as Williams secured the belts ... and this while the two were-raptors, who remained just beyond the high walls of the compound, yelped and yowled in the sun—a constant reminder of just how precarious their situation had become. As for Williams, he was still just as confused about Ank's history and intentions as he had been the night before.

"So let me get this straight: When you woke from your tumble into the ravine you had total recall ... that being that you were a rocket scientist—"

<*A nuclear munitions expert ...*>

"—and that you had contracted with the Department of Defense to design the next gen of soldier-mounted tactical backpack nukes ... even though they'd been outlawed since 1994."

<*The law was repealed in 2004; but yes, that's the jist of it.*>

Williams hopped onto Ank's tail and clambered to the top of his shell, where he positioned his rifle against the ceiling-less wall and began sighting the yowling were-raptors. "Fine. And that you were assigned to this place in spite of your age—S-4, they called it—but were vacationing in northern California when the Flashback hit: where you were attacked by a pack of raptors and died next to a pond before being lifted into the sky and brought back to life by aliens. Is that about it?"

<*I didn't say they were aliens. I said—*>

"At which point you were returned to bodily form but as an ankylosaur, not a man. A little higher—can you arch your back or something?"

Ank groaned as he straightened. *<Look, what can you see? We've got precious little time and if we don't—>*

"Just hold on. And that this device is what you were working on before skedaddling off to wine country for some much-needed R&R; even though it's as big as a refrigerator—"

<It's a prototype, dammit, I told you. Now what can you see?>

Williams squinted along his barrel. "Two were-raptors; one's Katrina ... the other, I don't know. They've retreated to the fence line—probably to make it harder for me to sight them. Wouldn't be a problem except for one small detail ..."

<You refuse to shoot Katrina.>

"No. I've only got one bullet left."

Ank was silent. At last he communicated, *<You left without any additional—>*

"It seemed like the right thing to do at the time," Williams exclaimed. "God's been talking to us while you were out of the loop, in case you didn't know, just as sure as you're talking to me now, and—"

<Then we're in real trouble, because I can't fight with this thing strapped to my back. And we don't have time to try and wait them out ...>

Williams moved his barrel from one animal to the other, past the steel fencepost between them—then back to the fencepost, which was bound up in razor wire.

<Did you hear me, Will? I said I can't fight with this—>

"Ank, just ..." Williams lowered his head. "Just shut up a minute. I'm ... trying to think."

The ankylosaur stirred beneath his boots and he almost lost his balance. *"Steady, dammit!"*

He refocused on the fencepost.

And it hit him all at once—just hit him with the force of a rock: The Travelling East Meets West Show and a smiling Ngoc Tran. Their final performance in sunny Fresno, California.

The red balloons.

The mounted knife.

The adoring crowd just instants before the Flashback.

Sammy wasn't sure how long he would have slept if not for the choking smoke, which waked him in a fit of coughing sometime around 9 am, at least according to his nicked and battered watch. Nor was Sheila still with him—although he wasn't particularly surprised; she had her son to think about, for one, and who knew how Williams would react if he were to return from his sojourn to find them suddenly cozied up in her—in *their*—own tent?

Poor Sammy, came a voice, *her* voice, his ex (not the younger woman, Annie, with whom he'd absconded shortly before the Flashback). *'Have Dick, Will Travel' reads the card of a man. Your work is just never done, is it?*

He sat up and ran a hand through his hair, trying not to think about it. It was only after several moments that he realized Erik was standing just beyond the flap, looking every bit as disheveled as Sammy felt.

"Have you seen my mom?" he asked, simply, quietly. But there was no mistaking the fearful expression on his face.

"She's not with you?" said Sammy.

"No, sir." The boy frowned as though slightly embarrassed. "I haven't seen her since last night. The way you were dancing, I thought ... I thought she was with you."

"Well, I ... We ..." He glanced at where Sheila's bra lay helter-skelter in the corner. "Look, give me just a minute, okay? We'll go find her."

"Okay." The boy just looked at him, waiting patiently.

"Yes, sir, just one minute and I'll be right out," said Sammy.

"Okay," Erik repeated.

And then, when it became clear the boy wasn't going to budge, Sammy held the blankets against himself and zippered the flap shut, after which he stuffed Sheila's bra under the pillow and hurriedly dressed.

It wasn't until after they'd checked everywhere, virtually everywhere, from the thriving common areas to the sandbagged and razor-wired battlements to the radio station itself, that Sammy hit upon the idea of using the plane to search for her—an idea which was well-received by both Bella Ray and Peter, for they were each of them eager to see if the Cessna would still fly and if the former airline pilot could accommodate himself to its streamlined and mostly manual controls.

As it turned out, the answer to both was a resounding 'yes,' and before Sammy knew it Peter and himself were jouncing along the crude airstrip and swooping into the air, even as Erik and Samantha looked on from the sidelines and the residents of Barley threw up a cheer. Then they were circling the fortified town and its surrounding areas at increasingly higher altitudes—Sammy grinding the binoculars while Peter worked the controls—until that, too, proved fruitless; at which point Bella requested they broaden their flight pattern to include the nearby highways and towns, lest they be unprepared to welcome any new arrivals (or, worse, even miss a threat), and it was at precisely that moment that Sammy realized what should have been obvious to him from the start: that Sheila had not merely disappeared but rather left in search of Williams—probably racked with guilt.

At least that's what he was thinking as the mile-long caravan of vehicles came into view and Peter muttered "Holy shit" into his headset, prompting Bella to say, in a somewhat alarmed manner, "What is it? What do you see?"

But Peter didn't respond until he'd swung around and had a better look, flying low over the column until it was obvious there were precious few military vehicles and that it couldn't possibly be the armada described by Felix the Fixed-wing Wonder. Indeed, the people in the wagon train waved at them as they passed, appearing even to hoot and to holler, at which point the pilot laughed and said into his headset: "No worries, Bella. Looks like the cavalry has arrived, that's

all. I'm gonna push on for Missoula and have a quick look-
see."

And it was there that whatever celebratory impulse they
might otherwise have had was quickly extinguished ... for the
city had been surrounded by the real caravan (the one Felix
had so aptly described only a few days ago) and was being
shelled mercilessly even as they approached—enough so that
the municipality virtually glowed like an ember ... even in the
sun.

"Turn back, Peter, immediately," said Bella with the
utmost urgency. "Don't let them see you." —although it was
hardly necessary, for the pilot had already begun the turn.

And then they were on their way back, Sammy using the
opportunity to scour the landscape for Sheila even though he
knew by this point there was very little hope. And while he
saw no signs of her and his eyes had begun to fail from
squinting, he did notice something he had utterly missed the
first time—a series of what appeared to be tank tracks, no, not
just tank tracks, but therapod prints, of the kind a
tyrannosaur might make, or an allosaur, along with others he
did not immediately recognize. And he noticed, too, that they
stretched both backward toward Missoula and forward
toward Barley, circumnavigating it—as though someone was
attempting to mount a rear assault. As though someone had
been planning all along to catch them in a pincer movement.

Sheila waited until the Cessna was well out of sight before
reemerging into the glade, still feeling the ground vibrate—
which she had first noticed upon crouching so near to it in
the bushes—still sensing that something was coming, and still
only half aware of where she was or how she'd gotten there.

It was, in a sense, as if she still dreamed (certainly the air
was still choked with smoke as it had been in her vision of
Bozeman), and yet, beyond that, the clearing had about it a
slumberous quality all its own, one she could only liken to a
cathedral or other place of worship, at least until the M1-A1

Abrams tank appeared at its opposite end and began rattling toward her.

Holy Mother of God, she thought, as it was joined by another ... and another ... and yet another still; nor did they travel alone but were accompanied by foot soldiers, themselves armed with flamethrowers. And that was just the first tier. For behind them lumbered a collection of dinosaurs—a triceratops and stegosaurus were easy enough to spot—less obvious were the legions of velociraptors which flitted between the trees like wraiths. And behind all of it strode an allosaur such as those they'd encountered at the Santiago— except this one was mottled red and black and bore a kind of saddle—upon which the Bandana Man sat, perched.

Like a king, she thought. Or a bizarro-verse paladin ... who raised a hand, and, without so much as a word, somehow caused the tanks and the animals to stop.

And then there she was, alone against an array of idling tanks and grumbling animals, as the Bandana Man trotted his steed around to the front and simply stared at her, his gaze such that it seemed she was being penetrated rather than merely looked upon, and penetrated by not just two eyes but many, as though the man were not a single being at all but legion.

And she found she wanted to run more than anything in the world but couldn't. Wanted to turn and dash for Barley and the arms of Sammy and Erik but was paralyzed. And it was at that moment that the man in the bandana swung a leg over the saddle and glided—yes, *glided*—to the earth, where he touched down like a fog, and she wanted to scream, tried to scream, but couldn't—and not because her body had become paralyzed but for the simple reason that she no longer had a mouth to do so.

"*Shhh,*" he whispered, placing a finger against his bandana. "It isn't a time for speaking but for listening."

And then he used the finger to pull down his scarf, revealing a face that was at once rugged and serene. "See?" He smiled warmly, beatifically, revealing teeth just as straight and white as a movie star. "I'm just a man, I assure you. Don't let the parlor tricks fool you."

He touched her between her heaving breasts gently. *"Shhh,* it's okay. Breath through your nose. Try not to hyperventilate." He leaned forward and scrunched up his neck, smiling at her as though he would a child. "It'll be returned to you, don't worry ..."

She focused on her breathing, trying indeed not to hyperventilate, but feeling as though her heart might punch through her chest at any moment. The spot where he had touched her seemed to burn and freeze at the same time.

"You don't remember ... do you?" His brown eyes suddenly twinkled and he shook his head. "No? You don't remember calling on me in the depths of those first awful nights, when you were at your most exposed, when you were at your most vulnerable?" He stroked her long, brown hair with an almost impossible gentleness; it was as though a cool-warm breeze rifled it rather than his fingers. "When it was just you and the boy ... alone, scared. Cold. Hungry?"

She began to shake her head almost violently, her breathing and heartrate accelerating once again.

"Oh, yes," he said, squinting, smiling. "You did. All the world did. It's nothing to be ashamed of. You called on many during that time, in those hours and days and weeks after the Flashback—you wouldn't have been aware of it. And you cursed the One who had brought it upon you ... who had taken your husband and your daughter; who had taken so many husbands and daughters. It's okay. We—we don't judge. Not like them," He looked at the hazy sky and the alien-colored lights, at the sun itself which was a white disk in the smoke. "Not like Him."

He placed a hand over her face suddenly and not particularly gently, and the next thing she knew they were standing on a hill overlooking Barley—or rather, what was left of it. It was covered in snow and ice as though a brutal winter storm had swept through—snow and ice amidst which hundreds, perhaps thousands, of bodies lay entombed. He took her hand abruptly and they glided like wraiths over the necropolis ... until they were standing again but this time over a pair of individual corpses—a woman and a child. Herself and Erik.

"What you see is the future," he said simply, softly. "What you see is what will remain after the tip of the spear and its shaft meet—when all your efforts have resulted in nothing but needless suffering and chaos." He didn't speak for several moments.

At last he added, "You have an elemental among you, that is good. But she will fail in her bid to counter our own," He laughed so softly it was almost imperceptible. "Our little bald sage. Our He Who Commands the Freezing Dark. And she will fail, in part, because of you."

He waved his hand almost desultorily. "Now let me show you an alternative—one in which the end result for Barley is the same ... but the fate of you and your son is not."

She blinked and the ice was gone, replaced by the hardscrabble trailer home in Anchor Rock. "Let me show you what is possible in a world without them ... a world without Him. A world in which all, even the Dukes of Hell, simply do what they wilt ..."

And then Stephen was there and Tammy too, both her husband and her daughter; and they all the four of them were a family once again—together beneath a stormless sky, undaunted by anything but their worldly troubles—free of the Flashback. Free, even, of Time itself.

"We'll camp here tonight," he said amidst the vision, and when again she blinked they were back in the glade.

"Yes, my lord," said one of his lieutenants—and scrambled off to make preparations.

And to her he said, "Stay with us."

To which she responded, finding she had a mouth again and could speak, "Okay."

There was a single, sharp tap of the drums followed by a rapid succession of beats as the crushed velvet curtains spread and the audience gasped: for Tran had taken her position in the box and was even now being secured as Williams struck a gunfighter pose and his hand hovered next to his weapon.

"Ladies and gentlemen, I think it goes without saying," said the announcer over the speaker system, "Do not try this at home."

Williams relaxed his entire body even as his mind cycled through the calculations—altitude, the breeze, humidity, temperature, the curvature of the earth, the spinning of the earth ... It was, like music, a largely mathematical proposition; a cold equation he'd had a gift for ever since he could remember, ever since he was a boy with a Daisy BB gun in the backyard of their southern California home.

He focused on the knife blade as the balloons to each side of it warbled in the breeze. It was a funny thing, sharpshooting, so utterly unlike music, in that each time he did it he felt like he was doing it for the first time, felt like he was starting over from scratch. With music his fingers just automatically found the frets, just instantly knew where to begin and where to end; he never felt as though he were lost in a vortex of potentialities, never doubted his ability to perform. But sharpshooting was a different beast altogether. With sharpshooting he had to call on something outside of himself as well as from within—something which was not his to control. Something which either kissed him with its ghostly lips or turned away with perfect indifference—like love itself, he supposed. Or God.

And then the drum taps stopped and he was alone with the breeze, and it was time to make the intuitive leap which would set the bullet in motion. And as he breathed out and drew his revolver and squeezed its trigger softer than he would a daisy, he knew, even before the *crack!* and the *ka-chink!* and the pop of the balloons, that the projectile had found its target. That it had found the slim blade and split like an atom—becoming two loaves rather than one—two soft but lethal slugs, which had spread like shrapnel in the Fresno heat and ruptured the red balloons—releasing their air in a vacuum-like rush and causing the audience to gasp and to cheer.

And then his wife was there, having loosed her mock bonds and scrambled out of the tall wooden box (with its crushed velvet curtains and bulletproof glass), and she'd bowed to the audience before embracing him like the wind, and he had kissed her as he always did after completing their final act—when air raid sirens sounded and he looked at the sky, which had darkened with a stormfront as fast-moving as it was inexplicable ...

For the Flashback had come to southern California—come with its otherworldly weather and pterodactyls which circled like tornado debris; its time-scrambling phantasmagoria, its erasure of both the living and the dead—just as it had come to all the world.

He batted his eyes and came out of it, saw two corpses spread out amongst the sage. Katrina and one other, having reverted to human form. Birds tweeted obliviously as their nude bodies lay broken beneath the sun.

<What happened?> asked Ank as he stirred beneath Williams' boots. *<Did you get one or not?>*

Williams looked at the razor wire and at the steel pole to which it was attached. "Yeah. It's—it's all done. Both of them. I—can you let me down, please?"

The ankylosaur groaned and knelt upon the broken pavement, after which Williams hopped off and crouched by his head.

"Those people were good to us, especially her," he said at last, before falling into a sullen silence. The birds continued to tweet obscenely.

<It—it wasn't meant to be. Let it rest, Will. Let them rest. We've ... we've got work to do.>

Williams swept his hat off and ran a hand through his hair, sighed. "We'll never make it ... you know that, don't you?"

<And yet we may, Will. We just may.>

And then they were off, pausing just long enough to pile stones upon the bodies.

IX

Peter had been right: The cavalry had arrived. Or so it seemed as the motor homes and semi-trucks and construction equipment and motorcycles and even a couple armored personnel carriers rumbled into Barley. And yet introductions had been kept short and celebrations to a minimum as the drivers sought position and the smoke roiled in from the southeast, for it was clear to everyone now just how close the Enemy had drawn ... and how near the confrontation was.

Still, Bella felt an optimism she hadn't felt in days as she inspected the crowd of what amounted to new soldiers and helped her big assistant take stock of the heavy equipment, and by the time she and the wagon train's leaders met for an initial consultation by the hot springs she had largely beaten back the depression which had so dogged her the first part of the day.

Mostly she was just relieved at what a hardy and experienced bunch they were: from the hand-less man named Roger to the strapping former convenience store clerk (whose name she couldn't remember) to the tough little woman named Charlotte to the steady and stoic man named Red—they were seasoned survivors, all of them, and had seen their share of blood and conflict long before they'd ever heard of Radio Free Montana or the Enemy in the East.

That experience would be needed, and soon, thought Bella, as she inspected the perimeter's booby-traps and fortifications—its sandbagged pillboxes, its trenches full of gasoline—for she was now convinced, after consulting with Sammy and Peter, that an attack could come at any time ... and from any direction. And she wondered: Had they done enough? For something still tasked her—she couldn't quite put her finger on it. Something ghostly and ephemeral. Something which had first arisen in her dreams and now dogged her every waking step.

Something was missing ... something that, in her single-minded purpose, she had overlooked completely. She thought of the albino girl and what she'd said immediately after their arrival: *But this isn't all of us. There's also Will and Ank ... but we don't know where they are right now.*

Will and Ank. Why did the names sound so alien and yet familiar at the same time?

Ank's been gone awhile ... but Will went looking for him.

Just today, Sheila had said. *Heading south on something called the 'Redneck Highway.'*

Bella stopped in her tracks, staring along the battlements but no longer actually seeing them. *Of course,* she thought. Her dreams ... the visions ... The mirror and the Paladin. The Paladin and the Brute.

And like that she seemed to understand the thing—its rules and its perimeters, its use of proxies and doppelgangers, its need to conjure counterparts in every single aspect ... and she knew, also, just what she needed to do to fulfil her part.

They sprinted, galloping and swerving around the hardscrabble landforms of the steppes, Ank's tail undulating and swaying, Williams' poncho flapping in the wind. And at first it seemed they might keep that pace indefinitely—for they had both experienced a burst of raw energy since leaving the compound and its night of delicate terrors behind—and yet it was not to be as Williams began to lag and Ank grew concerned with his wellbeing and they at last trotted to a stop next to a pair of rusty railroad tracks, the man panting and gasping while the dinosaur used his snout to brush against him affectionately and to communicate, without judgement, *<It's okay, Will. If you need to rest ... do it. Just—don't take too long. Please.>*

Williams lowered his head, breathing heavily, clutching his chest. "It's—it's no use. I'm just not going to make it ... not at this pace, Ank. Not in time to—"

<Yes you can, Will. You can and you must. Look, Will ... everything comes down to us getting this bomb there. And to doing it before the Enemy has gotten too close for us to use it. Luna, Sheila, the kids ... they're all counting on us, even if they don't know it yet. You can ride on my back if you have to.>

Williams shook his head. "I'd—I'd never be able to hang on ... and ..." He took a deep breath. "You've got enough burden as it is." He shook his head again. "No. I've ... I've done my part in all this. This is on you now ... it's always been on you. Just—leave me here, buddy. We haven't seen a predator since we left the compound. I'll be fine, really. I'm just going to keep plugging along. And I'll see you in Barley."

The wind blew and Ank didn't say anything. At last he gazed down the tracks forlornly, thoughtfully, as if by doing so he might divine the likelihood of Will's survival ... and then froze, fixated on something in the distance.

"What? What is it?" Will followed his gaze to where the watery-looking tracks met their vanishing point. He squinted in the sun. "There's nothing there, Ank. Just some old tracks—they probably didn't amount to anything even before ..."

But there *was* something. Just the smallest rectangle of color, yellow and red, wiggling amidst the convection waves. And when he realized what it was he very nearly fainted. "You've got to be fucking kidding me ..."

At which instant he heard two things that he hadn't heard in a long time: Ank's laughter, which was a stranger thing to hear in one's mind even then his speaking voice, and the booming, throaty horn of a diesel locomotive—which was bearing down upon them at a shockingly rapid clip. "Get off the tracks, Ank. What are you doing?"

<I'm flagging us a ride on the Post-apocalypse Railway, destination Barley, Montana.> He swung his great head to look at Williams, who was looking on in stunned disbelief and starting to laugh himself. <And I could use your help, if you don't mind.>

And then they were both standing on the ties and making a ruckus, Ank roaring and rearing up on his hind legs while Williams jumped up and down and waved his hands, having laid his rifle next to the tracks.

His name was Szambelan and at first he'd had no memory of who he'd been before the Flashback—only that he had walked the earth for approximately thirty-five years before the winds and the storms and the crackling, killing bolts, which had changed the world forever.

"I was reborn that day," he said almost casually as he began stripping away his accouterments in the silk-draped rear of the tent, which was palatial in comparison to the one she had shared with Sammy the night before. "Oh, I remembered the world and its earthly machinations; its geography and its politics, its toil and petty motivations. What I could not remember was anything of myself—the face of my mother, the face of my father ..."

Sheila watched as he pulled the dark tunic over his head and dropped it to the floor, revealing back muscles which gleamed with sweat and scars beyond her ability to count, some of which had healed and crusted over while still others seemed as fresh and angry as if they had happened only yesterday. "I only knew that I should head east. That it was only there that I might ..." He paused, his hands on the waistband of his trousers. "Well. I still believed there were clear answers then. Now I'm not so sure."

He dropped his trousers and she turned away, stepping toward the tent's door—toward the haze of smoke which enshrouded the world, the ashen dust which threatened to suffocate the life out of everything. There was no guard save the mottled red and black allosaur, which slumbered, twitching, seeming almost to dream.

"No answers," she said in what was very nearly a whisper. "You've killed thousands—hundreds, at least—and left nothing but desolation. And you say," She turned to face him again. "You haven't any answers?"

He'd put something on, thankfully, a pair of wide-legged silken pants of the kind a monk might wear, and yet the sight of him revealed so completely startled her nonetheless. For he was, physically, at least, perfect in every respect: from his wild mane of unkempt dark hair to his handsome but queerly eldritch face to his chiseled and ropy arms and abdominals. "I have no absolutes, if that's what you mean," he said, and held out a garment, the deep green color of which matched his own.

"Put this on."

She hesitated, her somber brown eyes locked up in his. At last she moved forward and took up the attire, trading places with him as he paced so that she was in the back of the tent and he stood near its door.

"What did you expect, some kind of answer to the suffering or even the great and terrible riddle?" he veritably hollered. She listened as she undressed and it sounded as though he opened a bottle. "As though I were the sage himself, I suppose ... and not merely a duke of war."

She emerged at last wearing the garment he had provided—causing him to pause, a flask of dark liquid in one hand and a pair of wine glasses in the other.

"So it *is* you, after all," he said, and set the goblets down. "Our seer had been so confident—far too confident—it had caused me to doubt him, I confess." He poured a glass for her and offered it. "Will you drink with me, then—you who in this world are Sheila Were of Anchor Rock?"

She froze suddenly feeling as though she could both nod solemnly and laugh out loud—if this were the truth behind the combined phantasmagoria of their dreams and visions then how absurd it all was! Then she took the goblet and quaffed it, deciding, in that instant, that she would no longer fear this mortal man who was as beautiful as he was ridiculous—and that the time for fear was over, in any case.

They both felt it at the same time, even as the train lurched forward and the cars jolted thunderously—a tremor in the very fabric of things, like a ripple in a foam of potentiality which contained in it the threads of all their possible futures. Something, somewhere, had just happened—something directly related to their current endeavor of delivering the bomb to Barley and detonating it amidst the Enemy.

<*An attack, you think, maybe an ambush? So soon?*> communicated Ank, still smarting from his struggle to climb onto the flatcar with the added weight of the weapon.

"You felt it too? Like one door closed and another had opened, but with disastrous consequences, for us all ..." Williams looked at him, rattled and bewildered. "Ank, how could we know that?"

<*It's possible that whatever this—this thing is, this event horizon, this convergence of power dynamics ... it's speeding up as we get closer, growing stronger. Meaning that the psychological link between us could be expanding to incorporate others. Regardless, it also means that our window for getting there has narrowed still further, possibly to the point of impossi—*>

"Ank, *don't.*"

<*It's something we need to prepare ourselves for, Will. At any rate, I'd suggest just now that you encourage our friendly engineer to step on the gas a little, or a lot.*>

Williams leaned forward until they were almost nose to nose. "Our friendly engineer, in case you haven't noticed, is clearly insane!"

<*All the more reason to give it a shot. Just do it, Will. He may actually listen.*>

And then Williams was leaning over the side using one of Ank's spikes for a handhold while simultaneously yelling at the engineer, who poked his head out the engine's side window, his long, gray hair flying, and shouted, "You want speed, you got it, ha-ha! The world, she's a comin' back, yesiree!" He sounded the horn suddenly and Williams covered an ear, even as his hat blew off and fluttered away behind them. "The New World Special is back in service— and it's taking its passengers to the Promised Land! Ha-ha!"

He thrust into her again and again, gripping her waist harder with each ramming motion of his pelvis, seeming to knock the wind out of her over and over. It was all she could do to simply not pass out; to grip the green sheets in her slim, pale fingers; to will herself back to the present and close the deal, even if it killed her.

Yes, by all means, close the deal, she thought insanely. *Oh, sister! You've most certainly done that!*

Szambelan, meanwhile, continued to fuck her from behind. *You wanted an answer, yes?* he communicated to her suddenly, telepathically, penetrating her on a whole new level, veritably splitting her in two with his thoughts. *This is it, then, in part. The First Realm—which is the true realm, the only realm, the everlasting realm praise be to Iblis and Ahriman, to Azazel and Mastema, to Al-Shaitan and Samael and Kölski and Der Leibhaftige—this realm both loves and hates you, and always has. Hates you because you are a grotesquerie, an abomination, a treasonous act of an out-of-control God; loves you because you are feeble, and brutish, and mortal, and thus deserving of compassion, and mercy, the kind of mercy we bring ...*

He stopped stabbing at her long enough to change his technique, choosing instead to penetrate her slowly, deeply. She ground her hips against him as if to concur, welcoming the respite, attempting to catch her breath. But it was difficult to do for he seemed to grow more powerful with each push— seeming literally to expand, to get bigger and bigger.

He continued: *What did thou thinkest Creation was if not the animation of dead matter from the simple infusion of conflict? Aye, so you've sculpted a homunculus and there it lay—how then to get it to raise its little arm? Why, give it Free Will, of course! For first and foremost it has to CHOOSE— that is the secret behind every act of creation. 'I will lift thine arm,' the homunculus says, and in so doing pits one muscle against the next—pushing thine blood to thine heart and thine eyes.*

Again he increased the tempo of his thrusts—as if to emphasize his point—and her breath came and went in ragged gasps.

That is it, of course, the whole of the secret in one simple shell. And thus you mistake your wars and disease and mortality for misfortune; when in fact they are but Life itself—material life, which is to say life as He reinvented it; not us. This is the reason for which we came when they instigated the Flashback—they, the judgers and the experimenters, the scramblers of Time, the halflings between this world and the next. For we shared with them a common goal: the complete eradication of your kind—by which I mean not your First Realm doppelgangers but your material manifestations, which mock us. And now it must all play out, even though the end is no doubt presumed. For if we know anything of Him and His followers, it is that they—

He stopped communicating abruptly and finished in her powerfully and voluminously, seeming to fill her at once with both ice and hot oil. Then it was over as quickly as it had begun, and she could only lay there shuddering ... wondering if he would, or even could, honor the deal, and wondering, too, just what in God's name she had done.

He stroked her hair with a hand which had become massive and a curved talon snagged in the locks. *So tell me, you who in this realm are Sheila of Anchor Rock. Given that your Creator has merely invented pain ... and called it the Second Realm ... do you see now why we resist Him? And why we would end His experiment once and for all?*

But Sheila saw nothing save a universe even less sane then she'd presumed—not her family reunited nor her former enemy vanquished nor her son miraculously spared. And when sleep came at last it was fitful and incomplete ... and long with dreams in which she wandered alone.

Williams half-slept—his back propped against Ank and the wind in his hair—dreaming, remembering.

They had been running, was all he knew for certain: running with hundreds of others as the storm fell upon the fairgrounds and the dinosaurs scattered the crowd—entire swaths of which simply blurred and vanished completely, as though they'd never existed, as though they'd never been more than figments of his imagination. And then they'd been swallowed by a group none of whom had disappeared, and carried along by its current to the slow-moving train, upon whose flatcars throngs of parents had begun placing their children, and Williams had let go of her—of Tran's—hand, and begun assisting them. And he hadn't been but a few minutes—three, at a maximum—when Tran had called out ... for someone, meaning well, of course, had picked her up and sat her upon one of the railcars.

And then the locomotive had begun picking up speed, its horn blowing, its diesel engines pounding, and he'd no choice but to run along next to it, reaching out to her desperately, grasping her hand once before having to let go, unable to find a place among the throngs—which now included adults—until the train began to pull ahead and he was forced to double his speed in an awkward and dangerous fashion, at which point he tripped over an obstruction and fell hard upon the pavement, striking his head so that blackness overcame him and he was lost to her—to the world—even to himself.

He stirred even as Ank stirred—as the train rattled and clacked and swayed, passing over a crooked section of track— and the dinosaur regarded him closely, almost clinically. *<I experienced part of that, Will. Just now. The throngs of terrified people ... the one you called 'Tran.' I saw her just as clear as I'm seeing you now.>*

"My God, Ank," Williams began—as bewildered as he had been before. "What's happening to us?"

He watched as Ank looked on, scanning the landscape, it seemed, trying to gauge their location.

"She's *alive,* Ank. Did you feel it? Alive, now, somewhere north of here. Canada, maybe. Jesus, she's been waiting for me all—"

<It's an adventure for another day, Will. This is our stop.>

Williams smiled as the train jostled them, his head hanging to one side, his cheeks suddenly rosy. And then he came out of it and once again hung over the side, calling to the engineer, "Conductor, it's been a pleasure riding with you! But here is where we must depart!"

At which the engineer merely gave him a thumbs up—and, as evidenced by the shrieking of the wheels, began applying the brakes.

X

Bella Ray very nearly threw up her hands as the crowd devolved into chaos, wondering what more she could possibly say that might organize them and steel them for the inevitable—what more she could possibly do to prepare them for what was coming ... and soon. Indeed, it could come at any moment.

"Order, order!" cried her big assistant—Gorjira, someone had dubbed him, and it had stuck—shoving back those closest to the stage, adjusting the strap of the rifle at his back so that it would stop sliding off his shoulder.

"What good is order if we're all going to die anyway?" someone hollered—a young woman with cobalt hair and a plethora of tattoos, whom the newcomers called 'The Acolyte of Blue'—something they'd yet to explain to Bella or to anyone else.

"Maybe you should broadcast the Lord's Prayer again," shouted someone else, referring to her decision to engage the listeners of Radio Free Montana in a group prayer just hours before the meeting—and a large percentage of the people laughed.

Bella looked to the newcomers' leaders in what appeared to be total exasperation—as if to say: Help me, please?

At last one of them took to the stage—the man named Red—followed by his girlfriend, Charlotte, and finally the others: Roger, Savanna, and the convenience store clerk (whose name Bella still couldn't remember). And yet the bedlam only intensified ... at least until Red raised his arms and began shouting, "Enough! That's enough! Everyone just settle down!"

He waited until the ruckus began to peter out.

At last he said, "This bickering will get us nowhere. Believe me, I know. I've seen this movie before. I know everyone is scared ... that's understandable. But, *dammit*—

we've come this far without turning on each other's throats, why now?"

Bella looked out over the crowd, at the faces of the survivors both young and old. *Why now, indeed,* she thought. *When the Enemy draws near and his influence spreads ...*

"Maybe you'll *mansplain* it for us," cried the Acolyte of Blue—and Red just stared at her, thinking of the Shambhala and realizing that some poisons, once they'd polluted the groundwater, just never went away.

"Maybe it's because none of us ever recall holding an election," shouted Someone Else, which was met with a round of raucous applause. "Or giving our permission to broadcast our whereabouts to the entire world."

"That's where it all started," yelled still another, and pointed at Bella accusatorily. "If not for her they'd have never even known we existed ..."

"We should burn her goddamn radio station!" shouted the Acolyte.

"Yes, and topple its tower," added Someone Else.

"Topple its tower!" someone shouted instantly, and began repeating the sentiment: "Topple its tower ...!"

And then approximately half the crowd had begun chanting, and Red looked at Charlotte who looked squarely back at him—and began to shake her head. *We're in over our heads,* she seemed to be saying. *This is no longer the Shambhala.*

That's when a series of shots rang out and everyone looked to the back of the mob, where Williams stood next to Ank—having commandeered a pistol from someone in the crowd—and began lowering his gun hand slowly. Gasps quickly followed as more and more people took notice of the bomb on Ank's back and the mob gave them a wide birth.

"Are you done now?" said Williams at last. He handed the gun back to its owner. "Because if you'll kindly screw your courage back up, we've got a way to end this. To end the Enemy. For good."

She moved through the forest like a ghost, uncertain of her destination—other than that it was in Barley—but convinced, too, that she would know it when she saw it. Nor did she travel alone, for the voice of Szambelan now followed her everywhere: cajoling her to hurry—for the tip of the spear was about to strike—assuring her that she had made the right choice, reminding her that Erik was depending on her.

Not that she needed it, for the image of his frozen body had lodged in her brain like a bullet; it was at least possible that she'd never be free of it, not if she lived a thousand years. And so she glided through the trees and the shafts of sunlit smoke like a wraith, driven by her fear and animus, haunted by doubt—and yet knowing there was no going back; not for her.

Not for anyone.

The plane had no more than lifted off the runway with Peter and Sammy and the bomb onboard when the first missiles struck, rocking the air with concussions and causing everyone to hit the dirt—and Ank could only pray that he'd made the right decision.

Williams literally read his mind; they could do that now. "The altimeter was the right decision, Ank. Now they won't have to land and physically place the bomb and we won't have to fool with that remote detonator. All they have to do is fly over the target and *roll* the sucker out."

<*If it doesn't fail, Will, as I said. The bomb was never intended as an air-to-surface projectile—the altimeter was a last-minute addition. It hasn't even been tested.*>

Williams stood as even more explosions rocked the airfield and everyone scattered—rushing to aid the perimeter battalions, he presumed. "Will you know if it fails?"

Ank clambered to his feet and looked to where the remote detonator lay atop the radio on the command table—prepping and loading the bomb had been a frantic affair; the truth was he'd forgotten all about it. <If I'm close enough to the detonator, yes. Its screen will sound an alarm.>

"And you can still detonate manually?"

<In theory, yes. But I'll need someone to work the controls. And it can't be you.>

"Why not?"

There was the sound of automatic rifle fire. <Because you're needed at the front. You and that weapon of yours.> There were more explosions—followed by gunfire. <Go! If it becomes necessary, I'll find someone.>

Williams glanced toward the perimeter and did a doubletake. "Ank," he said—then grinned at his friend. "That's not going to be necessary."

And when Ank looked up he understood why: for Luna was running at them across the airfield, her pink dress trailing out behind her and her white hair flying.

They streamed out from the tree line in a veritable blitzkrieg, the guns of the tanks rotating and firing, the foot soldiers alternately taking cover behind vehicles and squeezing off bursts, the raptors and triceratops and stegosaurs charging—as Red and Charlotte and Roger and Savanna continued shooting and the children ran ammo and Bella lit the gasoline trenches, as Gojira and the clerk prepared shoulder-mounted rocket launchers. As hundreds of others joined the battle belatedly and began to kill and to be killed.

And then they were there; they were at the gates, and the triceratops and stegosaurs had waded into the burning trenches and begun serving as bridges—sacrificing themselves so that the raptors and the foot soldiers could cross—even as a column of bulldozers fanned out along the perimeter and prepared to break the lines for good: dropping their blades—which rattled and clinked against the hail of gunfire—revving their engines, spewing black smoke.

"Bayonets!" cried Red as the raptors fell upon them, thrusting his own so that it skewered one of the dinosaurs like a shish kabob even before he used its own weight and momentum to swing it over and behind himself.

And then, just as it seemed they would be overwhelmed completely, a strange thing started to happen: for the heads of the beasts began to *jolt* one by one; sometimes remaining intact—even while ejecting long streams of blood—but more often exploding outright ... and when Red and Charlotte and the others looked to see what was going on, they saw (with a rush of relief; for his fame as a sharpshooter had spread far and wide in his absence) that Williams had joined the fray at last, and had taken a position.

He'd found the M-16 and the 9mm pistol amidst the pile of surplus weapons near the armored personnel carriers, along with their attendant ammunition, and for that he was grateful. But that didn't change the fact that the Army-issue rifle was wildly inaccurate, at least compared to his own, and Williams found that he was missing as often as he hit even as he adjusted to its sights and the heft of it in his hands and the foot soldiers broke the lines—rapidly continuing on as though they had no interest in holding territory whatsoever and causing Williams to realize, suddenly and with perfect clarity, what their true intent had been all along.

For they'd targeted Ank and Luna just as surely as they'd crashed the defenses, and it was at precisely that instant, the instant he'd had this realization, that matters became a thousand times worse: for the Bandana Man had arrived upon his mottled red and black steed.

And before he'd even been able to react the dark paladin had dismounted and sent the allosaur forward, at which instant it bound directly for him and Williams held his trigger down—but was thwarted by the beast's winding movements and dizzying speed, so that he could only dive for cover as it trampled the sandbagged perimeter and continued on toward Ank and Luna.

And then he was facing off with the Bandana Man even as the battle changed direction—divining, in the same way he had divined almost everything since that faithful day at the East Mirabeau Drive-in Theater, that it was somehow his purpose to do so ... That it was somehow his fate.

Almost like clockwork, the altimeter had failed—just as Ank feared it would—raising an alarm as the detonator's screen flashed and causing him to scuttle closer ... even as the Enemy closed and Luna looked on—smelling suddenly of fire and smoke.

Now is the time, he thought, *to see how much the vergence has spread. To see if it can be done— how far one can project. To see if anyone can hear me besides Williams.*

And then he began projecting to Peter and the plane—saying, in essence: <*Listen to me and listen carefully ... there isn't much time ...*>

"What? What is it?" asked Sammy—even as Peter continued to gaze forward, clearly in a trance.

"I—I don't know ... It's like ... there was a voice. Inside my head."

Sammy looked out the window again as the plane's engine droned all around them—at the miles-long caravan of trucks and dinosaurs and military equipment, the totality of what they would face if their mission failed. "We're close enough. I'm going to open the door ..."

"No ... no, I wouldn't do that," Peter said, almost whispering. "Not yet. I—I'm going to take us down."

"Take us down? Have you gone mad? We're almost over the target!"

But the plane had already begun descending—rapidly, gut-wrenchingly—even as Sammy protested and the bomb rocked. And then they were skittering to a stop on the surface of the Interstate, Peter unbuckling his seat belt, saying to Sammy, as the pavement vibrated and the caravan rumbled closer, "Remember how Williams used to talk to his dinosaur and I'd laugh? Used to talk about faith?"

Sammy just looked at him, his long, dark hair hanging in his face. At last he moved to speak but hesitated.

"I'm asking you to have some right now," said Peter.

And then he got out and Sammy did likewise; and they met at the side door as Peter slid it open—the bomb gleaming within like so much black obsidian.

<Luna, listen, I'm going to need you to ...> And then Ank trailed off—unable, at first, to process what he was seeing. For the little girl's eyes had rolled back in her skull and become completely white, and she was even now raising a hand against the invading army—the fingertips of which began to catch fire one by one—as Ank watched disbelieving and a group of enemy soldiers simply exploded into a massive fireball.

And then the allosaurus was there, it was upon him, and the two dinosaurs were rolling like leviathan football players across the shoulder of the airstrip—their tails whipping furiously, their teeth gnashing—as Luna continued to target the soldiers and the missiles continued to rain down; as the white disk of the sun glowered at them through the smoke.

They paused at last, having approached each other slowly and surely across the terrain, discarding their rifles, unfastening their holsters.

Ank was in trouble, Williams knew; and yet he knew also that killing the Bandana Man was the surest way of saving him, of saving everyone ... that the mirror paladin and his red-black beast shared a bond not unlike Ank and himself, and that if he were to die the beast would surely follow—by having his concentration shattered at a pivotal moment in the battle, if nothing else. And so he stood with his hand poised near his pistol and stared the man down, knowing this was the way it was supposed to be, that each of them were but avatars of beings and forces beyond their control, and that it was too late to change tact, anyway. That it would be decided in a gunfight, a duel, a quickdraw. And that he was ready—as ready as he'd ever be.

"Draw," he said at last, simply, finally, even as the wind blew and the sounds of battle echoed across the plains.

"Draw," said Szambelan, mocking him, and then smiled coolly, serenely. "Surely you know that your bomb will not be detonated, regardless of this outcome, yes? That your army will be laid to waste, your loved ones slaughtered ..."

Williams didn't say anything, only continued to stare at him.

"Yes, yes, you do," said Szambelan, smiling, scrunching up his neck. "And if you didn't before you are sensing it now; as your companion fights for his life and your elemental deploys her power—only far too late. Yes, even as the altimeter proceeds to fail ..."

Williams blinked twice and Szambelan raised his chin, as if seizing on the opportunity to distract him. "It *has* failed, you know. Nor will it be detonated manually ... I've taken steps to ensure that." His dark eyes dropped to Williams' holster, lingering there. "I see you've adopted a new sidearm. Something, shall we say, more modern?" He looked him in the eyes again. "I must say, I am surprised by you. To go into a gunfight without your best friend ... It seems ... counter-intuitive."

When Williams still did not respond he added, "For it is a man's best friend—his weapon. Something he will live by and die by when all else abandons him. It is not woman. It is not wealth." He paused suddenly and looked away, as though he were looking inward—looking into the abyss. "Your companion animal, the ankylosaur ... he is not faring well."

And then he was drawing, his hand virtually a blur as it snatched up his pistol and aimed at Williams' heart, and he'd just begun to squeeze the trigger when a black hole the size of a dime opened in his forehead and a stream of blood squirted out the back of his head—once, twice, spattering upon the ground, three times.

And then he fell, his legs buckling like paper, his body convulsing.

"A dinosaur is a man's best friend," said Williams at last, and tossed the pistol onto the corpse.

And then he turned and ran for the airstrip, hoping he had made a difference. Hoping Ank was still alive.

As it played out, the battle for Barley, not to mention the battle between Ank and the red-black allosaur, had, indeed turned on whether Szambelan lived or died—for it quickly became evident that it had lost much of its focus immediately after his passing. Enough so that, with the help of Luna—who had stopped the foot soldiers in their tracks and literally melted the Abrams tanks—as well as the guns of Red and the other leaders of the wagon train, Ank stood victorious at last ... at least until he realized the remote detonator had been destroyed—utterly smashed to pieces, and by none other than Sheila, who had attempted to flee but been piled upon and apprehended in very short order.

Regardless, it had left everyone who had survived the battle (and been informed by Ank of the altimeter's failure) little choice but to gather around the command table and look on somewhat forlornly, for it seemed now their victory would be as short-lived as it had been costly. That's when Williams arrived without even a gun and was informed of the altimeter and of Luna's incredible power, after which he knelt beside the albino girl in haste, cajoling her to, "Let go," and to focus upon the bomb—to be the "magnifying glass beneath the sun," as they had talked about so many times.

"You saw it as we were loading it onto the plane, remember?" he prompted, even as Bella took his hand in her left while taking Gojira's in her right ... who then took Charlotte's ... who then took Red's, and so on until they stood in a circle around Luna with their hands conjoined, repeating after Bella: "Our Father who art in heaven, hallowed be thy name, thy kingdom come, thy will be done, on earth as it is in heaven. Give us this day our daily bread, and forgive us our trespasses, as we forgive those who trespass against us, and lead us not into temptation, but deliver us from evil. For thine is the kingdom, and the power, and the glory, for ever and ever. Amen."

And then, even as the plane skittered to a touchdown and the children came running to join them, there was a flash of white light—and they knew, all of them, that it was over at last.

It was time to go.

"Are you sure you won't change your mind?" asked Bella for the third time, finding it difficult to believe they were actually going to do it—that Ank and Williams were going to set out yet again, this time for Canada.

"Positive," said Williams, and threw more supplies onto Ank's back.

He turned to face her at last. "Maybe it's not true and she died a long time ago ... who knows. But the fact is ... I've got to try. Besides," He glanced at the others: at Red and Charlotte and Gojira and Erik—at Luna—at Peter and Samantha and Sammy (who'd been putting in double-time taking care of Sheila, who herself had no memory of leaving the camp or sabotaging the detonator) ... at Roger and Savanna and the clerk, whose name was Leon. "We're going to grow moss if we hang around here much longer." He swatted Ank's posterior playfully. "Isn't that right, Ank?"

Everyone laughed as the dinosaur grumbled.

"It's just that," At last Bella seemed to cede to his wishes. "Well, we hardly got to know ye, as they say." She looked up at him in the sun. "Safe travels, cowboy. And thanks. You know where we're at."

He tipped his hat to her—a gift from one of the residents to replace the one he'd lost.

At last Luna stepped forward and offered him her radio. "To remember us by," she said. She looked at Bella. "Maybe we can send you messages sometimes, so you don't get lonely."

Williams glanced at Bella as if to say, How about it?

Bella nodded. "Radio Free Montana will continue, stronger than ever. I—we've—got a responsibility. To give hope to those who may have none. To light the way."

Williams nodded and moved to go, then paused, looking at Sammy. "Tell Sheila ... tell her that He forgives. That he forgives anything and everything. Make sure the others do the same."

Sammy seemed to think about this before clasping his shoulder and nodding.

And then they were on their way, Williams taking point while Ank lumbered after him, pots and pans clanging. Nor did they go without fanfare, for the combined children of the Flashback cheered them on with gestures and homemade signs as they went.

And it was good, so very good, Bella thought, just to hear them be children again.

THE LOW RUMBLE OF DISTANT THUNDER (2020)

The cloud was like a wave, and yet not like a wave, like a storm, yet not like any storm we had seen (not since the initial Flashback, at least). Nor, in truth, could we be sure it *was* a cloud; for such was the distance that it remained as elusive and ephemeral—or nearly so—as when Maria had first noticed it: there beyond the cornfields near Sioux City, Nebraska (now an ashen necropolis); there beyond what had been our home before the arrival of the Flashback—but which now stood only as a gravestone and a cenotaph, a monument to the dead.

I looked at Caleb, who was still grinding the binoculars—peering at the racetrack. "Well? What do you see?"

He scanned left to right, slowly. "People," he said, adjusting the focusing ring. "Lots and lots of them. The stands are almost full."

When he didn't elaborate, Maria said: "Okay—but what are they doing? I mean, what's on the field?"

"Nothing," he said. "Nothing I can see. Not yet." He worked the ring with his index finger furiously. "I can't tell if it's a horse track or a dog track or—wait; okay, I can see enclosures now, horse-sized. They're—they're connected to the stables. That's weird ..."

"What?"

"It's like they're armored. Just really heavily-fortified," He handed me the binoculars. "See for yourself."

I pressed the rubber eyepieces against my brow and squinted, scanning the track, locating the enclosures. "Yeah, that is odd. Looks jury-rigged. Like they just sort of started welding plates on willy-nilly one day. And there's something else, almost like—"

I focused on a shape near the stalls that looked like a large steel cutout, which was attached to—

"Is that, like, a mechanical rabbit? With something attached?"

I handed the binoculars off to Caleb—but Maria quickly snatched them away.

"My father used to take me to the races all the time. Horses *and* greyhounds, if you don't mind." She peered through the glasses intently (which were huge in relation to her head). "And there's no way a horse track would ever have—"

But then there was a gunshot (or a recording of one; it was difficult to say from where we crouched on the hill) and the shape began *moving*—a shape we could now tell was that of a dinosaur, a gallimimus, to be precise—accelerating rapidly, wobbling precariously, as the gates of the enclosures banged open and the animals within burst free (revealing themselves not as eager thoroughbreds or even whipcord greyhounds but therapod dinosaurs of the *Allosauridae* family, juveniles, based on their size), who sprinted after the decoy like green cheetahs even as we looked on in disbelief and the stands erupted in applause; as the lights came on all over the stadium (impossible in and of itself) and a great neon sign flickered to life which read: WELCOME TO CHECKERED FLAGS; as darkness continued to fall and the cloud which was not a cloud—the very same we had been fleeing ever since dead Sioux City—continued to come, flashing, pulsating, rumbling.

As something moved at the corner of my vision and I turned: in time to see a man swinging a baseball bat directly at my head—after which, not surprisingly, there was a void black as night.

"... Hey, I said. Hey there. Are you okay?"

A voice, neither Caleb's nor Maria's, somewhere in the void, somewhere in the blackness.

"It—it was Luther, wasn't it? Uses a baseball bat—isn't that right? Hey there ..."

I blinked, trying to focus, saw a fleshy blur which resolved itself into a face; a face wedged between the bars of a—

I sat up with a start, hay clinging to my face and clothes, dangling from my hair. "Where in the hell?"

"Shhh," said Caleb, indicating I should look to my right, into a cage containing a single allosaur, which stood on one leg like a green flamingo, the other tucked beneath its great, bulbous belly, and seemed to sleep, fitfully. "I think we're safe; the bars seem pretty solid. But I'd rather not put them to the test, if you know what I mean."

Maria moaned as she sat up and rubbed her head. "Jesus, what hit us? Last thing I remember we—" She looked back and forth groggily between the allosaur on our right and the stranger to our left. "Where—where on earth are we?"

"I, ah, I can speak to that," said the stranger. "Although you may not like what I have to say. As for our scaly friend, well, while I am sure he would be happy to dine on us—you needn't worry. He has spent his entire life in that cage and would never challenge it. I'm Harry, by the way. Harry Hawkins."

We all turned and looked at him.

"Paul," I said. "Paul Barrett. This is Maria. And that's Caleb."

He pointed at each one of us in turn. "Paul, Maria, Caleb. How do. Well, then. Welcome to Checkered Flags—possibly the last place on earth you'd want to be. People are happy here; if your definition of 'happy' is waiting in line for peanut butter and rice and maybe a ladle full of water. And this, mind you, while Rudy De Santo practically swims in it. Up there," He nodded, possibly at the elevated restaurant we'd observed earlier (at least that's what it had looked like). "In his *'Winner's Circle.'*"

"I—I guess I don't get it," I said, unsure what he was trying to say. "I mean, if this—De Santo—is hoarding all the resources, why don't you just—"

"There's someone coming," said Caleb, after which everyone faced forward—in time to see a lithe form slink past the bars: a woman, coming to see Harry Hawkins. A woman with whom he began whispering heatedly.

I leaned close to the bars and listened, catching only snippets: something about the next race and the uppermost row of the bleachers ... about decapitating the snake, and a future free of want. Then she was gone and he had turned his attention back to us.

"You were saying? Ah, yes. Why don't we just—what? Take our fair share? Eliminate him, perhaps, so that we may divvy things up as we please? Nay, that's all well and good, but how does one do this when he is surrounded by bodyguards both day and night? Or when trying and failing would result not just in your own disappearance, but that of your family and friends, your associates, even your casual acquaintances?"

I was beginning to see his point. And yet—

"There must be some way to get through to him," I said.

"Short of a bayonet to the throat? I don't see it." He peered out at the stables, his eyes distant and glassy. "No. All that's important to him are these races. And betting on these infernal iguanas."

"Infernal? Iguanas?" —a voice, coming from the front of the cages, from the man with the bat himself; what had Harry called him? Luther. "Is that any way to talk about Rudy's Finest?" He looked at the allosaur next to us, then over his beefy shoulder—into the vespertine dark. "Did you hear that, Caligula? How about you, Lovely Bones? Man says you're 'infernal.' Calls you 'iguanas.' Now, you tell me: is that any way to talk just before dinner?" He looked at each of us in turn. "It's feeding time, you understand. Winner gets raw meat." His eyes landed on Hawkins. "Isn't that right, Harry?"

"No—no, I'm sure it isn't," stammered Harry. "Because—we're fresh out of livestock. Along with everything else. And that's ... That's—" The color drained from his face even as Luther began to unlock his cage. "You *can't* be serious. Not even De Santo—"

But they were already moving—Luther and his men—piling into his stall even as he desperately tried to elude them; counting and grunting as they heaved him above their heads; pitching him, as he fought and flayed and screamed, into the awakened allosaur's cage—where he vanished behind the partial wall only to rise again a moment later; as a red-black fountain of blood.

After which—calmly, deliberately, nonchalantly—Luther opened our own stall door; and said, not-unkindly: "By the way—you're invited to dinner. All of you. In the Winner's Circle. Follow me."

And then he was gone.

As it turned out, the "Winner's Circle" *was* the restaurant we'd observed earlier (a curious affair, indeed, for it was as if someone had chopped the legs off Seattle's Space Needle and simply mounted it above the bleachers, antennae, beacon and all). Nor could it be said that it—or our escorts—were unaccommodating; indeed, we were treated only with respect as they led us through its luxurious appointments and seated us, at last, across from De Santo himself (I knew it was he because he wore a polyester suit and yellow-tinted glasses—as well as a white cowboy hat as big as a serving tray—and who but the person in charge would dress such as that?). Neither was he alone, for Luther sat on his left side while someone I can only refer to as The Jockey (as he remained silent throughout the occasion and was dressed in full racing gear) sat on his right. And then we all waited—in a bonafide perfect storm of awkwardness—as drinks were brought and appetizers served, until De Santo sat back in his chair suddenly (which was more like a throne), and said, lackadaisically, "Okay—why not? I'll bite. Why has Hanover—with whom we've shared a perfect peace since the start of the Flashback, and, also, with whom we've never even exchanged an angry word—suddenly decided to start sending us, well, *spies?* Take all the time you need. Take your time—but don't waste mine. Go."

I glanced at Maria and Caleb, who looked as bewildered as I was. Hanover? As in Hanover Field?

"We—we passed an airport called that," I said, "right before we found you. Is that what you mean? There wasn't anyone there. In fact, it was completely abandoned."

Luther stiffened—as though he might pounce upon me at any moment—but was quickly quelled by De Santo, who gently tapped the table in front of him. "I warn you, Mr. Barrett—you insult my intelligence at your own risk."

I must have looked surprised.

"Oh, don't look so shocked; of course we were listening in on you. How else were we to determine your motives? I must say, however: we gleaned precious little before Luther arrived—*too early.*"

The two exchanged uncomfortable glances even as I cleared my throat to continue.

At last I said, "I would not lie about something so easy to disprove; nor risk all our lives in such a vain effort to deceive. Be assured—Hanover Field *has* been abandoned. Be assured, also, that the reason for its abandonment is clear: *something* is coming. Something we've observed for several days, but which Hanover, having aircraft, would have observed much sooner. Call it a cloud, a storm front, whatever it is you like. Call it another Flashback. But know this and know it well: *it is* coming. And you may not like what it brings. You may not like it at all."

And then I waited—waited as the three of them, De Santo, Luther, and the Jockey, glanced at each other and seemed to talk it over (without ever saying a word); waited as Caleb, Maria, and myself did the same. And I suppose my optimism that De Santo could be reached—although how I could think that after what had happened in the stables remains a mystery to me even today—got the better of me, because I was genuinely surprised when he said, simply, after a brief but pregnant pause, "Looks like rain, as they say." — before completely shrugging it off. "It's a dirt track—it shouldn't affect the race. And now if you're done with all this

... I'd like to make a proposal. That is, if you're curious at all as to what we intend to do with you?"

I'm afraid I could only stare at him in vexed disbelief.

"Really, Mr. Barrett. But what did you expect? That, on the word of a spy, I would just pull up stakes and abandon everything we have fought so hard to achieve here? That I would just—*hand it over* to you, and in the process displace, maybe, 2,000 people? My people?"

Caleb sneered. "You don't give a shit about these people. You heard our conversation with Hawkins—"

The table jolted, rattling the silverware, as Luther started to stand—only to be intercepted by De Santo, who encouraged him to sit.

"Easy, easy," said De Santo, patting him on the back, cajoling him. And to us: "Now *look* what you've done; you've upset Luther." He dabbed at some spilled water with a napkin and otherwise tidied. "You have to understand—it's Caleb, isn't that correct?—that Harry ... oh, dear, Harry ... was a bit of a disgruntled employee. He used to work in the stables, you know, although I don't recall him telling you that. The problem, of course, is that he was no good at it—had no knack for the animals—nor, and this is the important part, had he any love for the Race. And what you must understand about Checkered Flags, even if you understand nothing else, is that here, at last, the Race is *everything.*"

He licked his lips as though to savor the idea, and his green eyes twinkled. "It *drives* everything, you see. Decides *everything.* It will even decide what we do with you."

I had been looking at Caleb since he'd first spoken up— now I refocused on De Santo. "What do you mean?"

He sat back and smiled, smugly, over-confidently. "I mean the next competition—what we here in the Winner's Circle call the Post-dinner Dash—which will start in, say," He consulted his watch. "45 minutes? It involves you."

I glanced at Maria and Caleb—who only stared back at me, gravely—then again to De Santo. "What the hell are you talking about? What does that even mean?"

"It means four contestants in a win-only race: Caligula, Lovely Bones, Bromtide, and Mesozoic Nights. It means, Mr. Barrett, that you will place a bet; collectively, on one of the animals—truly, whichever you like—for a winner's purse ... the contents of which will be your unqualified freedom."

He lifted his glass of wine and sipped, daintily, as we looked on.

"Likewise, should you lose—well, let's just say, you'll be joining Mr. Hawkins. By the way—Luther. What ever happened to Harry?"

"He had sort of a falling out—with Mesozoic Nights. Seemed like there was some sort of beef between the two."

"Ah—well," said De Santo. "There you go." He looked straight at me—again, I have no idea why. "Loser loses all. So. Any questions?"

"I have some," said Maria, curtly, coldly, all business. "The first is: How can we be expected to place bets on animals that we know nothing about?"

I'm pretty sure Caleb and I just looked at her.

"And the second is: I counted three adolescent allosaurs present in the stables—one next to us and two across—not four. All of which begs the question: Where is the other one? And why is he being treated differently from the rest?"

Nobody said anything—for several breaths, at least.

"Ah, yes," said De Santo after some length, "you mean Bromtide. Well, that's the wild card, isn't it? Because, you see, Bromtide isn't a dinosaur ... he's a horse."

I looked at him quizzically and then at The Jockey, who just nodded, like he was fucking Boba Fett or something.

"As to the background of the animals, you'll find it all right here," He pushed a leather-bound binder toward us—I had assumed it was a menu. "Race results, pedigree, notes on health and temperament, it's really quite comprehensive. You'll even be left alone with it—before the race, that is—after which you'll dog-ear a profile and kindly leave it on the table, yes?"

Nobody said anything as we stared at the book.

At last I said, "And you're just going to pretend that cloud, or whatever it is, doesn't exist ..."

"Ah, that. Yes—bromtide. The low rumble of distant thunder. Like those rumors of an uprising, I suppose. Or my attempted assassination."

"I should think that would concern you," I said.

He tucked a napkin into his shirt as dinner was served. "You know what my father used to say? He said, 'Rudy, there's but two kinds of people in the world: those that are players, and those that are spectators. Don't ever let me catch you being a spectator.'"

He cocked his head as the plates were set down, seeming to study me. "You know what else? He said the worst thing about Hell is that you could still see Heaven, up there, just beyond the firmament, forever out of reach. Now—what do you suppose he meant by that?"

I stared at him numbly, utterly bewildered.

"I didn't know either—and still don't. It was just shit my dad said."

And then we ate—quickly, silently—and he left, followed immediately by The Jockey and then Luther, who remained just outside the door, watching us, guarding us.

I'll confess I jumped when the starting pistol fired—which seemed inordinately loud even from the top of the bleachers—mainly because I'd turned around to look at the cloud, which had doubled in size and now claimed nearly one quarter of the sky—spreading across it like a cancer, pulsing and flashing from deep inside.

"And here they go! They're on their way down the stretch. The break was good; every animal got a clean shot out of the gate. And as they come down here to the eighth pole, it is Mesozoic Nights and Caligula ..."

I peered at the announcer's booth, wondering once again what they were using for power, and so much of it—the stadium lights alone would have overwhelmed most generators. But then Maria nudged me and I focused on the action—seeing, to my horror, that Bromtide had already fallen behind; Bromtide, whom we had unanimously voted to support.

"Caligula is trying to force his way to the front and doing a good job of it as they pass the stands. Here on the outside comes Lovely Bones, in a good position. And as they go by me it is Caligula on the lead by one length. Caligula has the lead and then comes Mesozoic Nights in second place right along beside him. Going into the first turn is Caligula by a length. Mesozoic Nights is second and on the outside of him is Lovely Bones. Far back in the crowd, on the inside, in about fourth place, is Bromtide. They're going into the stretch; they've gone about half a mile ..."

"Jesus," I said, even as something like thunder rumbled and a flash of light illuminated the stadium. "What's wrong with him, you think?"

"Might be the T. rex piss," said Luther, leaning in, and chuckled. "Had to spray him down with it—otherwise the allos would be all over him. Guess we forgot to tell you that."

I glared at him before shifting my gaze to Maria and Caleb and finally to De Santo, at the very end, who looked like a kid on Christmas. "Oh, Caligula!" he cried, and clasped his hands above his head. "Beautiful! Beautiful!"

"They're turning into the backstretch with Caligula on the lead," said the announcer. "Caligula has a lead now of one length and a half. Right behind him comes Mesozoic Nights. And in there, slipping through on the inside, is—it's Bromtide! Bromtide is going up on the inside now and in a good position ..."

I refocused on the race even as Maria leapt to her feet and clapped—watching as the Thoroughbred accelerated through the dust like a thunderbolt and the allos' upright tails bobbed; as the mechanical rabbit with the steel gallimimus attached raced along its track, glinting and vibrating. That's when I noticed her, I'm not sure why—the concessions girl with the vending tray strapped to her shoulders, selling hot dogs—way down in the front, but moving our way. And it was the weirdest thing because even though her features were barely discernible I was certain I had seen her before, and in a situation similar to this—having to do with the races, that is—and in a flash it came to me, for she was the very same woman who had visited Hawkins in his cell and had spoken to him in such hushed, conspiratorial tones—about the next race and the uppermost row of the bleachers, about decapitating the snake and a future free of want. And then the sky was flashing and thunder boomed and I turned to look at the storm, and saw, with a mixture of wonder and terror, that it was not one cloud but two; one below the other, and more, that the lower cloud was ascending, not drifting—by which I mean it was being kicked up from the earth, and that, indeed, it wasn't a cloud at all but dust, great, billowing plumes of it.

"Jesus—Maria, Caleb, look at it," I said, even as the crowd went wild and the announcer related breathlessly, "And Bromtide is now moving up and challenging as they turn for home. It's Caligula and Bromtide challenging head-to-head as they swing into the stretch. And they've only got a quarter of a mile to go. Bromtide has got the lead halfway down the stretch. But here comes Lovely Bones challenging on the outside, challenging boldly. And the battle is on. And Lovely Bones may take it all. It's gonna be a photograph finish. It's anybody's race right up to the end ..."

Maria gasped, staring at the cloud of dust. "Are—are those what I think they are?"

I squinted and saw shapes beginning to materialize—large ones, little ones, shapes of every size and stripe—close enough now to identify, close enough even to—

"We're in trouble," I said—even as the dinosaurs herded directly toward us, like driven cattle, as the diplodocuses and brachiosaurs and tyrannosaurs and triceratops stampeded straight for Checkered Flags. "We're in—like—serious trouble ..."

And then there were screams and a great upheaval from the crowd, and we turned in time to see that the girl with the vending tray had produced a gun, produced it and was pointing it at Se Santo. Pointing it at him even as the sky boomed and Luther drew his own, shooting her in the arm; as the rumble of the approaching dinosaurs intensified and the announcer exhaled, catching his breath, and said, at last, "I think Lovely Bones got the money. I think Lovely Bones was first. It was an eyebrow finish. And Bromtide was the second. Bromtide was second and Caligula and Mesozoic Nights each tied for third. It was very close. That was an eyelash finish ..."

But by then, of course, the cloud was upon us. And as it turned out, I had been right. For it was the Flashback come again.

"The car!" barked De Santo, taking his eyes off the sky. "Get the goddamn car!" At which Luther hustled away and Caleb moved to intercept—until I blocked him with an arm across his chest and held him that way until both men were gone.

"Jesus, man! I could have stopped them."

"And we will," I said—even as the great herd crashed the gates and began stampeding onto the field: trampling the fences, toppling the media tower, crushing and goring bystanders. "But first let's follow them to that *car,* yeah?"

And then we moved—hurrying after them into the stairwell, ignoring the fact that, in a reversal of the first Flashback, the prehistoric creeper vines and overgrowth that pervaded the venue had started to disappear, to simply vanish without a trace, and so, for that matter, had the rampaging dinosaurs. Nor had we gone far when we came upon the car—one of those ridiculous Hummer limousines which was just as white as De Santo's hat and was already pulling clear even as Luther kicked its rear bumper and pointed his pistol, barking, "You bastard, De Santo! There was enough for both of us! There was enough for both!"

And then he opened fire, *Crack! Crack! Ca-crack!*— blowing out the rear window as well as the tires, causing the back portion of the vehicle to drop, after which the limo briefly continued on just sort of dragging its hind-end—like a dog wiping its ass—before getting stuck in a quagmire of tar and starting to sink; but not before De Santo climbed out and began staggering back toward us, reeling and stumbling.

Only then did what had occurred become clear: for the Flashback, or mini-Flashback, or controlled Flashback, or whatever it was, had *stopped;* and now two time zones existed where before there had only been one—the New Mesozoic, in which we had lived and breathed just a moment before (but which now contained only De Santo), and the Modern Era Come Again (in which we existed now). And yet that is not to say they occupied the same space; for between them, blue and opaque, ran what could only be described as a forcefield, a field which crackled and hissed as De Santo stumbled into it and blocked him—as much as any physical wall—from returning.

And, considering the world on our side had been restored to how it was before the Flashback—or at least, as we know now, a stretch of land from Devil's Lake, North Dakota through Checkered Flags, in Kansas—and its people and geography brought back from whatever phantom zone they had disappeared to, he must have wanted that very much. Dear God, how he must have wanted it. I could see it in his eyes as the race-famished allosaurs—who had escaped the storm in front of him only to come slowly creeping back—encircled him and cut him off, trapping him where he stood.

And I could see it as he died—as they ate him alive—still gazing at us (who, from his point of view, would have been rimmed in fire from the stadium lights) and at Checkered Flags; which, having been restored to its former glory, must have shined for him in that moment like Heaven itself.

THE ELEPHANT SLAYER (2020)

It was called Netherville, which wasn't too bad a name compared to some of the settlements I'd been to: places like Misery, Montana and Malaise, North Dakota; Grimburg, Texas; Forsaken Falls, Idaho. I guess you could say that American towns have always had ominous names—that it was part of our frontier heritage—but then, I wasn't in America anymore, I was in Canada. Edmonton, Alberta to be precise. The Big E, as they called it.

As for how I'd come to be there—I'd rather not talk about it, and it's not important, anyway. Suffice it to say I'd caught a broadcast on the radio of my new Cadillac Escalade (Thanks, Butte Auto Sales, I left a silver dollar in the break room) which had urged me to go north to a town called Paradise—a town I'd mistaken for Paradise, Alberta, and so overshot by about 500 miles. Luckily for me, I'd come to Netherville before running out of gas (the Escalade's tank had been completely full, go figure; that's why I'd chosen it) and found a friendly settlement in spite of my folly.

At least, it had been friendly so far. In my experience, these things could—and often did—change on a dime. Which is about what I had on me when I walked into the 'Goodbye to All That' Saloon and ordered a drink at the makeshift bar; a bar whose counter had been fashioned from the scorched wing of an airplane.

"Keep it," said the bartender, a largish man with thick stubble and bad teeth, as he pushed back the coins. "First visit's on us, always."

He moved toward the back door—which was propped open with a rifle; probably due to heat from the firepit—walking awkwardly, haltingly, as though he had a bad hip. "Beer's out back—in the snow."

I glanced around the room as he went: at the other patrons—bearded men, all of them—who had peeled off coats and hats; and at one who hadn't—a lone figure sitting in the corner ... with a pair of crutches nearby.

"That includes the mastodon; the mammoth. The roast elephant, whatever you want to call it."

He shuffled back, slowly, arduously, twisting the cap off a bottle of Molson, setting it down. "It's good—fresh. The meat, eh, not the beer. It was harvested only yesterday."

He laughed a little and shook his head. "Whatever he does with that ivory, I'll never know."

I looked at the bottle of beer, which had foamed over onto the counter—onto the Cessna's battered wing. "What who does with it?"

"What?"

"What *who* does with the ivory?"

He lifted the bottle and wiped around the rivets, fussily, fastidiously. "Oh, yuh. You're the new guy. Why, Gavin Carter, of course. Our mysterious and storied *Great White Hunter.*"

"Our Nanook of the North!" hollered a nearby patron, lifting his sloshing glass. "The Elephant Slayer of Alberta."

"Or at least the frozen shithole that used to be Alberta," said another.

I must have looked confused.

"Local hero," explained the bartender. "Big-time trophy hunter. Lives in that house up on the ridge; the one with the orange roof—the old Riblet Mansion. Just helped himself to it one day. But he's a hero because he hunts the mammoth—and I mean consistently, successfully—and keeps the town fed."

A patron leaned in abruptly, thoughtlessly—as drunk people are wont to do—his breath reeking of Molson. "Speakin' a which—I'll take some more of that, eh? The stew."

"Well, that depends, Liam," said the bartender. "Where is your bowl?"

The man looked around, dazed and confused, until his glassy eyes settled on the back of the room—and the booth next to the solitary figure.

"Never mind, Liam," said the bartender warily. "I'll get it for you. Just relax." He gave me a little bow. "Excuse me."

"Of course," I said.

And then I took my first drink and paused—savoring it. Savoring its bite and its body and its bitterness and its perfection. Worshiping it; and focusing upon it to the exclusion of all else. Because the truth of it was, drinking it was like drinking civilization itself.

The drunk, meanwhile, was just staring at me: as though he knew me, perhaps, or maybe not. As though he loved me, perhaps—but maybe hated me too. As though there was something on his mind that he just had to say—if he could just untangle his thoughts and find the right words. If he could just get his mouth to open and his tongue to—

"Don't," I said.

And he didn't—talk to me, that is—after which the bartender returned and fetched me another beer—saying, as he twisted the cap off and set it down, "Compliments of the young lady in the corner."

I looked over my shoulder and saw that the figure had unzipped its coat and removed its scarf and hat—revealing a woman with black, unkempt hair and harsh, asymmetrical features (and yet attractive, for all that) who couldn't have been more than, say, twenty-five. A woman who looked at me with such startling clarity and matter-of-factness that I almost averted my eyes—but didn't, because I didn't want to appear weak. Instead, I just smiled—confidently, breezily (at least that was my schtick), raising my beer bottle. As though I wasn't just Travis Hayes, UPS delivery driver from Denver, Colorado, but Travis-*fucking*-Hayes, Carefree Stud of the Apocalypse.

That's when it happened; when the fight broke out, erupting in a flurry of broken glass and expletives (and flying booze), toppling the nearby barstools.

"Hey, goddamnit!" shouted the bartender, as I scrambled clear of the melee—which, surprise! involved the man who had been staring at me— "Hey, hey, hey!"

And then everything was noise and fury as others joined in and I turned to check on the black-haired girl (although *why* I am not certain; she could clearly take care of herself), but saw only an empty booth. Everything was chaos and confusion as I stared into her corner and noted the missing crutches—but couldn't for the life of me figure out where they—or she—had gone.

I looked to where a wooden door swung back and forth in the wind, letting in gusts of snow. The side alley, of course—!

And then I was moving—double-timing it, as we used to say in the corps—dodging a pair of brawlers, bursting into the alley; pausing by a heap of garbage as I noticed there were no footprints in the snow and thus no way to—

At which my vision winked out and I could see only stars, like scratches in space-time itself. At which I saw only comets—which darted and swirled, ember-like, as I fell.

"Ah, ah! Here he comes. You see now, Eska? You didn't hit him so hard after all. Our sleeper has awakened."

I blinked, clearing my eyes, as the room swam into focus: as the floating spheres of light resolved into candle flames and the hovering pink blur became a face, which smiled—patiently, fatherly. Elusively, like a wolf.

"Welcome to the Roc's Nest," said the face—its skin cracked like bleached leather, its teeth straight and white. "Please, have a look around. I'm Gavin Carter. And this—this here is Eska. My adopted daughter."

I looked at her even as I became aware of my pounding head: at her strange, harsh face and dense, un-manicured brows; her large, stout teeth—which were *not* straight and white—her eyes like chiseled obsidian.

"Go on, Eska," said the man—Carter—who appeared to be in his late 50s. "Be a dear and give Mr. Hayes a smile.

Show him some of that primal charm you have; and in such great abundance. Come, come, now."

I watched as the corners of her mouth crept up, slowly, hesitantly. Indeed, she *could* be charming—even beautiful—when she wasn't braining you with a board, that is (or whatever she'd used).

I looked around the room, which was more like a great hall—at the pillars made of immense tree trunks and crossbeams carved from maple or walnut; at the astounding collection of mounted animal busts which adorned every wall and flat surface.

At last I managed, "How—how do you know my name?"

"It wasn't difficult," he said, taking a sip from his wine glass, dabbing at the corners of his mouth. "You still had an I.D."

I slapped my back pocket—my ankle catching on something as I shifted—but it was gone, of course. My wallet. That's when I looked down—having heard the *ka-chink* of metal—and realized I was shackled to my chair.

He frowned almost sheepishly. "An imposition, to be sure—but a necessary one." He looked at something on the table which I recognized as my old military ID. "Can't have a trained killer just wandering about the house—now can we?" He paused, studying my face. "I must say ... you don't exactly look the part."

"Well, people can be full of surprises, can't they?" I glanced at Eska, who just stared right back. "Your 'daughter' is certainly capable of a few. Wouldn't you say?"

"Oh, most certainly," said Carter—and added: "People, I mean. *People* are full of surprises. Not Eska. Not from me."

I raised an eyebrow.

"I know her too well ... having reared her since she was a pup." He paused, appearing wistful—even morose—before changing the subject; abruptly, I thought. "I, ah, couldn't help but to notice you appreciating my collection. Do you hunt, Mr. Hayes?"

I looked at the nearest mount, a triceratops head with a broken horn (and a frightful visage), wondering what the circumstances of its death had been. Had it been charging—with the Flashback in its eyes, perhaps—and thus *aware* that it had an opponent? Or had it been unaware, just mulling its soft grasses, until the bullet entered its brain?

"No," I said, finally, turning my attention back to him. "Can't exactly say as I am. It—it's never seemed like a fair contest to me." I jerked my leg against the chain—twice—to make a point. "Does it to you?"

"Pshaw," he protested. "You speak as if we're enemies. As though this were some contest between you and I, personally. On the contrary, Mr. Hayes. *It's a collaboration."*

I'm afraid I just stared at him.

At last I said: "Okay—why not. I'll bite. What are you talking about?"

"I am talking, Mr. Hayes ..." He stood and began pacing the length of the table. "—about *legend*. About myth and memory—and the securing of one's place in the natural order of things." He withdrew something from his housecoat as he walked—a pipe; but didn't light it. *"Posterity* is what I'm talking about. A place at the table of the gods. That, and endings. Inevitabilities."

He paused and struck a match. "One last and penultimate hunt."

He lit the pipe and waved out the match, then turned, slowly, regarding me through a cloud of smoke. *"Atatilla,* is what I'm talking about. Queen of the Mammoths. The, ah, Leviathan of the Steppes, as they say. I intend to kill her. And you, my lost and wayward friend, are going to help me. By acting as my driver."

"Your *driver?"*

"Yes. I'd normally call on Eska, but, as you've no doubt observed, she is—at present—incapacitated." He glanced at her across the table. "Isn't that right, Love?"

She took her eyes off me long enough to nod at him, stoically, silently.

"She, ah, understands, you see." He moved around the table toward her. "And not only the language but, how shall I say it? The lay of the land."

I watched as he took up position behind her and placed his hands on her shoulders.

At length I said: "What is it, Carter? And what is she? Cro-Magnon? Neanderthal? What do you mean— 'the lay of the land?'"

"I mean, she understands who she is ... now. And also, where she belongs." He fussed over her as she stared straight ahead—straightening her collar, repositioning her hair. "More importantly, she understands who *I* am. She can even say it— can't you, Love?"

She looked up at him with what seemed like respect, even reverence.

"Go on," he cajoled—gently. Softly. "Who am I?"

"Ma—ma—master," she managed at some length. "You are ... Master."

He veritably leapt with joy. "Very good, Eska! Oh, very good! Oh, that is absolutely wonderful. Most excellent. Now tell me, what I am the master *of?*"

She hesitated—as though searching her memory.

"E-everything," she said at last, the words seeming to come easier, if not any faster. "M-m-me. The animals. All—all the world."

"Yes, yes," he said, and practically capered. "Very good ..."

He looked at me as though he assumed I'd be impressed. "Well? What do you think? Does she pass the test for *Homo sapiens sapiens?*"

But by then my anger had boiled over and I'd stood, abruptly, jerking the chain on my ankle as I moved toward him, dragging the chair after me.

"Look—you indoctrinate all the *Cro-Magnon fucking girls* you want ... If you don't have me out of here inside of *60 seconds* I'm going to—"

"Genghis!" he shouted, and snapped his fingers, the sound of which echoed in the hall. "Come along, now. *Right now.*"

And before I could do much of anything he—*it*—was there, entering the room from a nearby corridor and snarling as it advanced, crouching and tensing as its foreclaws splayed; tapping its retractable sickle claws over the smooth, polished floor.

Stalking me as I fell, tangled up with the chair; and blanketing me with its shadow—as only a Utahraptor could.

"Freeze!" barked Carter—and the mottled orange and black Utahraptor froze, its knife-shaped head only inches from my own, its breath smelling of fish and rotted meat. "Hold."

And the Utahraptor held: snarling and growling—hissing, even, like a snake.

"There, see? There's nothing to be afraid of," said Carter, calmly. "Now, if we can avoid any further outbursts— let's continue, shall we? Where was I ..."

"Call it off," I said, shrinking away from the thing's muzzle, staring at its yellowed teeth (between which I could see bits of decaying flesh). *"Call it off, Carter."*

"Ah—well. So much for the vaunted bravery of the U.S. Armed Forces, eh?" He snapped his fingers quickly, crisply. "Kennel." But the Utahraptor didn't budge—indeed, I was pretty sure it only moved closer. "Genghis!" he barked. "I said, 'Kennel!' *Now!"*

At which the predator *did* move, although grudgingly, defying its master to the extent that it circled me quickly before breaking off and vanishing the way it had come, its tail whipping after it.

"There, you see? I can be reasonable." He paused as though he were looking at me. "Good heavens, Mr. Hayes! You look as though you've seen a ghost."

I pulled myself together as my breath came and went in ragged gasps. "What was that? Your hunting dog?"

"If you like." He paced over to the far wall— which wasn't, in fact, even a wall, but a towering black curtain—and stood to one side of it. "I want to show you something." To Eska he said: "Leave us. Tend to Genghis."

And she was gone.

He drew open the curtains.

"Behold, if you will, the Terror of the North—Ursus Maritimus Tyrannus, otherwise known as the Pleistocene Polar Bear."

My jaw dropped a little as the massive thing came into view—mounted not in a pose but as an enormous rug, which had been affixed to the wall, itself painted black.

"Magnificent—isn't she? 'There 'mid grand icebergs slipping *from* the cliffs, or on the drifting floes that choked the tide ... gigantic Polar bears, so grim and gaunt ... in solitary majesty abide.'" He turned to face me in the semi-darkness. "Isaac McLellan."

"Look, Carter. Would you just get to the—"

"But she wasn't solitary, Mr. Hayes—not this one. Nor did she have a sleuth of cubs. And yet she was—indisputably—a mother. No, what she had, my wayward friend, was *a* cub. A cub who was but an infant then but has since matured—at an accelerated rate, of course—into adulthood."

My eyes must have grown large as awareness dawned. "Eska. You're talking about Eska. But how could—I mean, the Flashback only happened less than—"

"Come now." He looked at me with something like pity. "Surely you've encountered it; that aberration in the Flashback by which a person— seemingly at random—begins to age—rapidly, I mean, exponentially—out of all context with their surroundings? Well, that's what happened to Eska. As for the hows and whys: such as why that process halted at her current state, or how she came to be living with prehistoric bears in the first place—who can say?"

I stared at the massive hide, at the flattened body and carefully preserved claws, and at the great head, which was big as a T. rex's. "How much does she know?"

"As with everything, only what I have taught her, of course. That I found her mother already slaughtered—by a cold-weather predator mightier even than she." He drew the curtains and walked toward me. "A story that was true—if not entirely factual."

I got up slowly, shaking my head. "And that was you ... The Great White Hunter of the Wastes. How ironic."

"Ironic, Mr. Hayes?" He paused and lifted his chin. "How so?"

"Because you seem so prissy and effeminate. I guess it's just hard to—"

And I lunged at him—chair and Genghis be damned—before something struck me in the head (a fire poker, as it turned out; wielded by Eska herself) and rendered me unconscious, if only for an instant.

"Really, Mr. Hayes," he said, circling me where I lay. "These outbursts will be your undoing. Irregardless, there you have it. Everything you need to know in order to help us with our hunt. You've even seen the bar we must surpass—the gold standard, as they say; the mount stuffed by Fidelio himself—my taxidermist, God rest his soul—before he showed Genghis an affection at the wrong time and place, and when the animal was in the wrong mood."

He removed a coin-like medallion from beneath his shirt and studied it, wistfully. "Dear Fidelio, who fashioned this."

He leaned close to show it to me and I saw a gold disk with an engraved bear on it—Ursus Maritimus Tyrannus. The Terror of the North. Eska's adoptive mother. "A reminder of my greatest prize to date."

He turned toward Eska. "Thank you, by the way. Although I must caution you; do not enter the room without my permission again, eh?"

I looked back and forth between them.

"Y-yes, Master," she struggled to say. "Eska is s-sorry."

He looked down at me. "Well, there, see? She learns. No need for another confrontation at the top of the stairs ... isn't that right, Eska?"

I looked at the splint on her ankle and the single crutch she was using.

At last I said, "I'll help you with your hunt, Carter. We—we'll kill this ... Atatilla. From the truck, isn't that right? Like cowards. But I'm going to kill you too, you bastard. Somehow, someway. You just watch."

Again, he looked at me with pity—or something like it. "I'm sure you'll try." And then he shouted down the hall:

"Genghis, my boy! Snap to, old friend! It's time to release the hounds and hunt again!"

I guess I don't know what I expected when Genghis—having paused outside the vehicle's windows to sniff at the crisp air— leapt forward suddenly and vanished into the gloom. I suppose I was expecting the same result as the last twenty times he'd done this; which was nothing (although he had, at one point, emerged with a dead possum in his mouth). What I was *not* expecting was the wooly mountain that emerged— with Genghis clinging to its back—a thing easily the size of an industrial dump truck; which thundered past us on our left even as Eska pressed the knife to my throat and Carter readied his rifle—indeed, even as I put the Jeep into gear and prayed, having already been nicked once, that I wouldn't displease her, the fucking driving critic, again.

"Very well, Mr. Hayes—that's it," said Carter, aiming his rifle—a .460 caliber Weatherby Mark V he'd been droning on about since we left—squinting into its scope. "Now draw alongside—that's right. Step on the gas."

I stepped on the gas, disturbed by the lack of visibility— the lack of *road*—terrified we might plummet into a ditch (or even a chasm), *knowing* I had to do something—anything—to stop the madness.

"Faster, Mr. Hayes," he persisted, as the Jeep bounced and jolted and he struggled to maintain his aim. "Faster, damn you! Align us with her head. *Quickly,* or we'll lose them both."

I went faster—the great mammoth thundering along beside us as Genghis tore at her flank and the snow continued to fly; as Eska held the knife to my throat; and, due to the truck's jouncing, nicked me again and again.

At last I shouted: "You don't have to do this, Eska—all right? Can you understand that? You don't have to do what he says. *Nobody does.* Listen to me."

I stared at her through the rearview mirror: at her strange, dark eyes and sharply-chiseled features; at her tangles of black hair and large, uneven teeth, until she diverted her attention back to Carter, who was focused, exclusively now, on the stampeding elephant—and appeared almost to ask his permission.

"Ah, don't worry about him," I said, re-concentrating on my driving. "Can't you see he's busy?" I glanced at Carter—who ground his rifle scope silently, intensely. "He's too focused on that pachyderm." I jerked the wheel once so that the Jeep rocked violently and he lost his target. "Isn't that right, Carter?"

"Eska!" he snapped.

I stiffened as her blade—having relaxed briefly—re-pressed against my throat; only harder, sharper, drawing new blood, then nodded, quickly, indicating the mammoth.

"Look at it, Eska," I said, having to raise my voice over the sound of its trumpeting, "Look at *her*. Look at how mighty and beautiful she is—how unspoiled and magnificent. What does she remind you of—Eska of the Great White Bears, of the animals who found you when you were lost and without hope; when you needed food and shelter and compassion—what does she remind you of and who in all the world could kill such a unique and powerful beast?"

I glanced at her in the mirror even as a shot rang out and she jumped—her dark eyes looking at Carter as he worked the bolt and ejected the casing; her focus shifting to the elephant at it cried out thunderously and increased its speed.

"Who, indeed, Eska," I said. "But the *Master of All?*"

She looked at me through the mirror and we locked eyes immediately—even as I continued to drive, blindly, recklessly.

"*Yes,* Eska. *M-M-Master.* The master of you—and of all living things. Who but he could have—or would have—killed your mother?"

I reached out suddenly and yanked the medallion from around Carter's neck.

"Your mother, Eska," I said, shaking the engraving—forcing her to look at it. *"This, right here!"*

And she took it; even as I faced forward briefly and began to slow down, and the giants, still at war, quickly pulled ahead—vanishing at last into the snow-speckled gloom.

Carter was enraged, incensed, speechless.

"What—what is the meaning of this?" He gripped his rifle, trembling with anger, then looked from me to Eska, his face swollen and red. "What have you ..." He exploded suddenly, violently, pathologically. "What have you *done, you animal?*"

I watched her in the silence.

"M-mother," she managed, staring at the gold coin, processing, it seemed, in the still, dark vehicle. "M-master.*" She looked at me as though struggling up from dream—and finally back to Carter. "Master ... *kill* ... Mother."

Carter shook his head, desperately, I thought, even fearfully. *"Pshaw!* This is nonsense! Killed your mother! What *rubbish.* Come here, child. Let me—"

And then the knife entered his throat and he gasped—gasped and choked and gargled—as the blood bubbled up and he wretched on it; as Eska twisted the blade.

He opened his door and fell to the ground, dropping his rifle which discharged—the sound of it echoing along the hills—prompting me to get out as well.

"Hold on, man!" I shouted, slipping and sliding around the hood, unzipping and yanking off my coat—crouching over him as he rolled in his own piss and blood. "We'll tie the sleeves together; make a tourniquet ..."

But he only got up and staggered further away: holding his throat, hemorrhaging into the clean, white snow, crying out as he slipped and fell and struck his head ... even as the ground shook with mighty footfalls, with the approach of something like a god.

That's when she emerged, the mastodon—*Atatilla* herself, having defeated Genghis—and lumbered to within a few feet of us, her shadow falling over us like a shroud.

"Easy ... easy," I said, stepping back slowly, gazing up at her face (which seemed positively ancient, positively eldritch). "It's all over now. It's—everything's done. You've won, old girl. You've survived."

The wind blew and the snow fell, clinging to her trunk and the folds of her face, sticking to her eyes, like cotton lint.

"I—I ..." Carter managed, the blood bubbling up like Karo syrup, like thick, black ichor, congealing on his chin and at the corners of his mouth, pulsing from his throat like little bursts from a squirt gun. "I ... am your master," he wheezed at last, and stared up at the thing in defiance, in cold-stone obstinance, smiling red, smiling like a lunatic, which I suppose he was, refusing to concede—to give even a centimeter.

And then she lifted her great foot and brought it down, missing me by just a few scant feet, and smashed Carter flat—raising it a couple seconds later to reveal a body thin as a bear rug but with its head and limbs intact. Leaving him like a trophy, like a warning to all who would challenge her, before lumbering back into the gloom and receding like a ghost, a legend—Atatilla, Slayer of Carter—master to all she surveyed.

You might say we made a strange couple, Eska and I. It's certainly possible, considering the odd looks we garnered on our return to Netherville.

Whatever the case, I saw no reason to part now that we'd established a means of communication (Carter had begun to teach her American Sign Language, which I was familiar with from my days as an interpreter). More to the point, I could never have simply abandoned her; not to the snowy wastes, and not to Carter's empty mausoleum (whose fuel stores for the generators were nearly depleted anyway).

And so we just went, stopping in Netherville only long enough to refuel the Jeep and to stock up on supplies, before beginning the long drive to Paradise, Montana, and also, more specifically, a place called Barley's Hot Springs.

For we had caught the broadcast again (the same one I had heard earlier) on our way in from the wastes. A broadcast calling itself Radio Free Montana—which had promised, among other things, a climate utterly unlike other settlements, and that, and I quote: "Here, indeed, is where civilization begins!"

It seemed worth another try.

As for this document and my need to put it to paper—and deliver it to the town repository—who knows? Maybe I just wanted to make sure history was recorded right. God knows, it rarely is.

And finally, for whoever may find this and wonder at its context—in a future, perhaps, where that context has become mere dust and memory—I offer this:

Welcome to the Big Empty, the world after the Flashback, a world in which most the population has vanished and where dinosaurs roam freely. You can survive here, if you're lucky, and if you're not in the wrong place at the wrong time, which is everywhere and all the time. But what you'll never do is remain the same, for this a world whose very purpose, it seems, is to change you, for better or for worse.

I recall watching Eska study the engraving on the way in, her face full of sorrow and yet complexity too, realizing, even then, that I need never fear her again, in light of which, I'll add:

It is my most fervent hope that it change you for the better.

It shone lustrously, feverishly, sun-painted red and gold, as though it were on fire—the Gateway to the West (although for us it opened eastward); the towering landmark that meant we had arrived at our destination, our Court of Pelles and Eliazar. Even so, it wasn't the great arch of St. Louis that had compelled us—Sirs Mortigen, Black Duncan and myself—to ride some 1,500 miles (all the way from Ambergard in Coeur d'Alene, Idaho to the Missouri/Illinois border, on unshod horses), but, rather, the edict of King Craxis—who, having listened to the newcomer's account (about what he had seen in St. Louis) had, at the behest of Mercurius, dispatched five of his knights—two of whom were now dead—to return physical proof of what the vagabond had (supposedly) seen.

And yet it was "supposed" no more; for what the man had spoken of—with a tremor in his voice—now lay before us like a mirage (if it could be said to lay at all; for it had stabbed into the Mississippi at such an angle that its rear quarter hovered above the far bank like a cloud).

"'As though God Himself had shot an arrow into the earth,'" said Black Duncan, quoting the vagabond. "I must say, it's bigger even than I expected—easy now, girl."

He wrestled with his reins; all of us did. The horses had become nervous.

"And he was right about another thing. It stinks. Of *Them.* Positively reeks. Like sulfur mixed with ozone; or like when its little brother was hovering over Lake Coeur d'Alene."

"And set the mosasaurs against us," I muttered. "Or so Mercurius believes."

Mortigen laughed. "The beasties? Nah, they were just hungry. Lake Coeur d'Alene couldn't sustain them, that's all.

Old Merc loses himself in the part—it doesn't always have to be *aliens*. Plus he speaks in riddles. You know that."

"And yet he has performed miracles," I said.

We were referring, of course, to our oracle, our wizard, or at least the physics professor from Evergreen State College who had played him since before the Flashback (and continued to do so); someone who now claimed to have real gifts—an effect of the time-storm, he said; a supposition for which there was some evidence. As for who we were as a group—as an enclave of survivors—we *had* been the Northwestern Branch of the Society for Creative Anachronism (covering Oregon, Washington, and the northern tip of Idaho), otherwise known as the Kingdom of An Tir. At least, until Craxis—an outsider whose real name was unknown—had taken over and consolidated his power. Now we were Ambergard, a fully-functioning city-state with real weapons and a real stronghold (Castle Hagadone, formerly the Coeur d'Alene Resort and Marina, on Lake Coeur d'Alene). And we were not, despite Mortigen's flippant tone and demeanor, to be trifled with. Nor were the considered theories of Mercurius to be taken lightly.

"What the hell are those?" mumbled Black Duncan, his voice muffled. He was chewing some jerky from his saddlebag, peering at the top of the arch. "Are those—*people,* or something?"

I followed his gaze—to where three dark shapes hung suspended from the monument (they were small enough in comparison that we hadn't even noticed them earlier), then quickly fished out my binoculars.

"They are," I muttered, adjusting the lenses. "People, I mean."

I focused on the figures' faces: on their blue, lolled tongues, their blank, bulging eyes. "What's more, I'll characterize them. *Hanged people.* Just kids, really. Teenagers. All boys. They hanged them from the windows."

I handed the binoculars to Mortigen.

"Weird that the vagabond didn't mention it," said Black Duncan.

"They probably weren't here then," I said. "The decay hasn't set in."

"He's right," said Mortigen. "They're too fresh. Probably hasn't been a week." He ground the eyepieces. "Their clothes are clean—casual. Did you notice that? Like they're crisp from civilization. The tall one's even got a slipper—"

"It's a good bet we're being watched," I said. I unhooked my helmet from the saddle and held it in my hands; then scanned the area to where a nearby bridge crossed the Mississippi. "We should get moving."

"Eh?" Mortigen lowered the glasses and looked at me, surprised. "And test our virtue so soon? That isn't like you, Galaren."

I'd started to move away; now I curbed my horse—his name was "Scar," due to an old jousting injury—and cantered back.

"By which you mean you know me to be as prudent as I am faithful, of course," I said—and drew slowly along beside him. "Ah, but you flatter me too much."

He looked at me tentatively, calculatingly, his face bathed in sweat. It was the same look he gave me when I bested him on the field: one part submission, one part guile.

I extended a gauntlet to him. "We are blood brothers, Sir Mortigen, never forget—forged in battle; tested on the field. But be assured: when it comes to Lady Emeline—I am as eager for the contest as you."

Upon which—hesitantly at first but then with surprising enthusiasm—he clasped and shook my hand; and we went. Toward the nearby bridge and the other side of the muddy, orange Mississippi. Toward the sleek, dark, (possibly) alien ship—the anomaly—with its hideous smell and trail of crepuscular, yet somehow iridescent, debris—like shards of stained glass.

By the time we'd trotted close enough to the wall of semi-trucks and other vehicles (which were positioned midway along the bridge), as well as the massive signpost which had been attached to the side of one of the trailers—the sun had crept below the horizon and the sky begun to turn a bare, brooding mauve. Still, it was enough to read by, and what we read was as clear and succinct as anything I'd encountered: ILLINOIS IS OURS ... DO NOT PROCEED. VIOLATORS WILL BE SHOT. —a chilling message made more so by the number of bees buzzing and crawling about the sign.

"What's this?" asked Mortigen, and cantered closer. He indicated a hive, a massive thing, which lay on the roof of a nearby car and yet, somehow, was wholly independent of it. "They're busy, for twilight. Look."

I nudged Scar up beside him and looked (finding it highly unusual that a colony would build their nest in such an exposed way), saw a broken branch sticking out from beneath its papery mass. "This didn't form here—not naturally. Not at random. It was placed."

There was the *clop-clop* of hooves as Black Duncan joined us. "Yeah, but, who on earth would do that? I mean, if you're trying to scare people off, wouldn't that sign—not to mention those bodies—be enough? It doesn't make sense."

I stared at him, dumbly. "Beats the hell out of me," I said. I studied the small hole in the nest's bottom, which was a riot of activity. "It almost looks like they're fighting ..."

"Or fucking—more likely," said Mortigen. "See the ones with the big eyes? Those are the drones; the males. All the others are female." I must have looked at him queerly. "My uncle was a beekeeper," he said.

I watched as a drone with an injured wing struggled free of the mess—and promptly fell to the pavement. "They're outnumbered—whatever they are."

I shifted my focus to the barrier. "Okay. So. Obviously they were more concerned about vehicles than foot traffic—because it's pretty porous. We can get through it." I indicated a gap. "How about there—between that ambulance and the UPS truck? What do you say?"

"I say we're going to meet a hail of gunfire the moment we cross that line," said Black Duncan.

"We don't know that," said Mortigen. "Guns have gotten scarce; ammo even more so. Besides, it's getting dark." He looked at me as though he were making a pitch. "I say we ride for the opposite side as fast and hard as we can—weaving in and out of each other, winding between cars. If there's snipers, they won't know what to focus on. Then we get lost amongst all those railroad cars, fortify one for the night, and, in the morning, test our virtue against the shards. Every one of us." He looked at Black Duncan and then back to me. "And may fortune favor us all."

I stared at him with something like pride; he was, after all, however competitively inclined, however filled to the brim with guile, a Knight of the Lake—of the Heart of the Awl. And we would meet this Truth together; just as we had so often met on the field (and would again—only with un-blunted tips—should both of us prevail).

"Aye, Mortigen," I said, and clasped his gardbrace. "A wise plan." I looked back and forth between them. "We'll use our riot shields—just like the charge on Post Falls. I'll take point, followed immediately by Mortigen; Black Duncan, you bring up the rear. *Do not stop* until you reach the rails—then get off the bridge as fast as you can. With luck, they'll be little to no resistance." I crossed myself even though I wasn't Catholic, or even Lutheran. "May God be with us."

"May God be with us all," they repeated, and took up their shields.

And then we went: approaching the opening and cracking our reins; thundering forward as the dusk trembled and yielded before us (and no gunfire erupted), weaving in and out of the empty vehicles and time-displaced cycads—and leaping over fissures—like clanking ghosts.

Until we'd gained the opposite side and made our way down a collapsed section of the bridge—laughing, capering, carrying on. Until we'd unfurled our bedrolls in the cold, empty railcar (having forwent a campfire so as not to reveal our position) and curbed our banter (so as not to betray our fear); and, slowly, reluctantly—for tomorrow we would be judged—let slip our grip on the world.

Comfort. Warmth. Sturdy, clean-smelling sheets. It was still dark out.

I sat up with a start.

Silence, or nearly so. I blinked and rubbed my eyes.

The room was simple, sparse, nondescript, like a hotel room. And yet two things were immediately apparent: The shower was running—or had been, for I could now hear the sound of taps turning; and my armor and weapons were gone.

Not just removed—not, say, draped over a nearby chair—but *gone,* vanished. Vanished and replaced with ...

I rubbed the silken material of the tunic between my fingers. Whatever this was.

I threw off the blankets and stood even as the bathroom door opened and a woman wrapped in a towel stepped out—and immediately froze, as though she'd been unprepared for what she saw. "Oh, my," she said.

"Oh, my?" I must have looked bewildered. "Wouldn't that be my line?" I took a step closer. "You act as though you're surprised to see me here. Why?"

She seemed to relax and to regain her composure. "Surprised? No. No—not really. And yes. A progenitrix is always a little shocked; by the reality of it, I mean. The directness. At least, at first." She moved toward the kitchenette. "Would you like a drink? Something to take the edge off?"

I watched as she took out a bottle of wine and paused, checking to make sure her towel was secure—then fetched two glasses. "I still want to do my hair, if you don't mind. I know it's silly, but—"

"Enough! Where are the others?"

"Oh, they're here. They're with their pro—they're with their partners."

She approached and extended the decanter—but hesitated before giving me the corkscrew. "How do I know you're not going to gouge my eyes out with this?"

"You don't." I snatched her by the wrist suddenly and yanked her against me—the bottle falling and smashing against the floor—then brought my face close to her own. "I want you to take me to them—do you understand? Now."

"Easy. *You're hurting me ...*" She shook the hair from her eyes as she struggled. "You'll be with them soon. Besides, Hespa won't allow it—not before fertilization. Please, don't—"

"Who is Hespa?" I squeezed her wrist tighter even as she yelped. "What do you mean, 'fertilization?'"

"He—Hespa is our Administress, the viceroy of Matropolis. The one who established Progenistroika. But you wouldn't—" I shook her by the arm—too hard (she couldn't have weighed more than a hundred pounds). "It—it's a breeding program; designed to—oh, don't you see? There's *no men here,* only women. How else could we possibly—"

"Who are the men strung up from the Gateway Arch?" She recoiled as though in shock and disgust. *"Answer me. Who are the poor sods and why did you hang them? Or did they refuse to participate in your, your—"*

"Progenistroika," she said, still looking horrified. "The Multiplying; the Great Restructuring." She looked at the floor and the shattered glass—depleted, pitiful. "And I don't know who those men could be. I—I never leave the hotel. I don't even look out the windows."

I eased my grip on her, slowly, begrudgingly, studying her face. "I—I believe you, somehow. I'm not sure why." I let go of her wrist. "There's no deception in your eyes. No guile."

We stared at each other in the stillness of the room.

"Nor yours," she said. "Even in anger." She bowed slightly and re-met my gaze. "I'm Josephine, of the Holy Order of Progenitrices and Servants of Progenistroika."

"Galaren," I said, "of the Lake and Heart of the Awl."

She seemed to think about this, appearing distant, distracted. "Like Galahad ... the knight who found the Holy Grail." Her face lit up suddenly, beautifully, as though she'd had an epiphany. "That's what you were doing camped out in our territory. You're on a quest!"

I had to smile—at her accurate assessment, it was true, but also her effervescence, which was intoxicating. "Why, yes—yes, I suppose we are. A quest for a shard of the mothership—that great, dark shape which lies half in the river and half over the land, *your* land. Surely you're aware of ..."

Her blue eyes flicked up and down my body; it wasn't on purpose, it was just something she did. A tick.

"The Devil's Spade," she finished, seeming to shiver at its very mention. "The Ark of the Old Ones." She looked at the glass-strewn floor. "Aware, yes. Familiar with—no. Hespa says it is pure evil and that to touch it would be certain death." Her expression changed abruptly, from seriousness to outright horror. "But what on earth is it you intend?"

Again the eyes—bedroom eyes, with a life and animus of their own.

"I—we ..." I found myself hesitating, in part because I was unsure how to put it, but mostly because I was becoming increasingly intrigued, increasingly allured; to the point that I was losing my focus on what mattered—which was the liberation of my accoutrements (as well as my friends) and the resolution of our quest. Indeed, what was needed now more than anything was information, raw data. I needed to know where we were: the dimensions of the room, the layout of the building. I needed to know if there were guards—and if so, how many, and how were they armed?

"You said that—before fertilization—you wished to do your hair." I took a chance and placed a hand on the side of her head, an act of gentle dominance. "Do you still wish it?"

She closed here eyes and didn't move—and I thought for a moment I'd erred. Then she opened them and just nodded, slowly, resolutely. "I do," she said.

"Then go, Josephine. Make it so. And close the door behind you. I want ... I wish to be surprised."

"I have to tell you," she was saying, her voice slightly muffled by the door, "that if it's a piece of the Ark you're after—I think that's quite foolish. Hespa is right to call it a thing of pure evil; what else could something be that was seeding the clouds with those awful lights?"

I approached the door of the unit and paused, considering what she'd said, then reached out and turned the knob, slowly—only to find it locked from the other side.

"Because that's what it was doing—seeding the clouds; launching little replicas of itself, like satellites, like glowing arrowheads. At least, until we came out the next day and found it half in the drink—with a trail of wreckage behind it ... your shards." She laughed, brusquely. "Better be ready, though. Because the dinos *love* that thing—*and* its shards. They're everywhere out there. Hespa says it's because they're connected; the saurians and the ships—the lights, whatever—that they share a bond and can recognize each other. As for me, I don't know. What say you?"

I approached the sliding glass door at the opposite end of the room and peeked between the curtains; saw a small balcony on what looked to be the third floor—then rushed back over to the bathroom door.

"She," I had to pause to catch my breath, "She may be right. I can't really speak to it other than to say our own oracle has spoken along similar lines; although he believes, also, that what power they possess—the visitors—can be offset, even neutralized, by human faith and virtue; something he says unlocks the power of God."

There was a *ka-click* as the bathroom door opened and swung inward—revealing Josephine resplendent in high heels, thigh-high stockings, and a black garter belt and matching bra, her face made up like a movie star, her long, blonde hair curled and coifed.

"I'd like to hear more," she said, simply, and approached, her gait as smooth and sinewy as a show horse—her blue eyes fixed squarely on my own. "About what you said, for virtue means different things to different people, and about your quest. I mean, what does it require of you, exactly? Not the others, Galaren, not your fellow knights; but *you,* personally."

I stiffened as she made contact; as she ran her hands up the sides of my neck and cupped my cheeks; as my entire body seemed to crackle with electricity. "What—what the quest requires of one ... it requires of all," I managed—even as sweat beaded along my forehead and my teeth clenched; as my belly constricted like a nest of vipers. "Josephine—*please.*"

"What, Galaren?" She looked up at me dreamily, toothily. Carnivorously. "I mean: what does it require?"

"It—it requires we lay hands upon one of the objects—each of us. That is, each to a shard. And that we return that fragment—our fragment—to Mercurius, to be analyzed."

She only sighed, sensuously, smokily. "Why, Galaren. Why would you do such a thing—when you know it will result in your destruction?" She toyed with a lock of my hair, which had been washed and combed in my sleep (for I had been drugged, I was now certain). "When you know, or should know, by this point, that their hatred for us burns, it poisons, every single human thing it touches—or is touched by?"

I stared into her eyes, eyes which were now full of daring and decadence, passion, carnality, perverse promise, and shook my head. "No. Not if I am pure. Not if I am worthy. God will see to it. Besides, there is more at stake than just the quest. For whomsoever passes this test wins also the right to challenge for Emeline's hand. And I shall not fail her, Josephine. Not if you—"

And then she clasped my head in both hands and mashed her lips against my own: *mm*'ing and *aw*'ing, trying to slip in her tongue, as I moved to resist but instead lifted her off the floor (whereupon she wrapped her legs about my body and instantly cried out); as I gripped both sides of her ass (too hard) and strode for the bed—tossing her onto it like a bolster, like a body pillow; burying my face between her breasts and against her stomach (and finally beneath her garter belt). Pulling her panties down with my teeth before gripping them in my fists and working them free of her legs.

"Oh, don't you see?" she gasped. "This is what we wanted—only this, Sir Knight! And not just me; oh, no, we are all of us lined up—for you, Galaren, and your mighty friends;

173

to take as you will. Is it not wonderful? Oh, the sisters you will sire, the workers, the warriors!"

And something just snapped—like *that,* even as I was about to cross the line: something which sobered me like a slap in the face—or perhaps a cold shower. Something which made me get up immediately and sit on the edge of the bed, holding my face in my hands, aloof. Something I cannot explain—other than to say it was like God Himself had touched me; given me sight.

At length Josephine said, disappointedly, "It doesn't bring you much happiness, does it? This virtue." She covered herself with a sheet and sat up. "Nor anyone else, I think." She touched my slouched shoulder and rubbed it, gently. "What good is it, then?"

"I asked our oracle the same thing once," I said—a little disinterestedly, I confess. "Do you know what he said?"

I looked at her but she just shook her head.

"He said the rewards of virtue are less direct, but that a single chaste act creates ripples, which spread in unexpected ways." I removed her hand from my arm and lay it on the bed, gently, finally. "Likewise, one act of wrong does the same thing. And this would be wrong, Josephine. On my part. You are too young, for one; too young, too naïve, too unspoiled—however worldly you may come across, or feel. Further, I am betrothed—to an idea as much as a woman; which is to say that God has punished us for our trespass by sending us the time-storm—the Flashback; and that we must rediscover our virtue—our righteousness—if we are to have any hope at all."

And then she just looked at me, saying nothing: until she wrapped the sheet about herself quickly and, grumbling, scurried for the door—where she paused.

"I like you, Galaren. I really do. But I lied when I said I didn't know those men—the ones hanging from the Gateway Arch." She opened the door and whistled through her teeth— loudly, confidently—before turning to look at me again. "They were men like you."

And then she left and the guards poured in—like water through a dike. Then she left and I was clubbed and kicked and spat upon; as though I were less than an animal. As though I were less than human.

The questions began the moment I was alert; the moment I was cognizant enough to know that our so-called "dungeon" was in fact a powerless walk-in freezer in a St. Louis hotel.

"What the hell did they do," asked Mortigen, wrinkling his nose. "Drop you in a vat of dinosaur piss?"

"You kept saying 'Hespa, Hespa'—in your delirium, I mean," said Black Duncan. He offered me a cup of tepid water. "But who is it? Is she one of the progenitrices, a guard, their leader, what?"

I blinked as they swam into focus: remembering the pit and the fencing topped with razor wire; remembering Hespa in her elevated lifeguard's chair, like a queen. "They—they put me in a pool," I said, "you know, one of those rectangular ones, with the 12 foot deep end—only this one was empty. And then they, they—"

"They put something in there with you," said Mortigen. "Let me guess: A Flashback-crazed triceratops ... with spears in its back." He looked at Black Duncan and then back to me, knowingly. "Spears in its back and the Glow in its eyes—isn't that right?"

"Why, yes—yes, it is," I stammered. "But how—"

"My progenitrix—Rosemary—she told me about it. Said that's what they do to resisters; that they throw them to the triceratopses—which they anger by stabbing sticks in their backs—and wager on the outcome." He clasped my shoulder in solidarity. "What I can't figure is—how the hell are you still here?"

It all came back to me. The angry crowd—in which I briefly spotted Josephine; looking ashamed, I thought, even remorseful—the inadequate lance. The rhino-like herbivore swiping its foot on the concrete (like a bull) before charging me furiously and suddenly rearing up—falling on my braced polearm like a slab; voiding its bladder as it shuddered and bled and died.

"I—I got lucky," I said, looking up at a sound outside our cell—the sound of something heavy being set down; the rattle of steel. That's when it occurred to me that something wasn't right. "Wait, what do you mean, she 'told' you? You mean—they didn't put you in the pit?"

I looked from Mortigen to Black Duncan and then back to Mortigen. "But you were in contest for the Lady Emeline ..."

He frowned suddenly and glared at me—intensely, murderously. "Oh, I am, Sir Galaren. I am. The wench—Rosemary—never got close. You're a fool if you think otherwise."

He glanced from me to Black Duncan—anxiously, I thought. Uneasily. "Black Duncan, on the other hand, has a different story. Don't you now, good sir? Why don't you tell him. Tell Sir Galaren the Born Again what you told me."

And, indeed, he was about to do that when the great door of the freezer suddenly unlatched and swung open and we launched ourselves at it without hesitation—in time to see, not just a wheelbarrow piled high with armor and weapons, but a pale, lithe figure, a woman, a progenitrix, by the shape of her, vanishing in the dark.

A woman who, though I saw her only briefly—for a slim second, perhaps—bore a striking resemblance to Josephine.

"Come, Black Duncan, we must hurry," I said, sliding on my remaining gauntlet, picking up my red-plumed helmet. "Before they discover our missing gear."

Yet still he did not move, or make any effort to don his armor; even though Mortigen and I were already dressed. *"Gah,* it is ridiculous! Okay; we're breeders—so what? I, for one, see no cause for alarm. Nor, for that matter, to return to Ambergard."

I unsheathed Blood Zephyr and gave her a heft—relishing the touch and feel of her (even if it was steel on steel); appreciating her weight and balance. "No, Black Duncan. It is not possible. The Quest must not be surrendered—not for you or for anyone. You know that."

"And again, I ask: *Why?* Why, when everything a man could possibly want exists right here, *now,* and in such great plentitude? Bah. This shard and purity nonsense ... it's just that—nonsense. Why pursue it?"

I watched as Mortigen drew his own blade and paused to admire it, as I had done. "What would you prefer?" I snapped. "To live as prisoners? To wither away in this very cell but for the chance at some sexual gratification?"

Black Duncan guffawed. "They're not going to keep us here. Eve told me herself. It's only until they get to know us. Regardless, I think I should tell you, that, that ..." He lifted his chin and squared his shoulders, as though having made up his mind at last. "That I'm staying. That, indeed, I did lay with my progen—my progen—"

"Your progenitrix," I said, curtly.

"His hooker, he means," quipped Mortigen.

Black Duncan shot him a glance—one I wouldn't want directed at me. "I'm going to pretend I didn't hear that. No; she was skilled in the art of love, it's true—but she was no prostitute. None of them are. What happened between us was genuine. It was real." He looked at me almost pleadingly. "Don't you see, Galaren, *it was real.* It wasn't like Ambergard—or Craxis—or the way we talk—or any of this other faux bullshit we've immersed ourselves in. No. This was nature, this was truth—*real* nature, not some phantasmagoria dreamed up by—by *Them,"* He nodded toward the ceiling and the sky. "Like the bees we saw coming in. They are trying to *build* something here, Galaren; something based on reality, not fantasy. Something authentic. And I'm not simply going to walk away from that. I mean, surely you can understand—"

"What I understand is that we're getting out of here," I said. "And that the test of virtue will be met. And what I suggest just now is that you—"

"*Your* test of virtue, Galaren. Your test. I'm not leaving. I'll help you escape, but I'm not going to—"

"*Shh,*" said Mortigen. "Someone's coming."

I paused to listen—even as shadows began creeping slowly across the floor. "Back to the cell, hurry."

Black Duncan looked back and forth between us. "But you're—"

"We're *ill,*" I said.

And we went—trying not to rattle—Mortigen and I laying on the cots while Black Duncan covered us and quickly secured the door—which opened right up again.

"You are required once more," said a female voice, a guard (presumably), and added, "You. And—that one."

I assumed she meant Mortigen.

"I'm sorry, but," Black Duncan sounded agreeable, diplomatic. "They are both quite ill, as you can see. No, I'm afraid that just wouldn't be possible. But, ah, may I—I mean, if Eve is amenable to it, I'd be unopposed to a—a—"

"Come," said the guard, followed by a dry shuffle and clinking of accoutrements. "Leave the door; they're not going anywhere." And then they were gone.

We threw off our blankets.

"That was close," said Mortigen. "If they *had* shut the—"

"We'd be right back where we started," I sighed. I put my helmet on and cinched its strap, looked out the commercial kitchen's windows at the first light of dawn. "They're going to be all over us once we start clanking around out there, you know that. Plus there's the fact I'm not crazy about hacking into a bunch of women ... you know? We need a diversion."

"Yeah? How about a fucking stampede?"

I looked at Mortigen, who just grinned from ear to ear. "As in, 'men-ag-erie,' he said. "As in—they have one. And I know where it is. Our horses are there, too—not that they're happy about it. Come on."

And we went. Just as we had in the Post Falls War when we had singlehandedly attacked the command bunker and proven ourselves to be such a devastating dyad. As we had when Emeline had made public her private suitors—by asking them to approach the stand during Festival—and we had, each of us, learned our competitor was also our friend.

It would be difficult to describe the bedlam that ensued once we'd freed the animals: the brown, bucking triceratopses and the turkey-sized velociraptors (with their semi-transparent skin and pink, unblinking eyes); the Flashback-crazed iguanodons with their strange, false thumbs and even stranger patterns—the "tobacco" spitting dilophosaurs; the screaming pterodactyls. All I know is that by the time we'd mounted our horses and galloped away from the kennels (which were under the front awning of the hotel, the glass doors of which we'd smashed), the place was virtually crawling—both inside and out—with dangerous fauna; enough so that any attempt to prevent our escape would have proved not merely difficult—it would have been counterproductive. Nor did we stop or even slow down until we'd reached the river and the seemingly endless trail of wreckage before it; at which Mortigen came to a rest beside and slightly behind me (as I looked out across the field) and we were able, at last, to contemplate our next— and perhaps final—move.

Which, of course, was the touching of the shards; the testing of our virtue. The knowing, at last—after our long and perilous journey—if one, or perhaps even both of us, would perish or succeed.

"It's down to this, then," I said, fighting the reins (even though we were at a standstill), remembering the reluctance of the horses. "This is what it's all about."

"Aye," said Mortigen, and took off his helmet. "It's where the rubber meets the road, as they say."

He dismounted and approached the shards (having thrown his reigns to the bushes), but paused before kneeling. "Ah, but I forget. It's your move, Galaren. As per our coinflip—the one in Nebraska, if you recall."

I unbuckled the strap and removed my helmet, letting it fall to the ground; then dismounted and joined him.

"I do," I said, taking off my gauntlets, and knelt before a shard—a shard black as pitch, but which somehow gave off light. "Will you bow with me, Sir?"

"I will," he said, and rattled down behind me.

And then I prayed.

"Blessed be the Lord, my strength, which teacheth my hands to war, and my fingers to fight. Blessed be my goodness, and my fortress; my high tower, and my deliverer; my shield, and He in whom I trust; who subdueth my people beneath me. Amen."

I gritted my teeth and took the shard in both hands.

And nothing happened. It was simply cold, texture-less, inert. Anti-climactic.

I turned to Mortigen—for I was about to start laughing—and saw that he was no longer kneeling but had in fact stood; stood and was whipping the flat of his sword toward me—the weight of which hit me like an anvil, like a wrecking ball. Like a white-hot super nova on a starry, starry night.

There is little left to tell; other than to say I awakened to a pounding head and the smell of burnt flesh—for what was left of Mortigen lay next to me on the field: spitting and popping and sizzling—like so much frying lard—seeping back into the earth, like wine. Nor did I linger overlong with the grisly remains but rather dusted myself off almost immediately and located and mounted Scar ... after which, having tethered Mortigen's horse to us, we cantered along the water toward the bridge and promptly crossed it—pausing only after we'd reached the makeshift barricade, and this only because I'd heard a sound, a commotion, coming from the other side of the Mississippi, from the fortified hotel.

A commotion, I realized (having retrieved and employed my binoculars), that involved Black Duncan. For he could be seen struggling furiously even as the women forced him through the smashed front doors and into the parking lot, where he was beset by predators, velociraptors and compies, mostly, but also an allosaur. (Which I was pretty sure hadn't been part of the menagerie but had apparently been attracted by the ruckus; either way, there was nothing I could do for him). And I wondered—and still do—had they expelled him in retribution for our escape (and the freeing of the animals); or simply because he was no longer needed? And what of Mortigen? Had he failed because he too had lain with his progenitrix? Or was there some other reason; some mystery the likes of which only Mercurius could comprehend? Or God?

I gazed at the heavens and the enigmatic lights which may or may not have been connected to the saurians, the new rulers of the earth, the once and future kings. And why had I been spared?

And then I released it, having no answers but faith, and we cantered forward, toward the Gateway Arch and it's great, golden doorway to the West. Toward Ambergard and the bed I'd share with Emeline; and clean clothes that didn't reek of piss.

Toward and *away,* far away, from the crashed chariot of the gods and the men hanging by their necks; from the gray, papery hive of the rusted barrier car and the humming, swirling, undulating wasps.

1
Spears Out

My dad used to say, "It's amazing what you can see from the back of a pickup, if you're in the right place at the right time."

For him, it was watching ash from Mt. Saint Helens darken the sky from the bed of his own father's truck in 1980—when he was just 13 years old. For me, it was watching Mt. Hood smolder and spume at precisely the same age; sitting not with my back against a rusted cab, as he had done (I knew because he had told the story a thousand times), but on the hump of a brand-new Chevrolet's wheel well—so I could keep an eye on the driver.

"I told you this was a bad idea," said Jesse, watching the man carefully, suspiciously. He held his stocking cap down so it wouldn't blow from his head. "And why the hell does he keep staring at us—me in particular?"

I watched as the old man (he had to have been at least 40) glanced at us through the rearview mirror—again. "Dunno; we're probably the first people he's seen—look around." We glanced at the spare, hardscrabble pines and the blurred, yellowed sage; the great, brown piles of basalt which littered the plain like porous turds. "Probably hasn't seen anyone alive since the Flashback."

Quint harrumphed. "No way. He would have said something." He stared through the rear window at the driver. "Probably cooks kids and feeds 'em to the dinosaurs. Or he's a pedo. I don't trust him. Not around Jess." He looked at

Jesse as though the boy were fragile and needed special care. "Pretty, *pretty—*"

"Say it again," said Jesse, menacingly.

Quint hesitated. "Say what?"

"What you just said. Say it again."

Quint guffawed. "How can I say it again when I don't know what I said in the first place?" He looked at me as though he were completely nonplussed—all Quint Fucking Holloway: Innocent Man. "I don't get it. Seriously, though. What'd I say?"

"Ignore him, Miles," said Jesse. "He just wants to drag you into it."

Quint touched his fingers to his chest.

"Yeah, *you,*" said Jesse. "Peckerwood. Tornado bait. Son of a crawdaddy."

"Yo, lay off that."

"What's the matter? Your trailer wheels showing? Wood booger. Swamp Yankee. Inbredneck ..."

"Okay; it's not cute anymore," Quint growled. "Keep it up. And I swear I'll jam that stick right up your—"

"All right, knock it off, both of you. (I'd heard that in a movie once and had always wanted to say it in real life.) There's a sign coming up—what's it say? Is it Goldendale?"

The sign answered my question:

WEST 142
Goldendale
Klickitat
RIGHT ½ MILE

"Okay," I said. "This is our stop; he said he was continuing on 142." I reached for the thick, sharpened stick at my back. "Bikes ready and spears out—just in case."

We unslung our spears and stood our bikes upright. "I'll go first and you can hand the bikes down to me."

"And if he tries something?" Jesse looked at his weapon; at the clean, whittled point, which had been untested by

183

anything—the fresh, white wood. "I mean, are we talking fight or flight? Because I'm not sure if I'm ready—"

"Flight," I said—without hesitation. I adjusted the strap of the Thermos (because that's what the lead tube looked like), feeling the sheer weight of it, the awesome responsibility. "Because—what's Hal say about unsecured places?"

"Commotions attract predators," said Jesse.

"That's right," I said.

"Unless he has a firearm," said Quint. He waved at the cab, where we saw the driver craning his neck and smiling at us—folksily, fatherly. "In which case, we *kill the son of a bitch.*"

2

Until We Meet Again

It would be incorrect to say that, without human intelligence, Goldendale simply 'lay' beneath the sun—stale, abandoned, lifeless; it didn't. To say that would be to deny what life remained: the foot-long Triassic dragonflies, for example, blue-green and iridescent, like 7-Up bottles, which erupted from the weeds as we pulled up to the market and scattered, like seeds, on the wind; or the slim, tan, almost stick-like Compies—hopping and foraging amongst street trash when we arrived—which did the same. Rather, it was that without human agency the town lived and breathed but simply *no longer knew it,* and so, far from being inert, it merely slumbered—silently, dreamlessly.

"Welcome to Goldendale," shouted the driver from his window, jocularly. "The time is half-past 65 million years B.C. and the temperature is hotter than a stolen tamale. I'd like to thank you personally for flying Hodge Worthington International and remember: the next time you fly, fly the International."

I lept out even before we'd come to a complete stop—holding my arms up to receive the bikes, snapping at Jesse and Quint to hurry.

184

"Whoa, whoa, *whoa,*" blurted the driver—ratcheting the brake, throwing open his door. "What's the big hurry here?"

I mounted my bike even as Jesse and Quint vaulted over the bedrail and did the same, and then we were riding away from the pickup just as fast as we could, standing on the pedals to increase our velocity, aiming for the corner of the building—the idea, I suppose, being to put its overgrown bricks between the yelling man and ourselves (in case he had a gun).

"I mean, for Pete's sake, you guys ..." He sounded wounded, exasperated. "Aren't you even going to say, *'thank you?'*"

I barked at the others to hold up and squeezed my brakes—skidding around to face him, staring at him intensely across the weed-infested, garbage-strewn lot.

"Thank you," I said. "Truly. You saved us—what?" I craned to look at Jesse, our map keeper. "About 40 miles?"

"More like 50," said Jesse. He adjusted the strap of his pack, which, like my own, had no doubt gotten heavier. "From Toppenish, and the start of 97, all the way to here. So, yeah. Thank you."

"Yeah, man. Thanks," said Quint. "Seriously."

The man moved to speak but hesitated. "Look. My name's Hodge—and I'm not a threat, all right? I promise you. I—I don't even own a weapon." He held up his arms as though to illustrate the point. "It's just that, well, I haven't seen anybody else out here. Not since Kennewick, at least, where I ... where I saw things. Terrible things. Enough to know that—whatever it is you're doing, *wherever* it is you're going ... it's a bad idea."

The wind blew, hot and cloying, and the trash skittered. Nobody said anything.

"Now you said when I picked you up that you're from a settlement; a place—a place northeast of here, up in Granger. A good place. Safe. Well, I need to tell you: there ain't no such thing as that in the cities—or out on the road—or anywhere. All right? It's just hungry lizards and hungry people, and I'd be hard-pressed to tell you which is worse.

And I really think you should consider just climbing back into the bed of this truck and letting me take you home to where you came from—after I complete my business in Trout Lake, that is." He looked at us plainly, compassionately. "I'm an adult, see, a father. And that means I've got to try. Gotta try to do right by you. So what do you say?"

I looked at Jesse as the wind ruffled his collar and then to Quint, whose shoulder-length hair danced, but neither showed any emotion—nor any indication at all that their minds had been changed. I shook my head.

"There's your answer, Mr. Worthington. I'm sorry. For us, it's the Garden of Oz—or bust."

He seemed to search his memory. "The Garden of Oz ... Seems—seems I saw something about that once ... on TV, I mean. A long time ago. By—by the Hollywood sign? In Los Angeles?"

I nodded, gravely.

"What's there?"

"Our business," I said. "Just like yours—in Trout Lake."

At last he exhaled and slapped his arms against his sides, appearing to give up. "That's a thousand miles, you know; I guess you understand that. And those motocross bicycles will never make it—you understand that too?"

"We've got innertubes," I said. "And we can pick up other bikes along the way."

"Yeah, well." He scratched at his high forehead and thinning hair. "I guess you've thought of everything. Except that you're sitting ducks on those things: for highwaymen, for one—those are a thing again, you know—for raptors, for pterodactyls. But I don't suppose you're worried about any of that—being young and invulnerable, after all."

Again, nobody said anything.

The man—Hodge—looked at Jesse, appearing almost to well up. "There's a reason I kept staring at you, you know. Because you look like someone; my first son, gone long before the Flashback." He paused, seeming to choke on his words. "Like his mother, too."

I looked at Quint, who looked at Jesse—who frowned.

"All right," said Hodge. "Well. Until me meet again."

And then he climbed back into his truck and put it into gear and was gone, rumbling toward 142 which he would take west toward Trout Lake, leaving a cloud of dust. After which we thought about what he'd said—for it was obvious Jesse and Quint were doing the same—and I took out the Thermos, which we just stared at for the longest time before Quint handed me the key and I inserted it into the lid and began to turn.

3

Talon

We'd found the thing shortly after Jesse arrived at the camp (the one in Granger, a town full of dinosaur sculptures, go figure), back when we were still getting to know each other, still feeling each other out. Quint and I had already met and mostly hit it off—I'm still not sure why, he was from nearby Wapato (population 4,997) and I was from Los Angeles (I'd taken a Greyhound to spend the summer with my uncle, who had since vanished in the Flashback). We just had, same as we had with Jesse, who had arrived a short time after without so much as a knapsack—no family, no friends, nothing—and to whom we were introducing our favorite fishing spot (perfect and secluded and shady beneath the State Route 223 bridge, on the Yakima River) when the body washed up.

"Miles, what the hell is that? I mean, is that what I think it is?"

Quint sounded flabbergasted, incredulous. None of us had ever seen a dead body (aside from the disappearances, Granger had largely been spared). "Holy shit, man."

"Yeah—Jesus," said Jesse.

We laid our poles on the rocks and shuffled closer—to where it was caught up in a reed-filled shallow.

"Where's the top half of his head?"

I looked at the gaping, blue-gray mouth and plump, swollen tongue—like uncooked pork sausage—and the

187

horseshoe mustache; above which, above a serrated edge caked in dried blood, everything was gone. "I don't know," I said. "But he died screaming."

Quint was the first to point it out: "What's *that?*"

He indicated a dull gray canister which was slung from around the thing's neck (it didn't seem proper to call it a 'man' anymore). "Look. It says something."

I inched closer, stepping into the water up to my ankles. "'Radiation Products Technology,'" I read. "It—it's like a brand-name, or something."

"Get it," said Quint.

"I'm not *touching* that thing!"

"Get it—you're right there. Don't you think Hal's going to want to look at it?" He was referring, of course, to Hal Keller, the brains behind Camp Courage's makeshift electrical system—among other things.

"Well, then Hal can come and get it," I said—and didn't budge. "What part of 'radiation' don't you understand?" I looked at the body: at the swollen tongue and horseshoe mustache—jet-black on blue— and the thing's one visible hand, which was contorted in a crook.

"I'll get it, you candy-ass," cursed Quint, and stepped into the water.

Jesse, meanwhile, had begun to stir. "Ah, guys ..."

"'Candy-ass?' What are you, my grandpa?"

Quint reached for the canister. "Hey, if the shoe fits ..."

"Ah, guys. You need to like—not move. Okay? Like, *at all."*

"Here," said Quint. "At least keep him from floating away while I—"

"If you don't shut up and hold still," growled Jesse, "we are all *going to die.* All right? Just, look south, okay? *Slowly."*

And we looked south: toward the bend in the dark, lazy river and the gray, rocky sandbars further down—and froze.

"Oh, shit," rasped Quint. "Just holy fucking shit. Is that— is that a ...?"

I waved him to silence as I studied the thing's physical makeup: the brown body and distended belly, held horizontally over the ground, like a side of beef on a spit, and the balanced tail; the wrinkled, S-curved neck; the long snout and brow horns.

"It's not good, whatever it is," I whispered. "Everyone get in the water—it hasn't seen us. *Quietly.*"

Quint demurred. "But what if—"

"Just do it. It'll help mask our smell."

And we did it, wading into the cold, (seemingly) slow-moving water, moving out deeper and deeper, something my mother had warned me against—because of the undercurrents—time and time again.

"What's the hell's it doing, anyway?" asked Jesse at last, shivering. "There's no big game around here."

I watched the therapod as it stared into the water. "It's fishing, just like we were. Probably got one in its sights. Look, see how—"

And it raised its head ... then swung it around to face us.

"Oh, shit," whined Quint. *"Oh shit-oh shit-oh shit ..."*

Nobody moved.

That's when I heard it: a kind of whisper—a *suggestion*—not vocalized *but in my mind;* as though I were thinking it to myself, as though I were imagining it.

Release us, it seemed to say. *Release us and we will protect you.*

I looked around: first at Quint and then at Jesse, both of whom seem bewildered—until my eyes settled on the corpse and its awful, gaping mouth, its frozen scream—like something from *The Thing*—and finally on to the canister, which floated and bobbed, like a buoy.

Do it, Miles.

And then it was coming—the therapod, the allosaur, *whatever*—slowly but surely; padding toward us along the bank with its eyes focused on us like laser beams, like heat-seeking missiles. Like a great cat stalking its prey.

"What are you doing?" It was Jesse—sounding alarmed. "Quint—what is he doing?"

I reached the body and gripped the canister, worked its strap up and over the corpse's partially-eaten half-head.

"Miles? What are you doing, man?" Quint, I think. "Because it's a bad idea—whatever it is. Come on. Give it to me."

"It'll protect us," I said—dreamily, dazedly. "It'll make it so that it thinks we're one of its own." It had a pin in it with a ring attached, like a hand grenade— which I pulled; but with no luck. "More, it'll let us know when there are others—other predators. We just have to release them ..."

"Jesus, stop him!"

But it was too late; I'd already twisted the ring and pulled the pin, which had opened the tube; opened it so that a weird, emerald light spilled forth even as I reached in with my fingers and felt an object—something smooth, cold, metallic, like a necklace—which I snatched up by its chain and quickly held aloft.

Something which burned like green fire as the predator entered the water but paused, snarling. Which reflected from its eyes like an emerald sun as it sniffed at the air and seemed to change its mind; as it cocked its great head—which was the size of a jet ski—in curiosity, before swinging it away like a wrecking ball and bounding from the river, back into the woods.

Something whose glow quickly faded as the threat diminished and became lifeless and inert in my hand; just a small chain with a medallion attached—which was black as coal; just a curved piece of an unknown metal (or glass) which was cold to the touch and looked like a velociraptor's scythe-like, retractable toe-claw.

Or a talon.

All of which brings us back to the present, and the fact that as Hodge drove away and I opened the Thermos a green light spilled out which painted our shirts; a light which told us—in no uncertain terms—that there was a predator (or predators) nearby. A predator—or predators—who might even then be preparing to rush us: from behind the overgrown ruins of the store, perhaps, or the Mesozoic rock formation in the street.

Or just from out of nowhere, I thought—as Hodge's truck disappeared finally down the road—*in a place that was in the middle of nowhere.*

4
Wolves of the Jurassic

I looked around: at the Les Schwab Tire Center and its sun-bleached ads (FREE BEEF WITH ANY TIRE PURCHASE!), and its block walls covered with vines; at a crusty, two-tone mobile home (beige and peapod-green) and a ruined café; a partially-collapsed house. It wasn't just that we felt like we were being watched; it was that we felt like we were being watched from every direction.

"I got a bad feeling," said Jesse—as the Talon continued to glow, to tremble. "We should—we should take cover."

"Yeah," I mumbled, warily. I resealed the Thermos and swung it around to my back. "I think you're ri—"

"That Les Schwab," said Quint. "How about that?"

I looked at its bay doors—one of which was open. "And become the free beef? Dude ... it's wide open. The market's right—"

Something rustled and we jumped—but it was just a tumbleweed, skittering across the road.

"Better think again," said Quint. "Look. Its roof is collapsed."

I looked. "It'd keep the raptors out, though. Don't you think? Maybe."

"Maybe. But it might not be raptors. It might be one of those things from Granger. Or a *whole pack.*"

"The café," said Jesse, suddenly. He indicated the overgrown—but intact—building: *The Alienated Heifer,* whatever that meant. "It'll have food—canned stuff, bottled water—if we have to hole up. Plus they'll be a walk-in—one of those big industrial freezers—in case anything gets in. Like a panic room."

We both just looked at him. The dude definitely had a knack.

"Okay," I said. "We're splitting for the diner. We are not gonna pass GO; we're not collecting 200 dollars. We're just gonna—"

"Oh, fuck," said Quint, stiffening like a board.

And we followed his gaze.

It's never easy; coming face to face with a predatory dinosaur—even one as far away as this one—especially when it just stands there like a psycho killer with its dark tail swishing slowly and its white face cocked; coldly, dispassionately—like Michael fucking Meyers. Hal says it's because they release a pheromone that causes panic and disorientation in their prey, but I think it's the eyes—which gleam like the Flashback itself (or at least the weird borealis the Flashback left behind) and can give you the heebie-jeebies. Regardless, I knew once we'd seen the Nano-A (or *Nanoallosaurus,* for I remembered its wide skull and narrow snout from Mr. Jones' science class) that we were in serious trouble; for it was, or had been, or was again, amongst the deadliest of predators: a smart, lithe species Jones had referred to as—because of its sophisticated pack behavior—"the Wolves of the Jurassic."

"Nobody move," I said. "Just—don't even breathe." I reached for the Thermos and brought it around. "There's something about this. Something—"

"Forget it," said Quint. He indicated the Nano-A. "I don't want to get close to that thing. Besides, we don't even know if it'll work—the Talon, I mean. It could have been a fluke. No way, man. We need to run, *now.*"

I opened the canister and took out the Talon, which glowed, fiercely.

"He's right," said Jesse. "You're putting too much faith in that." He shielded his eyes and looked at the diner. "We can make it but only if we get a head start. And that means getting a move on it; like, right—"

He jumped as something cried out—we all did—like a fisher cat at night; or a drunken woman shouting unintelligibly.

"Jesus," said Quint. "What the hell was *that?*"

"It came from the other side of the market," said Jesse. "Whatever it was."

I put the Talon around my neck. "It's what I'm trying to tell you, there isn't just ..." I trailed off, suddenly, looking for the Nano-A. "Where'd it go?"

We all just looked at the spot.

"Okay, fuck this," said Quint—and dumped his bike.

"Yeah," said Jesse—doing the same. "For once we agree."

"But don't you see, running might be just exactly—"

And then Jesse was grabbing my arm and I was dumping my bike (as well as the thermos) and we were all of us breaking into a sprint—just bolting toward the diner like lunatics, like frightened children, which I guess we were, leaping across the pavement in bounds—even as I glanced at a nearby fence and saw the tumbleweed from earlier pushed right up against it—rocking and vibrating and shaking, as though it were alive—deposited there by the wind; trapped.

5

Wane

They say your entire life flashes before your eyes right before you die, but that's not what happened—not to me, anyway. Instead, I found myself thinking about all the people closest to me that weren't actually there (not including my parents, oddly enough): people like Hal Keller, who would have been sitting down to a cold lunch of hot mustard sardines and boiled water—if he bothered to eat at all—at Camp Courage about then; or Macey McNeil—who was probably so worried about us she *couldn't* eat, much less teach, or Colby Higgins, listening to the Stones' "Hang Fire" on his shitty cassette deck (for the millionth time) while sipping that godawful herbal tea of his and tending his marijuana plants. And it seemed to me these images all had one thing in common—which was that they all showed just how wonderful otherwise mundane post-apocalyptic life could actually be; how smooth it could run if one just had the good sense to accept things and to appreciate them and to let the dead or disappeared or just plain missing lie; to not tempt fortune on some foolish, ill-conceived, even suicidal, errand; *to stay put.*

To live to see one's 14th birthday—which seemed unlikely now that the animals had begun appearing from everywhere: from corners and recesses and stands of dry, prickly hawthorns; from the dark between buildings and the cover of stalled, faded vehicles. From everywhere and nowhere at once: triangulating us, boxing us in, choking off our every escape—until one of them tripped over a toppled motorcycle and, falling on its saurian ass, provided us the opening we needed.

And then we were through; we'd threaded the noose and piled through the café's front door, closing it behind us, and the dark-blue predators with their ghostly white faces could only howl and gnash their teeth as we braced it with red vinyl booth benches and finally a cigarette machine—which, to our surprise, held the thing firm; even after they'd started butting it with their heads (at least, I assume that's what they were doing).

"See? *See?*" Quint sounded manic, unhinged; hysterical. "If we'd relied on the Talon we'd be *dead* right now ..."

I looked down and closed my hand about it, wondering why it felt different (at least from before), why it shone dimmer. Why it died completely even as I touched it.

"All right, never mind, spears out," said Quint—as if from a million miles away.

Maybe they weren't close enough, I thought. Sure; the thing at the river had practically been on top of us. Or maybe—maybe it *attracted* them first; that is, before finally repelling them. But that wouldn't explain the loss of—

"Come on, come on!"

I looked at the shaking door and the red, vinyl booth seats; the rattling, old-fashioned cigarette machine with its clear glass pull-knobs and LUCKY STRIKES masthead—like something from the '50s. Or maybe its energy had simply had a lifespan—like everything and everyone else—and was just gone now; extinguished; like my parents, most likely, like the world.

"Goddammit, Miles!"

And then I was awake; I was back in the moment—holding my spear, standing with my friends. Then I was ready to die fighting as the glass of the door shattered and a swinging head wormed in and its jaws snapped open and closed and its teeth gnashed; as Quint drove his spear through its maw and out the back of its skull—where it ran with blood and brains—and another took its place; and hand-like talons, white as the things' faces, began to reach and grope and feel about—like the arms of cats, I supposed, so eerily articulate and human—like shambling fucking zombies.

6

Interlude

I don't how long it took to finally ward them off: maybe 50 seconds, maybe 5 minutes—all I know is that by the time they retreated to their partially-collapsed buildings and stands of hoary hawthorns we were utterly and thoroughly wasted; I mean trashed, and just collapsed in heaps right there on the floor—on the black and white checkered tile of *The Alienated Heifer.*

"Jesus," gasped Quint. "Just ... I thought we were goners. Like, serious goners." He rolled over onto his back and exhaled, explosively. "I gotta hand it to you; you guys rallied like sons of bitches." He laughed suddenly, boisterously, which became a coughing jag. "Wouldn't believe it if I hadn't seen it myself."

I looked at Jesse—who was on his hands and knees next to me—in time to see his reaction, which wasn't pleased.

"Yeah? Well, sub-divide me and Kentucky-fry me, is that a backhanded compliment—from *you,* Quint?"

195

"Yo, *eat shit, man ...*"

"Yo, how 'bout we skip the catfight?" I rubbed the bridge of my nose and looked at them. "Until we know what's going on. Yeah?"

I dragged myself to the nearest window and pulled myself up, then peeked between the blinds.

"Well?" said Jesse.

I scanned the lot; from the hawthorn trees approximately west of us to the beige and pea-green shit-fest (the two-tone manufactured home) northeast.

"Nothing," I said. "Or at least, nothing obvious." I let out a sigh. "I think they might actually—wait; wait a minute." I studied the lattice fencing around what passed for a deck. "Right there. There's one behind that fencing ... real low ... sly." Jesse sidled up next to me as I reexamined the lot and the fresh market across the street. "And right there—behind that truck. See it?"

"I see it," he said. "Also there—behind the garden soil."

We turned and pressed our backs against the wall.

"We're not going anywhere," I said—even as my eyes came to rest on Quint. "Not for a good while."

"Yeah, well." He stretched and stared at the ceiling, as though he were thinking about something else. "We needed a break, anyway." He let out a sigh.

Nobody said anything.

"Jesse," he said, all mock earnest-like. "Tell me a story."

I glanced at Jesse—expecting fireworks—but he only shook his head: Forget it. And then we just stared ahead: close enough to kiss but saying nothing, as though we were straddling urinals.

At last, he said, "Do you suppose I really look like that guy's son—Hodge, I mean?"

I gazed at a framed print on the wall: a surprised-looking cow standing aloof from the herd—caught in a U.F.O's tractor beam. "I don't—I don't see why not. He seemed earnest enough. I mean, what do you think?"

"I don't know ..." He exhaled slowly, deliberately. "I didn't see any resemblance between him and me. I know that much." He leaned forward with his elbows on his knees. "It's funny; he could have been my own father ... and I'd have never known it." He laughed a little. "But then Hodge seemed to actually care."

I looked at him but didn't say anything.

At last, I said, "Must be tough, not having known your parents. But, you know, probably not a day goes by—that they don't think about you. You know?" I shifted and leaned forward—so I could see his face. "You ever think about that?"

He just shook his head. "Would that be before or after they dropped me off at the social services office?"

I locked his brown eyes up in my own. "Before *and* after. And every day after that ... for the rest of their lives."

He looked at me doubtfully and I raised an eyebrow. "Wanna bet?"

And then he smiled—even shoved me in the shoulder. "Yeah; how about a hundred now-worthless dollars?"

"Two-hundred," I said, and kept eye contact. *"Sand* dollars. When we get to the ocean."

I watched as his smile began to fade and he leaned back against the wall.

"Do you really think we'll make it—all the way to L.A.?"

I just stared at him and took a deep breath, then let it out.

"I do," I said. "I have faith ... in that much, at least."

"And your parents?"

But I just shook my head. "I don't know."

And then we let it go, as we had let go of so many other things, as Hal and Macey and Colby (and yes, even Quint) had let go; as had the billions who'd vanished, who'd died—as had everything; even Time itself.

7

Dumb like a Fox

"What about you? Why'd you come?"

I looked from Jesse, who'd asked the question, to Quint, who'd sat up on an elbow to watch us.

"What?"

"What about you? I mean, we know why Miles is here; he wants to know what happened to his parents. And we know why *I'm* here—I don't have anything else to lose. But why are you? I mean, you lost your parents, right? So are we here for the same reason; that we don't have anything else to lose? Or is it something else?" He added quickly: "I'm bonding with you, Quint. Help us read the entrails."

To my surprise, Quint actually seemed to think about it.

"I'm here to lend muscle," he said—determinedly, and sat up in a huff. "I mean, let's face it, you two—" He left off abruptly, as though reconsidering his words. "What I mean is ... we were just brought up differently, that's all."

"Oh? How's that?" But I knew what he meant: He meant he hadn't grown up with a silver spoon in his mouth, like me, or coddled by the state, like Jesse.

"Yeah," said Jesse. "Explain it."

"Look, I'd rather not, okay?" He shoved off the floor and began pacing—slowly, deliberately, like a tiger in a cage. "I mean, I didn't grow up in some blue heaven yupscale People's Republic of—*wherever,* if that's what you mean." He stopped and leaned against the lunch counter, facing away from us—toward the kitchen. "I grew up in Wapato; where the only education you get is the free trade and vocational school of high-toned son of a bitch old men, like my dad." He paused as though humbled, even ashamed. "You know ... the one where they teach you how to fly a flag and shoot at beer cans; or win an all-American fight, or tailgate old ladies while laying on the horn."

He stood straight suddenly and squared his shoulders. "I guess what I'm saying is, that I have some attributes. Ones that might just help us to stay alive—even if they're not always pretty. Miles—Miles seemed like he needed that. When he mentioned the trip, I mean."

Again, there was silence.

"How do you do that?"

He turned and just looked at me. "What?"

"How do you win an all-American fight?" I must have glanced at my shoes because I remember noticing how scuffed and threadbare they were, how worn out.

"You sucker punch him—and then you *just keep punching him;* just batter him like a hockey player, until he's good and down."

I looked at Jesse and he looked back. "And then—what? Do you help him up?"

"You start kicking. You just kick the living shit out of him. In the face, in the teeth—until someone tells you to stop."

"Oh. And ... and if he sucker punches you first?"

"He won't. Because he won't know he's in a fight." He hitched up his Rustler jeans and knelt beside the barricade—like a coach, I thought, or a drill sergeant, then tapped his right temple. "Because, *attributes.*"

"Yeah, well," said Jesse. "Thank you. But those attributes suck. And they're dumb."

But he just smiled at us rakishly, almost dashingly, and at Jesse in particular. "Yeah? Okay. So I'm dumb—just a dumb kid, really. Like all of us. But then, unlike you," He winked at him with a piercing blue eye—which struck me as unusual. "I'm dumb like a fox."

And the two just stared at each other—which, I have to say, was weird as shit. But, well, there it is. I reckoned that for Jesse and Quint, mere friendship just wasn't ever going to be in the cards (or the entrails).

And boy, was I right.

8
Demon and Machine

"Dude, Miles. Come on, man, wake up."

I stirred where I'd fallen asleep beneath the window (for I was still engaged with my mother, who had come to me in a dream), wondering why it was so bright out (it had been late afternoon when I'd started to nod), why Jesse was shaking me. "Don't. Just ... *Would you leave me alone?*"

I sat up with a start—having just realized where the light was coming from—and covered the Talon with my hand. "Holy shit. I mean, just, *holy shit. Dude. It's back.*"

I looked at Quint, who had fallen asleep beneath the lunch counter, and then at Jesse, who was beside himself with terror. "What—what is it? What's going on?"

He placed a hand on my shoulder and peeked between the blinds, which rattled softly. "I mean—you tell me."

I shifted around and joined him, still waking up, then peered through the gap. "I don't see anything. Just the tire shop and the fresh mar—wait. Something just moved. See that? Right there—behind that Subaru."

"That's Machine," said Jesse. "He's the Alpha. Mean bastard, by the looks of him, and a lot bigger than the rest. He's the one to watch—the 25th grizzly, as they say."

I must have looked confused.

"'The kind of bear that tolerates no man or bear; one that will maul without bias.'" He shrugged as though it wasn't important, just something he'd said. "I saw it on the Discovery Channel. And over there," He slid his finger along the dusty blind, toward a truck. "That's Demon. Because of her brow horns."

He shook the hair from his eyes and glanced at me. "I've been watching and naming them—while you guys slept. Most of them have been hanging back; Machine seems to want it that way, based on his vocalizations. But he and Demon, they just keep coming—ever since the Talon woke up. Like it's a dino magnet or something. Like they're attracted to it."

"They are," I said—not knowing how I knew it, only that I did. And then I reached for the Thermos—only to recall, quite suddenly, that I'd dropped it. That I'd dumped it in my panic just like my bike, and that there was no way to shield the Talon's power now. That—now that it was back on—there was no way to turn it off.

I looked at the door and the stacked red benches, and the cigarette machine, which had been pushed back by the animals (about six inches, but still). "Bigger, you say. Like, how much bigger?"

"A lot," said Jesse. "Like, 50 percent, at least. Like it's not even the same species."

I stood and began backing away. "We've got to find the walk-in, something with good, thick walls—or a basement." I kicked Quint in the feet—hard. "Get up."

"There is one—a basement, I mean," said Jesse. "Found it while you guys were sleeping. I—*oh, fuck.*"

"What? What is it?"

"It's Machine—he's on the move." He released the blinds and looked at me. "On the move and heading this way. Fast."

"Fuck ..."

"Follow me," said Jesse. "Hurry."

And we did, hurry, that is, dragging Quint who was barely awake and snatching up our spears; shoving through the swinging doors into the filthy, cobwebbed kitchen, piling downstairs into the musty darkness even as Machine collided with the front door and wood splintered and broke and there was a tremendous smashing noise which could only have been the cigarette machine falling over and its glass breaking.

Which could only have been the diner being breached as the sun continued to sink and twilight fell; as our hearts pounded in our chests like pistons, like drums, and I ran back up the steps to close the door.

9

Basic White Teenage Boy

I took the Talon from around my neck and dropped it in the dust. "Hurry up," I said. "Cover it with something, anything. Those bags of flour."

I started dragging the sacks from the shelves and letting them fall to the floor—as Jesse and Quint lifted the 50-pound bags together and threw them over the Talon, which cut off our light.

"Whatever happened to just letting it repel the bastards?" asked Quint, and grunted. "I mean, at this point, it's pretty much just a liability, don't you think?"

"Yeah, sure." I took off my pack and started digging for my lighter. "You gonna be the one to wear it? It's like you said: I don't even want to be close to those things."

"We should ditch it, then," said Quint. "That is, if we ever get out of this mess."

"No," I snapped, remembering the voice, and the way it had repelled the dinosaur on the Yakima River. "It—it's still our best bet if we get caught in the open. And it—it means something. I tell you. It's important."

"Yeah," said Quint. "Important at getting us killed."

I flicked on my lighter, having found it amongst the tools in the small pouch of my pack, even as pots and pans reigned down—clattering and clanging—somewhere above.

"It's in the kitchen," said Jesse. "Machine, I mean. And Demon too, I bet. Oh, shit—Miles. What are we going to do?"

I looked around the basement: at the industrial-sized cans of tomato sauce and 5-gallon buckets of dish soap; at the 50-pound bags of corn starch, the cans and cans of coffee beans. "Who am I to know," I said—and extinguished the lighter. It was getting hot. "I'm just your basic white teenage boy." I looked at Quint; or at least where I thought he was. "Why don't you ask 'Dumb like a Fox?'"

Jesse didn't miss a beat. "Hey, Dumb like a Fox, what do ya got?"

But Quint didn't say anything—only remained silent as the animal or animals above brushed against the basement door, snorting and sniffing and snarling.

"Quint?"

Which is when we heard it: a drizzling and a spattering, like a thin stream of water. A dribbling and a dripping—percolating in the dust. "I'm pissing, if you don't mind," he said at last—and added: "Back here, in a sort of cubby."

"Well, hurry up," I snapped. "We've got to figure a way out of this cluster—"

"Yo, Miles," he said. "Bring your lighter over here." I heard a rustling and a swishing, like small boxes being moved around. "Just—just follow my voice."

I gripped the lighter and followed his voice ... to where he was standing in the dark before a high set of shelves; shelves packed with a hundred different types of boxes and tubes—all of them colorful, all of them garish.

To be honest, it took me a minute to realize what I was looking at. "I don't ... I mean ... Are those—?"

He grabbed a clear package of what appeared almost to be shotgun shells and held them out between us. "And no; *you ain't imagining things.*" He gave the package a little heft. "How many sticks of dynamite in this?"

"None," I said, as Jesse joined us, and moved the lighter farther away. "That's—that's an urban legend. Those are just flash powder; black powder. They're not quarter sticks of dynamite."

Quint studied the cherry bombs, the M-80s. "Yeah, but—whatever. They'll make a big boom, won't they?"

I looked at all the boxes and tubes and other packages: shelf after shelf after shelf of them, like our own private fireworks stand. Our own little—or not so little—artillery depot.

"Oh, yeah," I said—and held out my free hand, palm up.

At which they slapped it; first Quint—way too hard, I might add—and then Jesse.

And we went to work.

10

Fuse

"All right, you dogs, *roll call,*" shouted Quint—gruffly, briskly, like a true leatherneck. "Alpha Battalion is 'go' for launch—and I mean *hot to trot.* I repeat: I am 'go' for launch. Bravo Company—sound off like you got a pair."

Quint and I waited: Nothing. Not so much as a peep.

At last, Jesse said, in a voice deeper than usual: "Yes—
yes, sir!" He laughed. "Bravo Company standing by! And hot
to trot, *sir!*"

"Better late than never," said Quint—like a disappointed
drill instructor—before adding, "Okay, faster now, more
intense: Forward-Battalion Charlie—*let's hear it.*"

"Sir, yes, sir!"

I took up my position at the base of the stairs—having
just come down from loosening the doorknob—watching the
entrance to the basement like a hawk; crouching over my
rockets and missiles like a villain, like Wile E. Coyote.
"Charlie Company—I mean Battalion, is ready to rock and
roll, *sir!*" I bumped the flashlight and had to reposition it—so
it again illuminated the fireworks. "And will fire on your
command—sir!"

I braced myself as the creature—"Machine"— snorted
and nudged open the door, which creaked and moaned.
"And that should probably come sooner rather than later—if
you know what I mean; and I think you do. And enough of
this 'sir' shit ..."

And then we all just looked at each other: Jesse and
Quint from their places at the window wells (they'd climbed
atop 5-gallon buckets to reach them), each with their own
rockets, and me by the stairs—by the Talon, which was now
covered with only a single bag of flour, for easy retrieval.

"Be sure to light *everything;* like, every fuse in your
arsenal," I reminded them. "Just—go all in. Then it's straight
for the bikes ... all right? Everyone got that?"

Jesse just nodded, somberly. "And then what, do you
think?"

"We put the Talon back in the Thermos and we *ride,* all
the way to the Columbia River and beyond—to the Dalles, at
least. And we don't stop until we're safe; like, in a hotel or
something. On the very top floor."

Quint seemed to think about it. "Yeah, but—we stop at
the river ... just for a while. You know—to hang out."

"To *hang out?*" I could see Jesse's exasperation from
across the room—even in the dark, or the semi-dark. "And do

what, exactly? In case you were wondering, there are, like, *dinosaurs* out there. Or haven't you noticed?"

"I don't know—maybe ... maybe swim, or something. I just—look, I've never seen a river. All right?"

The admission knocked me back—even though there were predators at our very door. And I remember thinking, *Jesus, I know there are people who have never seen the ocean—but a river?* It was slightly funny and somehow heartbreaking all at the same time. I mean, Christ; what kind of people had his parents been?

"Okay, we're stopping at the river," I said. "Biggs Junction, I think it was called, across the U.S. 97 bridge. We'll—we'll celebrate. Break out some cans of tuna, or something. For Quint's first river—and it's a doozy."

"What are we waiting for, then," said Quint. "Let's do it."

"Okay," I said. "On the count of three. You ready? One ... two ..."

There was a snarling sound and I looked at the door: saw Demon and Machine jerking and thrashing against each other violently (they'd poked their heads through at the same time and managed to get stuck; like Archie and Meathead). And now they were blocking the door completely—blocking our way out.

"Wait a minute," I shouted. "Wait a minute ...!"

Whereupon, to my complete and utter surprise, they pulled free of the frame, and—in a riot of busting glass and clanging kitchenware—began to fight; to just tear each other apart, right there in the kitchen—at which our pathway opened again like the gates of Heaven and I barked, vociferously: "Okay, do it; *do it, do it, do it!*"

And we began to flick our lighters—desperately. Frenziedly.

11
Finale

I'd be hard-pressed to describe the bedlam that followed—and rapidly doubled, tripled, quadrupled—other than to say that what started humbly, subtly, innocuously, with a chorus of staggered hisses and frizzles, quickly became a cannonade; a fusillade, a barrage of such sound and fury and color that, had I not been so focused on lighting fuses, would surely have blinded me, at least temporarily. As it was, I was able to launch virtually everything before ricocheting rockets forced me to shelter in place (which is to say, with one skinny arm thrown over my exposed head and shoulders); after which, cowering, I could only cough and hack in the stifling smoke—all while praying nothing detonated too close. Which, as it turned out, nothing did. And, also, that the warring dinosaurs had fled. Which—as it turned out—they had.

"Jesse! Quint! Long-fuses!" I rolled the 50-pound bag off the Talon. "And remember: Straight for the bikes!" (I was referring, of course, to the special fuses we'd made; which—it was hoped—would provide cover after we left.)

"That's a negative, hombre," shouted Quint. "I'm fresh out of lighter fluid over here." He quickly added: "Jesse! Get over here!"

"No!" I barked. "Belay that order! Keep up your barrage ..."

And I was on my way, bounding for Quint and holding up my lighter, shaking it, impatiently, as he turned and just stared at it—disoriented, shell-shocked. (Some of my rockets had—after ricocheting about wildly—blown up right next to him.)

"Take it!" I snapped—even as a ghost-white snout lunged at him through the window, lunged at him and crashed to a halt—snarling, gnashing its teeth; at which Quint spun upon it and clocked it in the nose, *hard,* and just kept clocking—until it yelped and beat a retreat.

"Okay," I said, "go, go, go!" And he took the lighter.

And then I could only return to the Talon and snatch it up off the floor, noting its fading color, its waning strength, before swinging it around my head and barking, "There's never going to be a better time. How much more?"

"Just about," said Jesse, and continued: "Just—okay!
Okay, I'm clear!"

I looked at Quint, who was still lighting. "All right, forget
it, let 'em go ..."

He moved the lighter from one fuse to the next. "Hold
on," he said, "just hold on ..."

At which we could only watch, rocking on our feet,
hopping up and down, until he lit the last fuse and jumped
down from the bucket.

And then we were hustling—double-timing it, as they
say—up the stairs and out of the diner, where not a single
predator could be seen. Then we were scrambling for our
bikes; our pinto horses of plastic and steel; which gleamed
like salvation even as the long-fused rockets began to explode
and the Nano-As, active but in hiding, began to whimper and
howl.

That's when I knew it; when I could feel it in my bones:
That we'd passed our first test; survived our baptism by fire.
That's when I knew that our journey would be complete—as
we sat on our bikes with our spears canted at our backs (like
the bows of Indian braves, I fancied) and, having returned the
Talon to its canister, watched the last of the fireworks as they
burst and boomed above. Watched, brooding, as they turned
the sky first white then green then blue, and finally, a deep,
lingering red, after which, taking a cue from our fellow
animals, we began to howl ourselves.

12

The Mighty Columbo

I think it's safe to say we all know the scene: it's the one in
Jurassic Park where Dr. Alan Grant—having just been
informed that billionaire John Hammond has successfully
recreated a T. rex—begins teetering about like a drunkard
before eventually collapsing in the grass and looking on,
dramatically—at the towering brachiosaurs as they wade across
a small, glittering lake; at a herd of parasaurolophuses

drinking in the shimmering, south American heat; at the birds fluttering about the sauropods' great bodies. Well, that's a little what it was like as we gazed out at the Columbia River from the Sam Hill Memorial Bridge: like something from the movies, from *Jurassic Park,* complete with long-necked sauropods (I think these were diplodocuses) drinking along the dry, rocky banks, and pterodactyls gathered on their broad, silver backs. Even the air was shimmering; I suppose because, although the sun showed only 10:00, it was already getting hot.

"So this is the—the Columbo River?" Quint tried not to sound too impressed. "But it's just a lake, like on *Fishin' with the Good Ol' Boys.* It doesn't even move." He added: "Fuck it—all the better to swim in, right?"

"It moves, you just can't see it," I said. "There are currents—trust me. Same as with any river." I looked at the brachiosaurs and then down into the silvery depths. "Besides, dude, seriously. Who knows what's down there."

"I'm not afraid of any currents," said Quint. "Or prehistoric fish." He stood and straddled his bike. "I'll jump in right here. We all should."

"Yeah?" said Jesse. "In what? Our birthday suits?"

Quint just looked at him. "Why not? What—you afraid somebody will see your weenie? Dude. Nobody cares. *Come on.*"

"I'm not getting in that water."

"But it's the great and storied Columbo Lake!" He glanced at me as if to gauge my reaction (I'd been talking the thing up for the last 13 miles). "I mean river."

I guess my smile must have faded (I had been studying him keenly in the hope he might experience some sort of epiphany: about crossing thresholds, maybe, like Joseph Campbell talked about, or just appreciating the beauty and splendor of the natural world—or unnatural, as the case may be—and our diminutive place in it). *"That's Columbia,"* I said. "It's called the Columbia." I peered down the length of the bridge to the rust-brown truss and beyond—all the way to Biggs Junction, which was just a smear of buildings. "And across the river is Oregon; the, ah, Beaver State. Which we should be getting to."

"The Beaver State?" Quint reoriented himself to face south. "Well—hell, why didn't you say so. I'm there, dude." He splayed his arms above his head as though worshiping a deity. "I have found my homeland!"

"That's not what he meant," said Jesse. "Besides, you won't—you wouldn't have liked it. At all. Neither you nor your old man. Before the Flashback, I mean."

"Yeah? Why not?"

"Big lib state," he said—and began peddling away.

He called back: "You couldn't even pump your own gas!"

And we just watched him—ride off, that is—not straight as an arrow, not aggressively, like Quint or I, but weaving, meandering.

"Is that true?" asked Quint, turning to look at me. "That you couldn't pump your own gas? Why?"

I shrugged, continuing to watch Jesse. "Beats me. Could have been a holdover—something from the '50s. How am I to know? Probably wasn't as safe back then—pumping gas, I mean."

"*Mm,*" said Quint, and laughed. "He's right, though. The old man would have had a heart attack; being told he couldn't pump his own gas." He added out of nowhere: "But he's wrong to just lump us together. Me and my old man, I mean. We—we weren't the same. Not really. He's wrong about that."

I turned to look at him, struck by his sudden candor—saw the same look in his eye I'd noticed at the diner, the same self-awareness. "Yeah, well," I said. "It takes two to tangle. Maybe you should—"

"So are you," he added—shutting me down. And then he kicked off for the truss, for the State of Oregon; for Jesse, at which I could only gaze at the river and wonder—again—at that weird moment between them (the one in the diner); that moment when they'd just stared at each other like they might kill each other on the spot. When reality itself had seemed to stretch—to warp—to shift its very meaning; and I'd felt as though I were seeing something which, like the change in my voice or the rapid growth in my legs, had only now been born—only now come into existence. A moment of rapid and unexpected change.

I looked at the weird borealis the Flashback had left behind—it was purple and blood-red today—and the strange lights that flickered deep within its depths.

Just a moment. Like a hologram, I thought, which changed depending on which angle you viewed it from. Or Schrodinger's Cat. Or the Flashback itself: indecipherable, unfathomable, non-sensical. Absurd.

And then I put my bike in gear and followed them—my traveling companions. My bickering quest-mates who would never change; whom I didn't want to change.

My only friends in the world.

13
Benson Bridge

I don't know why we stared at that dead pterodactyl chick so long—there wasn't anything particularly striking or even gross about it; there were no flies, for example, no maggots—just a couple of butterflies, one white and the other burnt orange, which matched the fading sunlight.

Maybe it was our nonstop ride all the way from Biggs Junction near the Washington border to Multnomah Falls, which was closer to Portland (I mean, it's a lot of work, peddling a BMX bicycle some 70-plus miles, even across level terrain). Or maybe it was how paper-thin the creature's exsanguinous, oyster-white skin was, how almost translucent, or the way its little talons weren't really talons at all but little hands, like a baby's hands. All I remember for certain is how contemplative everyone seemed to get while looking down at it—how funereal; even elegiac—like we were saying goodbye to one of our own. All I remember for certain is something akin

210

to holding vigil for a fellow traveler; which, in a very real sense, we were.

"For him, the war is over," I whispered—although I doubt anyone heard me over the crash and roar of the falls. "I wonder where Mom is ..."

"Not here, that's for sure," said Quint. "There are no nests."

I followed his gaze into the treetops and beyond, to the waterfall itself, which dashed and cascaded down the cliffs. "Weird. I mean—where the hell could it have come from?"

"Maybe it came from up there," said Jesse. "From the very top. There's—there's a platform up there, a wooden observation deck. We came here on a field trip once and hiked up to it. Be a good place to build a nest—real stable. And defensible."

I looked from one end of the concrete bridge—"Benson Bridge," the sign had called it—which was closed off with cyclone fencing, to the other. "Speaking of which, this bridge looks pretty defensible—don't you think?" I peered off the way we had come. "Only one side to protect; we can take turns standing watch ... I mean, it may not be the Ritz but—what do you say?"

We looked around and then at each other.

"Hell, I'm in," said Quint. "We can even build a fire and maybe eat something—something hot, I mean. It'll be just like—it'll be just like Camp Courage!"

I couldn't help but to notice he'd stopped short of saying "home," and a quick glance at Jesse confirmed he'd noticed it too; although whether he'd done so because his own home life had sucked or because he'd understood—in that moment—that, because of the Flashback, we'd never see home again, I don't know.

"Sure, why not," said Jesse. "We can heat up that beef stew, the one we were saving for Portland. We're close enough." He shrugged off his pack and spear and laid down his bike. "And besides, it'll lighten my load."

He dug out the can of Dinty Moore stew and paused, looking at it. "Seems ... almost wasteful, though ... doesn't it?

I mean ... you'd like to think, you'd like to think nothing was born ... just to lay there and rot, you know?"

We all turned to look at the bird.

"Yeah," said Quint. "I mean, it's like God laid it out there just for us, and here we are wanting to eat something from a can."

I got off my bike and reached for my pocketknife—touched its smooth, imitation-wood handle. "We're going to have to learn how to hunt eventually, I suppose. I mean—"

"I already know how to hunt," said Quint.

"And to clean and dress a—"

"I know how to do that, too." He held out his hand for my knife—which I gave over to him: slowly, reluctantly. "And since both you pussies missed man-school; I guess I'll be the one to have to show you."

Jesse looked at me and then back to Quint. "Let me guess. Because—attributes."

"Because—attributes," said Quint, and got off his bike.

14

Roast Pterodactyl

As it turned out—it was actually pretty good: closer to duck, I think, than anything else; more red meat than white, coppery and gamey, with a generous layer of fat. As for how it paired with warm Mountain Dew—well, you might be surprised; but then anything can be good with the right company and the right circumstances, which, as I took stock of the crackling fire and unfurled sleeping bags, the defensive wire comprised of cyclone fencing and canted spears, the raging waterfall, the serene moon—I knew these to be. You just had to be in a certain frame of mind; a certain mood; or to have survived something most people your age hadn't.

"And now," said Quint, letting out a belch, "a moment of reflection." He dug through his bag and pulled something out; something long and narrowish and wrapped in cellophane. "Brough to you by— Swisher Sweets!"

212

I looked at Jesse and he looked back—then back again to the package of cigars. I didn't know where he'd gotten them, probably from the bureau in Colby Higgins' pimped out, tie-dyed cabin tent; all I knew for certain was that a cigar sounded positively titillating at that moment—that slice of time not even the Flashback could touch—even though I'd never had one and had no idea how to smoke it; nor even what to expect.

"Hit me," I said, even as Quint mockingly cocked a fist, then held out my hand as he quickly tore open the package.

"Yeah'um," said Jesse. "Me, too. Hit me, that is."

And he handed us each a cigar.

Now, there is little that hasn't already been said about one's first experience with smoking, especially when one has the misfortune of accidentally inhaling, and I mean straight away. You could say that it stabs you like so many knives through the chest even as it bites deep into your lungs; that there's a sense of breathing and *not* breathing even as the smoke swirls and seems to expand; that there's a buzzing in your brain and your senses are dulled, like you've suffered a blow to the head. Most of that would be true, to a greater or lesser extent (it was certainly true for me, as I hacked and coughed and spit). And yet one of these was not true: which was that, far from being dulled, my senses had, in fact, been *heightened.* Sharpened. Indeed, after the wheezing had stopped and I'd grown accustomed to the buzz; after the stars and galaxies had snapped into focus (including the arm of the Milky Way itself) and a calm had settled over me like a down blanket in winter—and I'd learned how to puff (without inhaling) and even to make smoke rings—I dare say the experience became—*enjoyable.* Amiable.

Sublime.

"See?" said Quint. "That's what *I'm* talking about."

"Yep," said Jesse. He puffed and blew a huge cloud of smoke. "After a day spent fighting dinosaurs and riding, like, 73 miles—ain't nothin' like a good cigar."

I shifted to look at the Borealis, which was a deep, stunning cobalt tonight, a kind of alien, darkling blue, and the equally strange lights within. "They're vaguely geometrical—you ever notice that? Like triangles—sort of. Or arrowheads. I don't think they're intelligently controlled. Not by pilots, I mean."

"What's it matter?" sneered Quint. "I mean, anyone who could have figured it out is probably long gone by now; either disappeared in the Flashback or eaten by reptiles. Nah," He poked at the fire listlessly, lackadaisically. "We ain't *never* gonna know. No more than they knew how to cure cancer; or stop the aging process. Or cure a common cold. Forget about it."

"Forget about it, he says," I muttered, and reached for the Thermos, which I'd placed away from the fire. "Sure, why not." I turned the thing over in my hands, watching the firelight play across its curved, silvery surface. "But then, there's one thing I can't forget."

"Yeah?" He puffed his cheeks out and blew a series of smoke rings. "And what's that?"

I pitched the canister to him and he caught it, sort of, fumbling it in his lap.

"It's your turn to carry this."

And then I stubbed out my cigar and rolled up in my sleeping bag, not thinking about how the Talon had beckoned to me on the Yakima River or how it had referred to itself as "we" rather than an "I"—or that it had referred to itself at all—or about how it could burn so brightly one minute and lay utterly inert the next, or that I might just be fucking crazy, or about anything, really, not even my parents.

And then I just tuned out: curling up and shutting my eyes—clearing my thoughts; letting it all go.

Forgetting about it.

15
The Garden of Oz

It was funny: that I should have thought earlier on the fact that we could never go home—for when I awakened (or at least partially awakened), blinking my eyes and watching the curtains rustle, smelling the sweet lilacs in the Garden of Oz, well, I realized I had done just that.

Gone home.

"That's it, Miles," coaxed my mother, softly, encouragingly, urgently. "We need you to wake up; okay? Need you here, and present—and alert. Come on, honey."

I rolled to face her and found her sitting on the bed next to me—pensively, I thought; broodingly, her hair having fallen partly over her face. "I can smell lilacs," I said, and sniffed at the air. "But it's already late July."

She swiped the hair out of her eyes and regarded me. "And do you like it? The way their smell just sort of permeates the house and makes the sunlight itself seem lavender? Is that how you remember it?"

I lay and just stared at her. Then I nodded. "And the tourists ... laughing. Having a good time. Some of them from as far away as China. All of them having come *here*—to a place we already live. Or live next to." I studied her face, the faint lines around her eyes. "The Garden of Oz. L.A.'s oasis of beauty and whimsey and green, as Dad would say. The best place to have grown up in the world; even if it's in what President Tucker called a liberal—can I curse, Mom?"

"I know what he said."

I shrugged the thought away. "A place where people found something they needed. That's what I remember."

"Then what does it matter?" She cupped my cheek in her slim, soft hand; which was cool to the touch. "Late July, early May. In-season, out-of-season. It's just time, Miles. It isn't, and never has been, for us to hold to the task. Now—come. I need to show you something."

And she pulled away and stood—calmly, stoically, before gliding wordlessly to the door and vanishing into the hall, at which I threw off the blankets and quickly followed.

Nor had the house changed much—if at all—it was still as regal as it was airy with its eggshell-blue walls and whiter than white wainscoting; its wide backyard in which sheets fluttered restlessly—tempestuously—from the clothesline; like flags from a gantline.

"Mom ... *hey!*"

But she didn't stop, only continued toward the hung laundry, toward the undulating sheets, her pace quickening, her long, dark hair billowing—until she'd reached them at last and, to my complete and utter astonishment, passed directly *through them.* Just vanished without a trace.

"Mom!" I cried, even as I crashed into the sheets myself and fought them off; as I emerged onto the other side but could only look on in horror.

As I noticed sudden movement and looked toward the gazebo—where a pack of velociraptors had descended on my dad even as he'd tried to mow the lawn. Where they'd split him head to crotch and unspooled his entrails—and were eating him alive—as the sheets snapped behind me and the wind blew and I awakened again to find Jesse bleeding from the throat and hanging onto the side of the bridge.

Where I saw him trying to call out but only managing a gargle as the great, dark pterodactyl—its wings beating furiously—attempted to carry him off; to steal him away, even as Quint and I rallied but were too late and the thing rose into the purple dawn like a dragon—like some great vampire bat; gripping its struggling cargo like a vise, flying up and up and up.

Taking him to its massive nest—which, as we could now clearly see (and as Jesse had predicted), lie at the very top of the falls.

16
Left Behind

John Gardner once wrote, in deference to the human condition and its limitations (as well as its delusions), "But they rush across chasms on spiderwebs, and sometimes they make it, and that, they think, settles that!"

Well, that's essentially what Quint did when he swung across that ravine—having lept for one of the gnarled vines and somehow made it (even as I skidded to a halt at the edge of the cliff and teetered). He'd dashed across the chasm on a spiderweb. He'd done precisely what Quint Holloway always did: which was to seize an opportunity before anyone even knew it by acting without a care or forethought (nor the slightest concern for his safety) and with the gravest of intent. To the point that I felt feckless and impotent as he casually dropped the vine (which had broken off as he swung) and hurried up the trail, not so much as looking back. To the point that I could only curse to myself in frustration as I stood there looking at the remaining plants (all of which were too short and/or flimsy to even attempt such a move) and found myself wishing—not for the first time, and certainly not the last—that I, too, were dumb like a fox, or had fucking "attributes."

And then I was backing away in order to get a fresh start and launching myself at the crevice like a madman—like a fool. Then I was bounding over it like some kind of superhero even as my momentum flagged and I fell distinctly short—bouncing and sliding down the rocks like a rag doll, like a sack of blood and bone; tumbling into the pit like a cadaver—where I lay broken and bleeding; and still. Where I saw Quint helping Jesse out of the nest and the two embracing like lovers, like comrades (even as Mama-bird continued the hunt elsewhere and her chicks snapped and squealed). Saw them as though I were looking through the Talon itself, which I now realized Quint had taken out and put around his neck.

Where I saw and heard things I couldn't possibly have been able to experience—at least not from so far away—before finally passing out. At which, somewhere in the depths, I heard a cool, sinewy voice say, simply: *Now you've seen as we see.*

As it turned out, I wasn't nearly so banged up as I thought; which we found out after they'd fished me out of the crack in the earth and patched me up (we had a First-Aid kit in one of the bags, just a little tin box with Band-Aids, sterile pads, gauze, and gloves). Hell, I hadn't even sprained anything, which was pretty miraculous considering the tumble I'd taken. Quint, for one, was impressed.

"I gotta hand it to you, kid. You're as tough as a box of nails." He glanced at Jesse, who'd needed sprucing up himself. "And *you.*" He swung the Thermos—in which he'd replaced the Talon—around to his back. "I thought you were a goner. Jesus. What a ride."

"I ... it ..." Jesse pointed at the gauze wrapped around his throat. "It hurts to talk. But ... Thanks. Thanks for coming after me."

Quint just shrugged. "What are friends for—if not to rescue you from a pterodactyl nest at zero-dark thirty in the morning?" And they laughed—or at least tried to—after which Quint extended his hand. "No hard feelings, okay?"

"No hard feelings," rasped Jesse.

I watched as his thin, callow hand met Quint's— which was so much blockier, stubbier—before finally looking away: to the northern horizon and its craggy, basalt cliffs; to the silvery band of river and its overgrown parking lot—where a single vehicle could be seen through the framing of the trees; a vehicle I was pretty sure hadn't been there before.

A pickup, I realized, as I squinted and studied the truck. One that was oddly familiar now that—

"Jesse: How far is Trout Lake from Multnomah Falls?"

"I don't know," said Jesse. "About, what, fifty miles? I'd have to look at the map. They're in the same vicinity, I remember that."

I peered at the truck, which shone clean and new and unblemished, as though it had just been driven from the lot.

"Well, I'll be goddamned," I said. And then I turned toward the others. "Gentlemen—what do you say we go down there and say hello to an old friend?"

17

A Bigger Gun

Had the weather not changed so much after we passed through Portland—and Jesse and I not moved into the cab of the truck (while Quint stayed outside in the bed with an umbrella, because, in his words, he was an "outdoor dog"), I doubt we would have gotten to know Hodge any better than the last time we'd bumped into him.

As it was, we did a lot more than just get to know him; we fell in love with him a little, I think—or at least came to care for him in a way only those who have experienced a great hardship (like a World War, say, or a genocide, or a Flashback) can: by which I mean quickly and without hesitation; based on a bond rather than pure circumstance. By which I mean without any pretense or conditioning whatever—because there simply wasn't room for it, wasn't the time. There never had been.

None of which changed the fact that, after nearly five hours and 300 miles, his "Hodge Worthington Airlines" shtick—which had never been funny—was starting to grate: even if he only lapsed into it on occasion; like when we merged onto US Route 101 from WV 42 and he said, "And now, if you'll kindly look to your right, you will see the magnificent *Pacific Ocean;* or at least, you *would* see it—if not for the rain and fog."

I looked out my window into the great, gray void, and shook my head. "Tough break for Quint. His first ocean—and you can't even see the bloody thing."

Jesse only poured over his maps. "He'll have lots of time; we're going to be next to it pretty much the rest of the way." He glanced over his shoulder into the payload area. "But you know Mr. Attributes. He'll probably be disappointed." He lapsed into a serviceable impression of Quint: "Where's the big waves, like on *Hawaii Five-O?* Where's all the pirate ships?"

219

I laughed and looked around him, at Hodge. "So you really think you're going to find anyone in Wolf Creek?"

Hodge merely shrugged, focusing on the road. "It doesn't really matter if I do or not. You know? The point is, I have to try. These people were my friends; they were an important part of my life—right up until the end, right up until the Flashback. If I don't look for them now—when they might desperately need my help—how the hell much did I care to begin with?" He glanced through the rearview mirror at Quint; who was just the top of an umbrella. "I learned a long time ago: friendship's just a word—if it's never tested. If it's never put to the fire. It'll be the same with you: with you and Jesse, and with Quint. If you don't know that yet; you will."

"Yeah, but ..." Jesse scrutinized the map he was holding. "Didn't you say you were heading east—at Ophir? A little past Port Orford?"

"That's right," said Hodge. "On Skunks Misery Road—just a little past Prehistoric Gardens." He chuckled a little at the thought of it. "Prehistoric Gardens. Ha. Think about *that* one."

"Yeah, but. There's nothing there," said Jesse. "No road at all. Just the edge of a mountain range—the Klamath Mountains."

Hodge only laughed. "Not on your map, aye?" He smiled to himself warmly. "No, I guess it wouldn't be. Speaking of which,"

He slowed down as we approached a sign: a sign bearing a brown stegosaurus which read, in large, hand-painted letters:

HERE!
PREHISTORIC GARDENS
IN Oregon's
RAIN FOREST

"See the gift shop? You can ride out the storm there."

He pulled up next to a goofy-looking T-rex statue and came to a stop. "Unless of course you want to forget all this nonsense and just come with me. Because this is it; this is my last stop. After this, it's northeast to Montana, where I hear there's a settlement. But I can drop you in Granger along the way."

I opened the passenger-side door but paused, looking at him around Jesse. "This friend of yours—in Wolf Creek. He might just as well be alive as dead or vanished—huh?"

Hodge didn't say anything; only rummaged around behind his seat.

"Is it nonsense to want to find out which one?"

He dug out a black, hard-plastic case and handed it to Jesse; the weight of which lowered his arms. "Look—I get it. Okay? I'm not here to judge. But I do want you to have this." He patted the case where it sat in Jesse's lap. "If what you told me about Quint is true, he'll know what to do with it. Have him show you—*both* of you. Okay?"

He stared straight ahead through the wipers and the rain. "Now get out of here; before I start carrying on about my son—and about how Jesse reminds me of him. Go on. *Git.*"

And we got, climbing out into the storm even as Quint tossed out our packs and spears and handed down our bikes; taking refuge beneath the giftshop's eve as Hodge backed up and drove away and Jesse handed Quint the case; which he opened to reveal a large, scoped handgun and various accessories—including ammunition. Which he took out and gave a heft even as Hodge's taillights disappeared and there was a deep, guttural roar, a great, rumbling bellow; which rose up from the nearby trees like thunder even as we tried the door and found it unlocked, and quickly shuffled in.

As we huddled in the cold and dark and the gargantuan sound came again—vibrating the floor, rattling the panes; and Jesse said—in the most unwelcome attempt at humor *ever:* "We're going to need a bigger gun."

18
Exit Through the Gift Shop

"Okay, this is where the fun begins, so listen up," said Quint. "The first thing you're gonna do is to open the cylinder—like this."

He slid the cylinder lock forward and pushed the spindle out, which clicked, softly. "Right? Okay?"

"Got it," I said.

"Mm," said Jesse.

Quint moved to load the gun—a stainless steel Smith and Wesson which was so new it gleamed; I mean it positively shined—but paused. "Jesse? You got it?"

Jesse shifted in the doorway of the shop—which was wide enough to hold us all. "Slide the cylinder lock forward ... then push the cylinder out. Got it," he said.

"Okay." Quint turned his palm up—which was full of copper rounds. "Now we're gonna load it. Just slide each of them into a chamber—like that—rotate the cylinder ... close it, and lock it into place." He looked from me to Jesse, earnestly, gravely. "Now which of you is going to cover me?"

I stared at the gun before looking at Jesse—who only shook his head, slowly, solemnly—and then back to Quint. "I'll do it," I said. "If you show me how—"

"Let's start with your stance," he interrupted; and pointed the pistol at the ground. "But first I want to show you how to pass this thing." I watched as he reopened the cylinder and stuck his thumb through the revolver—then slowly handed it to me. "Got that? You don't just say, 'Here—take this,' and hand it over. Always make sure the cylinder is out and you're pointed at the ground. Okay? Now close it up."

I hesitated, acclimating myself to the heft and feel of the thing; wondering if I was remotely ready; keeping it pointed at the ground—then pushed the cylinder shut and locked the spindle in place. "Okay," I said.

"Now spread your feet ... a little wider, wider than your shoulders; good. Bend your knees—no, no, just a little. Stick your butt out. Just a little. Now bend forward ..."

Jesse laughed—and I shot him a look.

"Focus ... all right. Good. Now," He pretended like he was holding the gun. "The way you fire this beast is pretty simple: your shooting hand goes around the handle like—well, like that, actually; just be sure to keep your finger out of the guard until it's time to shoot; and your support hand goes—yep, just like that, over your fingers. And then you're going to extend your arms ... come on, bring 'em up ... and you're going to take your left thumb—no, no; *dude,* your *left* thumb—and you're going to *slowly* bring back the hammer—just nice and easy—until it locks."

There was a ratcheting sound as the cylinder rotated once and stopped. "Just like that." Then he laid a hand on my shoulder and gave it a pat. "And that—believe it or not—is all it takes. You're ready to unleash hell. Or at least to cover me while I place the Talon."

I squeezed an eye shut even as I sighted the T. rex statue; as I sighted its huge, green iris (just as Quint would try to sight whatever had made that roar later—if our plan worked, that is) and my body veritably trembled. As Quint guided my aim away gently but firmly and pointed me toward a pile of wood and debris. "No, bud. That rex is concrete; it'll ricochet. Shoot at the lumber. And remember—squeeze, don't pull. And get ready for the kickback. It's a Magnum."

But I didn't fire; choosing instead to hold the hammer with my thumb even as I squeezed the trigger and lowered the hammer slowly, carefully, so that the gun became un-cocked. After which I looked at Quint and said, "We shouldn't waste rounds. Besides, I'm good—I know what to expect. Go place the Talon. I got you covered."

And then I added (noticing the way he was looking at me, just sort of slack-jawed and flabbergasted): "Seen it on TV—about a million times—and wanted to try it myself. It—it works good."

At which Quint swung the leather strap of the Thermos over his head and moved out into the dirt parking lot—pausing once to look at me over his shoulder; speechless for the first time since I'd met him.

19

Giganotosaur

It's possible I'd heard them even before awakening—before fighting my way up from dream—the dull, cumbersome impacts; like the slack being taken up from a freight train; the *kroom, kroom, kroom,* like distant (but approaching) thunder. All I know for certain is that by the time I'd sat up they were literally vibrating the windows—rattling the glassware—enough that I found it hard to believe anyone (much less Jesse and Quint, who, like me, had learned to sleep light) could slumber through it.

Enough, I suppose, that I somehow knew what was coming even before it lumbered onto the lot and paused, sniffing. For what I saw there was nothing short of *Giganotosaurus carolinii*—which, like *Nano-allosaurus,* I remembered from Mr. Jones' science class. What I saw there was something so positively mind-bending; so very nearly Lovecraftian in its size and shape and scope, that I completely ignored the plan (which was to have Quint take the fatal shot) and reached for the pistol myself; all but ensuring that our goal of attracting the thing with the Talon (which now hung from a fencepost at the far end of the lot) before killing it straight away through its soft, supple eye— would fail. And fail it did; spectacularly. *Bloodily,* in a sense.

For that was the moment in which it approached the Talon and I scoped its eye—its keen, yellow, *lolling* eye—but then did something inexplicable, unforgivable; something Quint would never have done.

I hesitated. Worse; I *cowered*—even going so far as to lay the gun on the sill as the Talon slowly faded and the giganotosaur grew restless; sniffing the air. Even, I dare say, retreating—as the beast seemed to detect something and slowly turned to face us; then charged without warning, snarling and bellowing. As it collided with the gift shop and its walls began tumbling and Quint and Jesse were awakened—rudely; as it roared and the latter began shouting, hysterically, "It's me! It's me! Oh—*don't you see? It's after me!*" before fleeing—desperately, frenziedly, finally—into the damp, crepuscular, post-storm night.

And then we ran after him—just ran, through the moist rain forest and past the crude, gray statue of a triceratops; past an ankylosaurus and a trachodon, over a low, decorative fence into the woods. Nor was the giganotosaur far—for we could hear its breathing and the gnashing of its teeth even as it pursued us through the trees and the dripping ferns and shrubs; as we burst out onto a moonlit beach and saw Jesse entering the tide, advancing up to his waist. As the giganotosaur emerged with the sound of busting timber and roared too close behind us—too close, by far.

"Go, go, go!" I shouted, putting on a burst of speed, following Quint into the water, into the ocean, which breathed like a giant, advancing up to my neck in the freezing froth and spray. "It's all right! It's okay! I—I don't think it swims. Everybody—everybody just chill." I looked at Jesse, who locked his brown eyes up in my own. "It—it's going to be all right. *Okay?*"

And then we all looked at the giganotosaur—the tyrannosaurus rex on steroids, the beast to end all beasts, and saw that, indeed, it *had* avoided the water—and that it was avoiding it still; and more, that it was sniffing at the air randomly, almost blindly—as though it had lost our scent; as though it had lost our trail.

As though it couldn't see us—at which it swung its great head around to look behind it (as though maybe it had erred and we were somehow back there), and, after wringing its little hands in frustration (or a very close approximation) pivoted abruptly—and left.

At which, seeing that we were safe (at least for the moment), and still, remarkably, in one piece, we did what any self-respecting mammal would do: we capered and frolicked and splashed like fools—and tackled each other amidst the salt and foam. Or rather Quint and I did even as Jesse looked on: wary, silent. Demur.

20

Blood Brothers

Nor did Jesse leave the water when we did, choosing instead—inexplicably—to stay behind, submerged up to his neck, shivering.

"Dude, what?" I paused at the edge of the tide.

"Nothing," he said, and trembled. "It's just that—that thing could still be out there. Just—just waiting for us. You know?"

"Dude,"

"He's not worried about that," growled Quint, stepping up next to me.

"Oh, I'm not?" Jesse glowered at him. "Then what am I doing? Just, you know, catching hypothermia—for the hell of it? It's out there, I'm tell—"

"No," said Quint, flatly. "Because getting in the water took care of it—didn't it?"

"Jesus, Quint." I looked at him, surprised. "Cut the guy some—"

"He knows what I'm talking about," said Quint— and unzipped his jacket. "Don't you, Jesse? Or is that even your real name? Same as he knows that he can't leave the water because his clothes are wet. And we'll see his ... Look—forget it. Here, take this,"

He walked back into the tide, extending his coat.

Because getting in the water took care of it—didn't it?

Same as he knows that he can't leave the water because his clothes are wet. And we'll see his ...

And that's when it hit me. That's when the full extent of my stupidity and cluelessness came rushing in—came swinging like a sledgehammer (because, apparently, that's what it took to get my attention). That's when the *obviousness* of it struck

226

me like a bludgeon—a proverbial club upside the head—a fucking hammer.

Blood.

Menstrual blood.

Hadn't people believed once that it could attract predators, namely sharks and bears? And even if that had been disproven—and I was pretty sure it had—wasn't it at least possible that predatory dinosaurs might be the exception; especially since some species (like T. rex) were believed to have had exceptional olfactory capabilities? And if *that* were the case, how far-fetched was it, really, that giganotosaurus—and possibly others—might have been attracted to …

"Oh, Jesus."

I looked at Jesse.

"I mean, just …" And then I retched—harshly, repeatedly, as though I'd just gotten off the VelociCoaster at Universal (as in fact I had, retched, that is, when I'd gotten off the coaster—on that last trip to Florida, the one right before the Flashback).

Then I threw up—as though I'd been taken for one helluva ride.

"What?" Jesse spat. "Sorry I'm not one of the boys? Is that it?"

I shook my head. "No … I … it's just that …"

"Blame it on my mom; it was her idea," said Jesse—even as her teeth clattered and Quint approached with the coat. As the ocean roared and the moon shone, coolly, dispassionately. "Before she got divested of her intestines—by a pack of velociraptors. She, she didn't think a woman could be safe—after the Flashback, I mean. And she was right … from what I witnessed on my way to Granger. Before I got to Camp Courage." She looked through her wet hair at us. "Before Hal and Macey—and Colby. And you. Both of you."

I watched, disoriented, as Quint draped the jacket over her shoulders—then helped her toward shore. "But … I mean," I stammered. *"Quint.* How did … How long—"

"How long have I known?" He stooped to pick up Jesse's hat. "I didn't. Not until a few minutes ago." He wrung the hat out and handed it to her. "But I've suspected from the beginning—if you want to know the truth." He paused, staring at her hand, the palm of which was bloodied. "What happened?"

"Nothing," she said. "I—I fell in the woods. That's all."

"But it is something," I said, not really knowing what I meant, trying to figure it out. "Because you got that while trying to help us—while trying to lure the thing away; whether you were conscious of it or not. And the reason you did that was simple—you did it because we're brothers." I looked from her to Quint and then back again. "And when one of us bleeds, we all do."

And then I took out my knife and extended its blade—examining its edge, examining my friends. Then I drew it across my palm so that the blood welled up instantly and, staring into Jesse's eyes, held my hand out to her.

The tide rolled in and back out again.

"We all do," she agreed—and clasped it firmly, unwaveringly. "Together we stand. No matter what."

"No matter what," said Quint—having cut his own palm—then gripped hands with each of us in turn. "Together we stand—and may nothing tear us apart. That's our vow."

"Our vow," repeated Jesse, staring up at him.

And then it was done and we were heading back: back toward the gift shop—or what was left of it—and our packs which contained dry clothes; back to our bikes and spears and the Talon—as well as our quest to learn what happened to my parents—along the beckoning, barren Thunder Road.

The thing is, you can't anticipate everything, can't be 100% alert every waking second of the day: it's just not possible, especially when you've been walking for something like twelve hours. All we knew was that there'd be a bed for me and that the island of grass in the middle of the lot would work for Ank; and that we hadn't seen anything since Bowden, anyway (and *that* had only been a lone edmontosaurus grazing at the side of the road). It certainly hadn't occurred to us that by walking onto the lot of the Empire Inn and Suites—which was surrounded on three sides by strips of dilapidated units—we might be walking into a kill box.

And yet that's what it nearly became when the pickups squealed into position (effectively blocking any exit) and the men piled from their payloads—taking cover behind the vehicles like soldiers, like mercenaries, training rifles and pistols. That's when Ank rolled onto his side so that his armored back was facing them and I took cover myself; bracing the M4 on his wobbling cranium (as I aimed at where one of their fuel tanks would have been), firing a three-round burst—at which Ank shook me off emphatically and juddered his head.

<Dammit, Will—>

There was a *krack, ka-krack, krack!* even as bullets ricocheted off his armor. *<I've told you never to fire next to my—>*

"And I've told you—you have to lie still," I stepped back and sighted the gas tank again. "That's how we get out of these messes."

I fired a single shot and the truck exploded. "Unless you want to charge them, that is." I took out the other two trucks. "You know, with your big head."

I watched as a figure stumbled toward us that was completely engulfed in flames—a figure that fell, writhing, even as another tried beating him out with his jacket. And then I waited (for the other men had fled); sighting the would-be rescuer's left earlobe even as he attempted (and failed) to save his comrade; keeping it sighted as he drew his pistol and aimed it directly at—

Krack! I shot him through the left earlobe.

"Ahhh," he cried—but quickly re-aimed his pistol.

I shot him through the right earlobe.

"Arrrgg!" The pistol began to waver.

"The next one'll be between your eyes," I shouted.

At last, he dropped his weapon.

Ank grumbled as he righted himself, grunted as he stood. *<Tell him to kick it forward,>* he said. *<And ask him how many of them there are. Men, I mean.>*

"Kick it toward us," I demanded, focusing on the man's shiny forehead. "Hurry up!"

He raised his arms and did as instructed.

"Now, how many of you are there?"

He smiled slowly, stealthily. Gap-toothily. "Down here?" He nodded at the tops of the buildings. "Or up there?"

I froze and looked at Ank, who looked up at the rooftops.

"Go on, take a look," said the man. "You can count."

I scanned the peaked roofs and frowned—there were about twenty of them up there; all of them with scoped rifles and wearing helmets—their bodies protected behind dirty gray tiles.

I turned back to the man, who looked to be about thirty. "All right. So. What do you want?"

"Don't insult my intelligence, mister."

The wind gusted. The long grasses waved.

"Ank," I breathed at last. "You just can't bloody anticipate everything."

And I laid down my weapon.

"They work in *tandem?* But what does that mean?"

The man with the gapped teeth and bloodied ears stepped forward. "It means, m'lord, that, that—I don't know what it means." He lowered his chin as though ashamed—before straightening sharply. "Other than that the animal knew precisely what to do once we attacked; precisely how to defend itself—and how to defend the man too. And that the man talks to it—just as you and I are talking." He looked at Ank and then at me, gloweringly. "Calls it 'Ank'—when he isn't shooting at you. *Like the devil.*"

The old man on the throne (actually a threadbare La-Z-Boy recliner), who'd been introduced to us as King Archie Carrington the First, of Milwaukee—peered down at Ank from the stage. "So, not so much a brute as an intelligent creature, is that it?" He looked at the gap-toothed man—at old Bloody Ears. "And you're telling me this is how I lost several of my best men—and three of my war wagons—simply because you were faced with something inexplicable, something *uncanny?*"

The man nodded, grimly, solemnly.

"Very well. We must know the truth." He refocused on Ank. "Bow before me, then, intelligent creature. Or I will have you shot."

There was a silence.

<*Look, Will, I'm not bowing to anyone; much less—*>

"Just do it," I growled.

And he did it: bending his front knees so that his whole body tipped; touching his nose to the Asroturfed floor of the arena—at which I knelt as well.

"I see," said the king—rattled, taken aback. "Well: it certainly seems to understand basic commands—doesn't it?" He scrunched up his face. "Meanwhile, you acted as though you were—well, as though it were *speaking* with you. Actually communicating." He shrugged, perplexed. "I heard nothing."

"No, you wouldn't," I said. "Nor did I, at first. It takes time."

"But—"

"Call it telepathy; thought transference, ESP—whatever."

The king seemed almost to wince, trying to understand. "But—language itself—how ..."

"Because he was a man once; just like us. That is, until they, whatever they are, the lights in the sky, had their way with him. Until they took the essence of who he was and poured it into this, this behemoth, this ankylosaurus—as an experiment, perhaps, like the were-raptors. Beyond that, you know as much as we do."

"The—the *'were-raptors ...?'"*

"Look, it's not important." I stood and clicked my tongue, indicating Ank should rise as well. "What's important is that you release us—*now.* What's important is that we never meant to trespass and took only such action as was needed to defend ourselves and our right of way; and must therefore be allowed to—"

"Ah, but don't you see?" His sleeves slipped down as he raised his hands, revealing frail, liver-spotted forearms. "This is my quandary! How can I simply *release you* when you have killed so many of my infinite best; and more, when you have destroyed the very vehicles I need to—" He trailed off suddenly, looking at Ank. "He carries quite a load, this man-beast—doesn't he, now?"

I looked at all the packs and bags strapped to Ank's back: the fresh fruit and pemican and milk-jugs full of water; the bedrolls and camping gear and battered, black guitar case. "I don't see what—"

"Ah, ah! But you will!" He slapped the arms of his 'throne.' "Yes, you will! My God, how did I not think of it?" He paused as if to reel himself in. "Ah, but, how can we discuss business, discuss our transaction, if I don't even know your name?"

I looked at Ank and he looked back. *<What the hell is he talking about?>*

"Williams," I said, noncommittally—at which the king raised a beetled brow.

"*Williams.* As in, that's your surname, surely? And what of your—"

"Just Williams."

The king moved to speak but dithered. "I, ah, I see. Very well. 'Williams.' I do believe I have a proposal."

I glanced at Ank again—found him already regarding me from beneath a bony brow. "A proposal," I looked Carrington in the eyes. "All right. Okay. We're listening."

"Yes, well." Carrington hesitated. "It concerns my daughter, see, Princess Gisela—and the, ah, matter of matrimony. Which is to say that, now that she is of age, she will be expected to satisfy certain, ah, *familial obligations.*" He sat back in the La-Z-Boy, which creaked and moaned. "Certain duties. And for that, well, let's just say I am ill-equipped to instruct a debutant—especially when there's no proper society in which to introduce her; this being a—er, frontier outpost, primarily, and thus not a place where a suitable courtship might occur. Therefore,"

He squared his shoulders and breathed in and out, quickly. "I am ordering that she be transported to Edmonton Mall—the, er, realm of my former wife, one Amelia Issandra Chapman—to be versed in all things glitterati; to be trained in the ways of the crème de la crème—the, ah, *haut monde,* as they say. And I am happy to say that I have chosen *you,* Mr. Ank and Mr. Williams, to escort her to that end—knowing, as I do, that you will protect her diligently and faithfully, and above all courageously, even if it means losing your own lives in the process."

And he looked at us, first at me and then at Ank. And we looked back.

<Tell him to take a flying fuck off the nearest bridge,> said Ank. *<'Even if it means losing your own lives.' Go on, tell him—>*

But I wasn't listening, having been distracted by a figure above us, in the press box, a figure which hadn't been there before: a beautiful young woman wearing a Vietnamese long dress—the sight of which stopped my heart, if only for an instant.

Ank must have followed my gaze. <*Must be his daughter. Now look, don't go getting all misty-eyed; we're supposed to be looking for your lost wife, remember? And our lead said Sedgewick; which is east of here, closer to Saskatche—*>

"Your Highness," I said, looking up at the girl, or more properly the dress, "We accept this mission and will see to it your daughter reaches her destination safely." I shifted my focus to the king. "In God—and us—you can trust; *that's a promise.*"

<*Have you lost your mind? No, wait, don't tell me: the Phantom Hard-on strikes again. Okay; fine. But I'm telling you, right ...*>

But I was too focused on the dress to hear him: the deep purple dress with the golden, entwined serpents; the very dress we'd had made in Ho Chi Minh-Saigon in anticipation of the Split Bullet Tour in SoCal—the only one of its kind in all the world.

The one Ngoc Tran Williams, my wife (and co-star of the East Meets West Travelling Guitar and Trick-shooting Show) was wearing before we got separated, before the train carried her off. Before Time melted and the world went mad; lost to primordia—even as most of its people were lost; lost to the Flashback, which had given the world back to the reptiles.

"... and there you have it; from an abandoned lighthouse on the Oregon coast to Barley's Hot Springs in Barley, Montana, that was Francis Cope and a story of survival we're not apt to forget; at least not any time soon. All of which brings us to the bottom of the hour and more music; in this case, Johnny Horton with "North to Alaska"—and a special shout-out to Ank and Williams, wherever they may be. This is Radio Free Montana; take it away, John—*skishhhhhh ...*"

I looked up at the howdah strapped to Ank's back and saw 'Queen' Gisela fiddling with the radio. "What are you doing?"

"Johnny Horton is lame," she pouted. "I want to listen to something else."

I looked at Ank and he looked back, clearly annoyed.

"You're not going to find it," I said. "Unless, of course, you're looking for dead air."

At last, she circled back to the station. "I was looking for something like, oh, I don't know, music. Anyway," She waggled her fingers. "Let's go. Start walking."

<Will, either shoot her dead now or I'm bucking her off ...>

"Oh, hang in, Ank. It's only 95 miles."

"Hellooo, big, stupid animal? *I said you could go."*

<Will ...!>

"I'd get some sleep up there," I hollered. "There's not going to be much to see for a while."

At which she fell abruptly, blessedly silent—even as we embarked along the Queen Elizabeth II Highway and between the flat, green fields. As the stout backup singers chanted *Mush, mush, mush!* and Ank lumbered along and the howdah rocked; as I walked point gripping my M4 and tried not to think about Ngoc Tran or how Carrington had told me the dress had been a gift from his wife (and that it had come from one of her shops, a place called Eastern Market); as I watched for danger and tried not to get my hopes up, tried not to dream.

"Why are we stopping?" asked Gisela sleepily.

"Because *that,* your loftiness," I looked at the collapsed bridges and water coursing between piles of rubble, "is what I call a problem." I turned to Ank. "What do you think? Can you ford it?"

Ank moved toward the edge, taking care not to step too close. *<In a word, yes. I mean, I can walk on the fallen sections of bridge. What concerns me is—well, that.>*

I looked to where a wall of wood, mud, and stone—about 8 feet tall by 50 feet wide—divided the river. "What do you make of it?"

<What I make of it is: we don't want to threaten whatever built that. I'm trying to remember, but I seem to recall a beaver that populated this region during the Ice Age— Castoroadus, Castoroides, something like that. About the size of—>

"Well, if it's just a beaver—"

<... of a grizzly bear, with 6-inch incisors. Probably weighed about 700 pounds. And while it would have been herbivorous, like most rodents, the fact is, we go wading into that water we're going to be invading its territory. And I can't fight with this—>

"It's okay. Really." I looked up at Gisela. "It's okay! *I've got us covered.*"

<Sure, you've got us covered. But will you even see it coming when it's under the water?>

I went around to the rope ladder and began climbing. "All I can do is my best."

"I'm *not* okay with this," said Gisela—even as Ank lumbered into the river and I looked over my rifle at the water. "Not crossing the river; or being strapped to the back of this—this *beast,* or allowing you into my howdah, or any of it. Is that clear?"

"*Shhh,*" I whispered—watching the roiling water (as it rose to within a few feet of the howdah); trying to listen. "And keep your eyes peeled. If there's anything swimming toward us—anything at all—I'm gonna need to know about it. *And fast.*"

Several moments passed in silence.

"But water's gonna get all over the—"

"*Jesus, gods,* would you please just—"

<What was that?>

I jerked the gun left and right. "Nothing—it's nothing. Just a fish jumping. Stay on it."

<It's not easy. The pieces of bridge are slippery—some kind of algae ...>

"You're doing fine ... we're almost there."

Gisela stirred. "I think I saw something."

I scanned the surface with the rifle. "I don't see any—"

But then we *were* there; we were across the river—across it and climbing, leaving the water. Then we were breathing a huge sigh of relief as we looked back the way we had come and realized we'd overreacted; that there'd been no danger at—

<Look out, Will!>

And I ducked, pulling Gisela down with me, even as the albertosaurus' teeth clacked above us and Ank reared up: hurling us from the howdah, dumping us into the river. Even as the M4 slid from my fingers and began to sink, leadenly, rapidly, and Gisela, who had been looking toward the dam, began to shriek—at which I saw a huge, flat tail slip into the water.

"Jesus—*swim!*"

And we did: pumping toward the bank (where Ank was engaged in furious combat with the albertosaurus); lunging for its safety even as the beaver pursued; scrambling from the river as it caught the end of her dress with its teeth and began reversing—at which I drew my revolver but instantly lost it (due to one of her flailing limbs); then quickly reached for my knife.

"Okay; I got it, I got it," I grunted, as I sawed at the material. *"Okay, okay, okay!"*

And she was free—even as the beaver fell back into the water and I saw Ank's club tail bearing down on us like a wrecking ball (he'd taken a swing at the albertosaurus and missed), at which point I covered her with my entire body and we fell, *hard.* At which point the predator hesitated—opening and closing its little foreclaws—before turning and fleeing across the fields. At which we just laid there, gasping and coughing and thanking our lucky stars ... or at least I did.

"Yeah, ah, like, you can let me up now." She squirmed beneath me like a roped calf. "I mean, thank you and all that, but—"

"But the beaver. It's still—"

"The *beaver* doesn't care because we're no longer in its river." She bucked suddenly, violently. *"I said let me up, you bas—"*

"Okay, okay; your loftiness. Settle down," I stood and leaned against Ank, who'd approached with only minor injuries. "You'd think after our handling of that, that *situation,* you'd be more ... more ..."

She stood and glared at us, her thin dress—now more of a miniskirt—clinging to her revealingly; her flesh excited by the water. "Your 'handling of that?' Are you for real? I mean, *look at me."*

We looked at her.

"Doh!" Her teeth chattered as she went to the rope ladder and started climbing. "You're animals—*both of you.* Whatever my father was thinking when he asked you to—" She turned to look at me from the fourth or fifth rung. "Well—what are you waiting for? *Mush, mush,* as the song says. Let's pick 'em up and move 'em out. And faster this time; more intense. Unlike you and this, this *thing,* there's people waiting for me."

I stepped into the shallows and retrieved my pistol (the rifle, I knew, was gone). "Well, you heard her, Ank. Guess we'll have to pick up the pace."

Ank seemed almost to smile—it was all in the eyes. <*Like when we ran halfway across Montana in order to reach Barley's Hot Springs before Szambelan and his army of darkness could?*>

I twirled the silver revolver—to air it out—and sunk it back into its holster. "Yeah, Ank. Pretty much exactly like that."

And then I started jogging, slowly at first but increasing my pace, and he galloped after—faster this time. More intense.

And so we ran—like we had in the past, like it often seemed we were born to do—along the grassy strip between pavements (it was easier on Ank's feet) and past the patchwork fields; past Blackfalds and Kuhnen Park and the oil and gas town of Lacombe—I knew because I'd studied the guides the night before—past Lochinvar and Rosedale Valley and beautiful Barnette Lake—which shone like a mirror in the sun. Ran until we could see the small, white buildings of Ponoka; at which I looked up at Gisela—whose hair had dried and now fluttered behind her like a pennant—and thought I saw a smile—before she noticed me watching and scowled. And then it was over and we were done for the day and the only sound was the pop and crackle of the campfire (unless you counted Ank eating like a hog from the enormous tin he carried on his back; which seemed to make her physically ill).

"Got a long day tomorrow—all the way to Leduc-Nisku. You should eat." I scraped my can and took a bite. "Can't make a splash in Edmonton if you show up looking all, I dunno, stringy."

She watched Ank as he ate. "I'm not hungry—and I'm not a prize horse. They'll get over it. Besides," She shook the hair out of her eyes. "Some men like 'em stringy. You, for example."

I must have just looked at her.

"The dress," she said. "The one that belonged to your wife. It's a size 8."

I moved to speak but hesitated. "You've been talking to your father."

"Some," she said. "Enough to know your story. Enough to know you got separated from your wife during the Flashback and have been looking for her ever since. And that—that you and the animal share a bond; one he didn't understand and didn't elaborate on, but that made him feel ..." She looked at me with surprising intimacy. "I don't know. That you could be trusted." She laughed. "With his daughter, I mean. And, also, that you were someone who ... how did he put it? Was 'motivated by love.'" She dug around in her can of beans listlessly, disinterestedly. "Which I guess is what got me thinking ... about what I've been thinking. Which is—and I'm being, like, *totally serious,* so don't laugh—what's it like?"

"What's it like?" I raised an eyebrow incredulously. "You mean—love?" I looked at her doubtfully. "You've been thinking about that?"

She nodded solemnly, earnestly. "I really want to know."

I looked at Ank, who snorted and huffed his food. "Well, I mean, it's a big subject. Love. I really wouldn't know where to—"

"Start at the very beginning," she said, almost breathlessly. "At the exact moment you laid eyes on her. I mean, was it something she was wearing, or something she said ... was it her perfume—"

"No, no, nothing like that," I sat back and thought about it. "It's more that ... I didn't so much see her—as *recognize* her. I mean ... it was like I'd known her all along—only forgotten ... somehow. Like we were simply picking up where we left off, elsewhere—elsewhen." I gazed at the night sky—at the Flashback Borealis with its ghostly green glow. "It wasn't so much an introduction as an 'Oh, there you are!'" I tossed my empty can into the fire. "Leastwise, that's how I remember it."

Her jaw dropped as though I'd said something profound. "Oh, wow. Wow, wow, wow." She sat up suddenly. "What else? I mean, did she walk a certain way; or did she have one of those whiskey voices, like, say, Billie Holiday, or—"

"No, no, no, see, it's not about that, really. It's more," I thought about the last time I saw her, about the odd look on her face as the train pulled away and the crowd crushed in: a look almost of grace, of saintliness, as Time itself melted. "I mean, she was beautiful, of course—the most beautiful woman I'd ever seen—then or since. But this—this was something else; something at her very core. Water, I suppose, as opposed to waves. Warmth, as opposed to mere heat." I used a stick to poke at the fire. "Meh. It devolves into cliché."

She stirred her feet in the sand listlessly. "Yeah; you kind of lost me at water and waves ..."

"Of course I did," I said—sullenly, morosely.

"What I mean is, if it's the Buddhist thing you're talk ..." She trailed off abruptly. "What do you mean, 'of course I did?'"

"What?"

"You said, 'of course I did.' As though I couldn't possibly be expected to—"

"No, no, no, now that's not what I meant at—"

"Sure it is. It's just precisely what you meant. As though I couldn't possibly understand the higher, *abstract* thinking of *Jingo-fucking-Williams,* hotshot shootist and, *and eater of beans!*" She stood suddenly and kicked a log off the fire, scattering embers. "Well, have a good night, *Mr. Fucking Dinosaur Whisperer;* right here on the cold ground, while I'm up in my howdah—sleeping like a baby!" She stormed up the rope ladder as though she were laying siege to it. "'Of course I did.' Ha! And 'ha,' again! Because I must be an idiot; isn't that about it? Yeah, well, jokes on you, Gunpowder-head. Water not waves. Warmth not just heat. I've got your heat; good night, Mr. Williams! *Fuck you,* Mr. Williams!"

At which Ank just looked at me with slop dripping from his cobblestone beak and said, <*Well, that escalated quickly.*>

And we turned in.

We ran, even though we were tired (Ank had tossed and turned most of the night which meant of course Gisela had tossed and turned; which meant that between his farting and her griping I hadn't slept a wink); past former canola fields and dry pea fields and barley—all of it now overgrown—past Brightview and Wiesenthal to Southfork Landing/Leduc; where we came upon a car—a bright-yellow AMC Pacer, if you can believe it—which was headed in the opposite direction.

"Ho, easy does it," I said, even as Ank slowed to a crawl and the car pulled alongside.

"Eh? What sort of kerfuffle is this?" The driver looked at Ank disbelievingly. "Oat and aboat with the dinosaur, are you?"

I looked beyond him at the passengers: at the plain but pretty woman seated next to him and two others—a male and a female in their twenties—in the back. "Meh—tame as a Peep Toe mule, I assure you. And completely untouched by the fever. Carries our gear—and other things." I paused, noticing blood on the door. "We're heading up north—to Edmonton. To some sort of mall encampment. Anything we should be aware of?"

The driver's eyes flicked up and down; as though noticing me noticing the blood. "Din' come from there—hung a roger onto Highway 2 from Route 19; at the Petro-Pass. So I couldn' really say." He looked at the young woman next to him—who seemed markedly ill at ease. "I'll do ya a blunt tho an' tell ya: if you're look'n for a place to crash—that Petro-pass is tops. There's still stuff on the shelves: bottled water, toilet paper—"

"Have a safe trip," I said, with my hand close to the revolver. "Bridge is out near Red Deer. And thanks for the tip."

"Eh?" He looked me up and down again. "All right. Have it your way." He glanced through the rearview mirror at the young people, who just stared back. "Off like newlyweds, then. *Hooroo.*"

And they went—after which Gisela called down, "Why so *rude?*"

I exchanged knowing glances with Ank. "Because they were troubled—you couldn't see it from up there." I watched as they disappeared down the road. "The kind you can catch."

And then we continued—toward Leduc/Nisku and what I hoped would be our camp for the night. Toward the Petro-

Pass; which I assumed was a kind of Canadian answer to a truck stop.

We laid our cards on the upturned barrel as Ank looked on: a Five of Spades for me and a Five of Hearts for Gisela. War.

"All right, then." I staggered three cards face down on top of the faceup and flipped a fourth: a King of Spades. "Fitting," I said. "Ank and I being Kings of the Road—as it were."

She *hmphed* and did the same—laying out a Queen of Diamonds. "Also fitting." Then she sighed, accepting defeat. *"Fortun favet fatiis."*

I gathered up the cards and added them to my deck. "Losing—in your case—but fitting." I stood and faced the fog. "Now, if you'll excuse me, I've got to go spend a penny."

"Just don't spend it here," she said.

I wandered into the gloom to what would have been the edge of the Petro-Pass's parking lot. "What's that mean, anyway? 'Fortun favet fatiis?' Is that, like, Latin for, 'I am a big, fat loser?'"

"Why don't you ask your dinosaur—*it* seems to be the one in charge." She added: "It means, 'Fortune favors fools.'"

"Ah. I see." I exhaled and peered into the fog. "But then—"

That's when I heard it; just the faintest voice, the most subtle whisper—like a ghost. *"Eggsuckerrr ... P-p-p-pestilencsss ..."*

<What was that?>

I stared into the mists; into the swirling murk and brume.

"Nothing," I said—even as I unlatched my holster slowly. "It was noth—"

But it *was* something; something right there, silhouetted in the gloom. *Four somethings,* to be exact—poised like outlaws, gathered like crows. Four things that used to be human but were now obscenities, anathemas—abominations. Were-raptors.

"We're in trouble," I said, even as Ank interrupted and I drew and backed away. "We're in trouble!"

And then they came: hissing and cursing and clicking their forked tongues; as I stumbled into Gisela and grabbed her by the shoulders—switching places with her; I have no idea why—as something reared up behind her and I pushed her head down: firing into the thing's mouth, into its soft, pink palate; blowing its brains out—which bespattered the animal behind it.

"Go!" I shouted. "Get into the howdah!" I targeted the second animal's eyes in rapid succession: *kabamm, kabamm!*

"Pigfucker!" said the third, leaping into the air, trying to pounce; even as I dove and rolled and quickly stood—only to dive again as Ank's clubbed tail hurled at me from the gloom.

"Foot-licker! Guttersnipe!"

I watched as one of them slipped into the haze—completely concealing itself—then drew on all my experience, and a kind of third eye, to predict exactly where I thought it might—

Kabamm!

And its blood spread in a pool.

<I've got this; check on the girl.>

Which I did; seizing the ladder even as Ank whirled; ascending it as he reared abruptly and brought his weight down—all ten tons—crushing the remaining raptor like a gnat.

And then it was over and Gisela had thrown her arms about me—pressed her head against my chest. Then we looked at each other and finally into the sky, which pulsed and glowed.

Then we descended the ladder and inspected the bodies ... which had reverted back to normal, reverted back to human.

"Because they were troubled—the kind you can catch," she said, quoting what I'd said earlier. "How did you *know?*"

"I didn't," I said, holstering the revolver—which smelled of charcoal and sulfur. "I just knew we shouldn't get too close."

"But ... *why?*"

"I don't know. It's just ... it's just something you learn. Learn as you go." I removed her arms from my shoulders—gently, slowly. "Who to let in. Who to keep out. Remember that."

And then she just looked at me: enduringly, indelibly—perfect in her earnestness. Beautiful in her new vulnerability.

Again, we ran; unburdened by the howdah—which we'd left in a wreck at the Petro-Pass (at Gisela's insistence); into the metropolitan area of Edmonton—which shined like a city on a hill.

"How far is the mall," I shouted—unnecessarily, perhaps, as Gisela was right next to me. "And how exactly do we get there?"

"Not far; just a few miles northwest of here—by the Transit Centre. We'll be there in no time! Last one is a rotten egg!"

And she put on a burst of speed; at which I jogged to a halt by a dilapidated Toyota dealership and tried to catch my breath—even as Ank galloped past with pots and pans clanging and chided, <*You never were any good at the long run, Will!*>

Upon which, smiling, I just stood there and watched: feeling oddly content—oddly hopeful. Feeling as though I had not only regained my wife—or so I prayed—but somehow gained a whole family, a whole community. Feeling a sense of triumph, even giddiness, as I took a deep breath and ran after them.

Suffice it to say that, by the time we'd arrived at West Edmonton Mall and met Queen Amelia and dispensed with all the pomp and circumstance, I was ready to learn more about my wife; something which took care of itself when Amelia turned to me in the packed ballroom and said: "You've done a man's job, Mr. Williams; a hero's job, as promised. My husband was right about you. And that goes for your animal, too. Ank, as they say. And so. The question becomes: Given what you've accomplished—how on earth can we ever repay you?"

I didn't dawdle or mince words. "Your highness, I ask only that you take me to the shop where you purchased the purple dress: the one with the entwined serpents that you gifted Gisela—a shop called Eastern Market, and introduce me to its proprietor. Do this and no other payment is required."

She moved to speak but paused—looking at me differently, looking at me, frankly, as though she were looking at a ghost. "Oh, dear," she said, and placed a hand over her mouth.

"What is it?" I asked.

"It's nothing, I'm sure. It's just that the shop is no longer open—it is no longer in business. It—she left us about a month ago, before—"

"*What was her name?*"

"Well, I—I mean it ..."

"Her name. And how did she go; I mean, was she walking, driving, what?"

"Walking. With another. And we—we never knew her full name. Everyone just called her—" She hesitated, watching me closely. "We called her *Tran.*"

I must have just stared at her—doggedly, intensely. "Well, isn't that a coincidence? Because that's precisely who I'm looking for. And yet you say her name as though—as though it's loaded. *Why?*"

Again she hesitated. "Because I know now who you are—indeed, I realized it only a moment ago. She—she had a picture of you; one she never lost sight of—even for a minute. Said you were her missing husband—and that she'd find you if it was the last thing she did. That's why she left—to go looking for you. To look for you in the last place you were together. Somewhere in southern—"

"California," I said—thinking about the Split Bullet Tour and our last date before the Flashback; thinking about the seething mobs and swirling pterodactyls—the freight train heading north. "We were in California—in Fresno." I shook my head, marveling at the thought. "She's going to Fresno ..."

"Alas, Mr. Williams. It's been 30 days. It's likely she's long since—"

But I was already gone; already heading for the former sea lion lagoon (where Gisela was supposed to be giving Ank a much-needed bath). Already thinking about what I would say and how I would say it—as if it even mattered, as if he'd even care.

As if there'd ever be a trip he wasn't down for—not in a million, trillion years.

<I'm not down for it, Will. I'm just not.>

I looked at him where he stood in the pool, soaking, marinating—unable to believe my ears. "Now look, this is the best lead we've ever—"

<It's the best lead you've ever had, Will. You. I mean, it's your wife—am I right?> He used his tail to splash water on his himself, like an elephant. *<I'm getting too old for this sort of thing; this sort of galivanting—too old and too tired. I'm sorry.>*

I looked from him to Gisela; who was dozing in a nearby deck chair—wrapped in a towel. "Did you ... I mean, was she—"

<A dinosaur never tells.>

"I see." I moved around to face him directly. "Now listen; I see what's going on here—I really do. You're afraid that if we find Tran things will change—between us, I mean. And I suppose at some point they will; just not in the way you think. Look, Ank, I'm talking one more adventure here, one more for the road. I can't believe you'd rather lay around here with ..." I stared at Gisela, whose legs were like burnt gold. "With *society.* With people who seem to have everything and a mall full of ... of ..."

I gazed at the skylights and the high, arched ceiling; the two stories of shops and restaurants, the pirate ship with its sails. "Oh, to hell with it. You've clearly made up your mind. Well—have a nice life, Bone-head. I guess all our adventures didn't amount to much." I bowed to Gisela as she stirred. "M'lady."

And then I left; wanting to just rip the Band-Aid off and be done with it, to get out of Dodge while I still could. Then I walked the mall for what seemed like hours—days, months—looking for a car or even a scooter (hell, a bicycle would have worked; or a skateboard). Looking for a bloody ride.

The tire blew as I passed Brightview—or more properly, Bearhills Lake—exploding like a balloon; *frap-frapping* as I pulled onto the shoulder.

"Oh, for fuck's sake," I cursed, before lowering the stand and dismounting—starting to pace furiously. "Now what the ..."

I looked at the Yamaha, which gleamed in the sun, then at the horizon—which lay flat, green, featureless. "I'm hurtling through time and space ... and I'm driving at a record pace ... but the more that I drive, the later I'll arrive ... so it's time I did an about-face."

I sighed; not remembering where I'd picked up the limerick. Such as it was.

"Well, Ank. I guess you knew what you weren't getting into."

I looked around at the steppes; at the green tundra and patched highway, at the miles and miles of nothing—the Big Empty; the Lost Country.

"I can't do it, Ank. I can't do this. I mean; I thought I could—I really did. But this ... this is hopeless. This is just—"

"You'll always have me," came a voice—a voice which was smooth, reassuring. Mellifluent. "Look—*now*, back the way you came—you'll see me."

But I already knew, even before I turned: knew exactly who it was, who had come to tempt me. Knew it by the charge in the air and the smell of sulfur; the shadow along the road, a laughing sound on the wind. *"Szambelan,"* I whispered, and drew.

But the demon Szambelan only chuckled. "It won't work, of course—not against my true form. After all, you but killed the vessel."

And then he just looked at me, all 7 to 8 feet of him. Looked at me with his multitude of eyes and his white-furred ram's head; his spiked, deformed shoulders—which also had eyes; his sinewy arms. "Don't tell me you've never thought of joining me; or offered a silent prayer—I know what's in men's hearts. What's in yours, for example, is mostly anguish—anguish that you will never see your wife again ... and, also, that you have lost your one, true friend. And I can assure you, gunslinger ... these things are true."

I felt dizzy, disoriented.

"True? But how ..." My gun clattered as I dropped to me knees. "That's not possible. Ank needs rest—that's all there is to it. And Ngoc Tran—she's on her way now. On her way to Fresno; where we will be reunited. On her way back to my—"

"Lies," whispered Szambelan, melodiously, hypnotically. "The only truth is lead ... is copper and brass. The only truths are the bullet; are gunpowder and steel. No—no; you know what needs to be done. You have simply to pick up your weapon—and to put it into your mouth. Do it, Williams. Before—"

And then I was reaching for it; for my silver revolver which lay gleaming—for my one true friend who had never let me down. Then I was sliding it between my teeth as I looked through Szambelan's ghostly form and saw a cloud of dust rising in the north—just rising and drifting, like a signal spelled in smoke. Then I was beginning to squeeze the trigger when I looked below the dust and saw Ank: running like a stallion, galloping like an armored warhorse—charging over the strip of dirt and grass between lanes to close the distance between us like a blaze.

<You didn't think I was going to let you enjoy sunny California without me, did you?> he said, even as he tackled

me and began licking my face; began slathering my cheeks in slime.

"Okay, easy does it," I said, and laughed, then climbed to my feet. "So are we back, is that it? I mean, are we going to Fresno?"

<To Fresno and beyond—to Fresno and beyond! The Hollywood Hills, to be exact. Because, remember how, as we approached Barley, something sort of awakened in us—sort of opened like a third eye—and we could see and feel things we normally couldn't? Well, it seems to be happening again; seems to be peculating. And, well, we're going to be needed, Will. Needed as much as we've ever been. All of which is just my way of saying that I'm in this for the duration—in it for the long haul. And that—well, that I've got your back. You can count on it.>

At which I just smiled and holstered my pistol, looking down the road. At which I just walked and Ank followed, pots and pans jangling. At which we turned south and faced the future, faced the Big Empty—which, at that particular moment, didn't feel so empty at all.

And the Flashback continues ...

If you enjoyed this work of fiction, please consider
leaving a review at your point of sale. Thanks!

Wayne Kyle Spitzer is an American writer, illustrator, and filmmaker. He is the author of countless books, stories and other works, including a film (*Shadows in the Garden*), a screenplay (*Algernon Blackwood's The Willows*), and a memoir (*X-Ray Rider*). His work has appeared in *MetaStellar— Speculative fiction and beyond, subTerrain Magazine: Strong Words for a Polite Nation* and *Columbia: The Magazine of Northwest History,* among others. He holds a Master of Fine Arts degree from Eastern Washington University, a B.A. from Gonzaga University, and an A.A.S. from Spokane Falls Community College. His recent fiction includes *The Man/Woman War* cycle of stories as well as the *Dinosaur Apocalypse Saga.* He lives with his sweetheart Ngoc Trinh Ho in the Spokane Valley.